M000032741

THE
RELIANT

THE RELIANT

DR. PATRICK JOHNSTON

AMBASSADOR INTERNATIONAL
GREENVILLE, SOUTH CAROLINA & BELFAST, NORTHERN IRELAND

www.ambassador-international.com

The Reliant

© 2017 by Dr. Patrick Johnston
All rights reserved

ISBN: 978-1-62020-575-4
eISBN: 978-1-62020-650-8

Scripture taken from the New King James Version. Copyright © 1982 by Thomas Nelson. Used by permission. All rights reserved.

All rights reserved solely by the author. Except for brief quotations in printed reviews, no part of this publication may be reproduced, stored in a retrieval system, or transmitted in any form or by any means (printed, written, photo-copied, visual electronic, audio, or otherwise) without the prior permission of the publisher.

Cover Design and Page Layout by Hannah Nichols
eBook Conversion by Anna Riebe Raats
Cover photos courtesy of Charity Johnston, YourStoryPhotography.net

Printed in the United States of America

www.JohnstonFamilyMinistry.com
For bulk ordering deals visit www.thereliantnovel.com
To learn more about the movie being created from this story, entitled *The Reliant*, visit www.TheReliantMovie.com.

AMBASSADOR INTERNATIONAL
Emerald House
411 University Ridge, Suite B14
Greenville, SC 29601, USA
www.ambassador-international.com

AMBASSADOR BOOKS
The Mount
2 Woodstock Link
Belfast, BT6 8DD, Northern Ireland, UK
www.ambassadormedia.co.uk

The colophon is a trademark of Ambassador

"You are good,

and do good . . . "

~ Psalm 119:68a

PROLOGUE

"FAITH! HELP MY FAITH! SHE'S hurt!"

The cry was desperate, and the voice raspy, as if coarsened by a million cigarettes.

I was eleven, and Jimmy was nine. We sipped from cold soda cans as we sat on the bed in the doctor's lounge. Daddy had gotten off his shift at the Dover Memorial ER early because Mom had gone into labor. She was enjoying a much needed nap after the epidural kicked in, and Dad was fetching us some snacks when the frightful cry rang out, followed by the shouting of several nurses.

I turned my ear toward the commotion, which sounded like it was coming from just down the hall. Fear gripped my heart. "Dad?"

"Wait here." Dad stepped out of the room for a second, and then put his head back in. "No, come with me."

We entered the ER waiting room where two nurses struggled to get a little unconscious girl of about six onto the gurney. Her screaming father just didn't want to let go of her. He had a gash on his forehead and shards of glass sticking out. Blood trickled down the side of his head into the maze of his scraggly whiskers. His words were jumbled. "She hit her head, and cried for a sec. Then she was out . . ."

"Sir!" the nurse urged him. "Put her down so we can look at her!"

Reluctantly, he finally set her on the gurney. "Faith, Daddy's here."

Dad motioned Jimmy and me toward the waiting room chairs. "What happened?" Dad asked the man as he jogged near.

"But Dr. Ashcraft, your wife's in labor—"

"Only four centimeters, one floor up—"

"Dr. Seaborn can handle—"

"He's in a code in triage." Dad looked the man in the eye as the nurse took the girl's vitals. "Tell me what happened."

Jimmy protested. "But, Daddy—"

"Shh." Dad turned harshly to us. "Sit down until I'm done."

Jimmy and I sat in the chairs nearest him, awed to see him handle the situation with such confidence and finesse.

"Some motorcycles ran me off the road," the man with the raspy voice explained, "and I hit a sign . . ."

I turned to see an idling rusty four-door car in front of the double glass doors. Its engine smoked, and its right fender dangled.

Dad checked the girl's neck and eyes, and then he listened to her heart and lungs, and the man continued. "I came here right away. I know I told her to buckle up—"

"What's her medical history?"

The man shrugged. "I dunno." As the nurse tried to insert an IV into the crease of her elbow, the man staggered, and swatted away her hand. "What are you doing?"

"We've got to put in an IV, sir," Dad explained as he palpated the girl's stomach. Dad motioned for security to come near. "Does your daughter have any allergies?"

When the man didn't answer, Dad turned to him angrily. "Does her mother know? Can you call her? We need an answer, quick!"

The man hung his head as a nurse tried to dab the blood off his brow. "God took her from me." He swatted away the nurse's kind gesture.

"How much did you drink tonight?"

The man's eyes snapped up to meet Dad's, as if he was personally affronted by the inquiry. "Wha-?"

Dad turned to the secretary. "Call radiology. Tell 'em I'm bringing an unconscious pediatric patient for a stat head and neck CT . . . "

He started pushing the gurney away, and the man grabbed it. "No! I wanna be with her!"

Dad raised his voice to be heard over the shouting. "Your daughter's safe in my hands. Just, just let us do our job."

The security guard stood between the man and the gurney, but the man wouldn't let go of it. They began to yell at each other.

At that moment, a police officer entered the room beside us. He had one look at the man with the raspy voice, and spoke into his shoulder mounted mic. "He's here."

The guard tried to explain the situation as the officer neared, but he wasn't one for patient listening. "Hey!" The officer stuck a palm on the father's chest and pushed him away. "Did you leave the scene of the accident tonight?" The man glanced back at his idling car through the glass windows. "If I looked, would I find an open container of alcohol in that busted car? And green paint on the fender?"

He responded with a faint whisper, his eyes fixed on his daughter as her gurney was rolled down the hall. "That's my daughter. She's hurt. And she needs her—"

"You didn't answer my question!" The officer unveiled a pair of handcuffs. "If you want to keep these off your wrists, then you're gonna blow into this." He removed a device with a translucent tube from his belt. The man with the raspy voice took a step back.

I looked for Dad. He had rounded the corner and was gone. The man with the raspy voice suddenly exploded with a fit of rage. He pushed the officer's face with one hand and reached for his holstered pistol with the other. They spun. The security guard clamored to remove his club affixed to his belt, but he was too slow.

In a flash, the guard was sprawled out on the ground and the officer was nursing a shoulder with a grimace on his face. The man with the raspy voice screamed, "Take me to my Faith! Now!" He shook the gun in the officer's face. "Now!"

The officer extended a hand toward the man. "Think about what you're doing. You're never gonna see your daughter again if you pull that trigger . . . "

Someone from the corner of the ER stood up to run from the room when the man with the raspy voice turned his gun on them. "Sit down! Don't move!" His aim shifted to the secretary. "Put the phone down!" He aimed the gun between the eyes of the officer.

Out of the corner of my eyes, I saw Jimmy tremble. All this was taking place just a few feet from us. My head spun, like I was going to pass out.

Then he turned the gun upon me. "Nobody move!"

"What's your daughter's name?" the officer calmly asked the man.

A pause. "Faith," he whispered, his hands trembling.

"What would your daughter say if she saw you freaking out all these kids with a gun?"

Suddenly, the double doors burst open, and a crash cart pushed by several nurses whizzed by, oblivious to the man with the gun who stood by the entrance. They rushed down the hall where Dad took the little girl on the gurney.

"Oh no." The man with the raspy voice lowered his gun. "Oh, no."

"Put it down!" the officer urged. "And you'll see her again."

The man with the raspy voice turned to me, and for a long moment, we stared into each other's eyes. I could see in his face—feel it more than see it—a life of pain. Rejection. Rage. Rage against everyone. Against God mostly. I tried to imagine him as a little boy being picked on in school. A teenager being cursed out by his Daddy because he dropped a football pass on Friday night. A man weeping at his wife's grave.

His coarse facial features softened, and he crumpled to his knees. His grip on the gun lightened. "I'm sorry. I, I, I just want to be with my daughter, please . . . "

Four more officers suddenly burst into the room, guns drawn. "Put your hands up, now!"

"Drop the gun!"

Slow to follow their orders, one of them pulled the trigger, and 500,000 volts of electricity surged through the man's body over what seemed like a very long time. He seized, groaned, and writhed on the ground till the crackling stopped. Then the four officers descended upon him. The man gained the use of his extremities and jerked a hand away from the officer trying to cuff him. One of them pressed his knee against the back of the man's neck, and ordered him to "Stop resisting!"

"Faith!" I heard him scream beneath the pile of muscular officers. "Faith! Daddy's sorry! Daddy's so sorry!"

Out of the corner of my eyes, I saw Dad come back down the hall. We ran to him. Tears instantly streamed down my face. He dropped to a knee and embraced us. It felt so good to feel his arms about us. But he looked sad. Very sad.

"I'm sorry. I'm so sorry. Are you all right?" With his thumb he wiped a tear from my eye.

"He aimed a gun at us, Daddy." Jimmy seemed proud of it all, an out-of-place smile on his blush-cheeked face.

"NOOO!" The man with the raspy voice screamed out when he saw Dad. "You! Hey! Doctor! You told me she'd be okay! You told me she'd be safe with you!"

Dad grabbed our hands, stood, and took off down the hall as the man screamed out. "Doctor! You told me she'd be okay!" The officers pushed him against the wall as he began to resist again. He groaned in pain, and the chairs squeaked against the tile as they struggled.

1

THE LAST CHAPTER

GRINNING EAR TO EAR, I wave good-bye to the good-looking twenty-year-old young man driving away from me down our long driveway, the special one-in-seven-billion man who will be my husband in only thirty-nine days. I can't believe it! Adam Brands will be my husband. It blows my mind. He's perfect for me in every way—handsome, talented, homeschooled like me, and having aced college in three years, has already been accepted into med school. Adam enthusiastically waves his hand out of the open window of the two-door Honda as he drives away. I can just see the reflection of his broad smile in his rearview mirror. He *really* loves me.

Unbelievably, he's well-liked by both my parents. I never thought that would happen so easily, my parents being so different from each other. What Mom likes most about him is he comes from a stable Christian family, and he wants to have a large family, like his parents. Adam's a middle child of a dozen, whereas I'm the oldest of eight. I think Dad's more excited about him being a gun enthusiast and a fellow prepper than he is about him being accepted into med school and aspiring to become a fellow physician. My Dad is much more impulsive than Mom, and a dreamer, like Adam. They're always nudging everyone around them out of their comfort zones.

What I like most about Adam is something altogether different. The only thing Adam does better than talk is listen. Gazing into his deep blue eyes, I feel like we could talk forever. And he writes just as eloquently as he talks. Pages and pages of the loveliest cursive, launching butterfly after butterfly into my heart. He's so thoughtful. He's amazing. Since we're waiting till marriage to kiss, talking and writing is all we get to do, so we do a lot of it.

He so much enjoyed coming over to pour through the magazines and catalogs that just came in the mail, and my favorite websites, filled with pics of tuxes and wedding dresses, comparing prices. I've got my favorite dress picked out, but he doesn't know which one it is.

He disappears down the drive and over the hill with a twangy beep of his Honda horn. I stand and stare at the horizon, a faint smile upon my freckled face, longings and dreams bursting in my strawberry heart.

Under my left arm, I have one of the magazines rolled up. I open it to the page with the marker clipped to it, uncap it, and circle my favorite dress. I made him think I hadn't made up my mind which was my favorite. I want it to be a surprise. The first time he will see my wedding dress is when he sees me walking down that aisle with my dad.

"You gonna stare down that driveway and spin that ring around your finger all day, or you gonna come lose in a game of horse?"

I turn to Danny, irritated that he dares interrupt my euphoric moment. "What?"

"You're always messing with your engagement ring." Danny bounces the ball toward me. "Come lose to your little brother."

I catch the ball and bounce it back to him, ignoring his invitation. Mom comes out of the side door of our house holding Joey on her hip.

"Mom, do I really have to wait thirty-nine more days to get married? We've waited so long."

"You better pick your dresses and tuxes quick, or you're gonna wait longer than that." She hands one-year-old Joey to eight-year-old Gracie, who takes him to the swing set in the back yard. Taking the Ziploc bag of Oreo cookies from her clenched teeth, Mom says, "It'll be here before you know it—"

"But if I know he's the one, why wait?"

Mom unscrews the cap on her spring water and heads toward her lawn chair. "Your Dad and I asked the same question a thousand times during our engagement." I cross my arms over my chest and turn back toward the driveway. "Be patient," she says. "A good catch like Adam is worth waiting for."

"Let's pretend," Danny proposes, bouncing the basketball toward me again, "that if you beat me in horse, you can get married tomorrow. But if you lose, you've got to wait till you're nineteen." Danny, for all his over-bearing boyishness, knows how to push my buttons.

"You're on, loser."

Within ten minutes, I am one anxious shot away from losing this lousy game of horse. Danny bounces the ball toward me for what he teases will be my final shot when I hear the roar of Dad's SUV barreling down the driveway. I turn and gasp at the sight of his shattered windshield.

Danny sees him and exclaims, "What in the world!"

Dad's beeping horn and damaged SUV intrude as uncomfortably into our otherwise lovely day as a curse word in an Easter sermon. Mother, who has been enjoying her Oreos and the playing children from the comfort of her lawn chair, is alarmed by the honk of Dad's horn and the strain of his engine. She stands and walks slowly to the driveway, the little ones approaching cautiously in her wake.

"Sophia, Danny, back away from the car." She waves Danny and me off the driveway and onto the grass.

Jimmy, who is fifteen and the oldest of the boys, comes running up out of the woods, his survival knife on his right hip and his orange-tipped air soft rifle in a sling over his shoulder. He arrives just as Dad skids to a stop underneath the basketball hoop.

"Whoa!" Jimmy exclaims, running toward the vehicle.

We are aghast at the cracks of the windshield spreading across the glass like lightning across a threatening sky. A rectangular hole punctures the right passenger window—the shape a brick might leave. There are several dents in the hood the shape of a hammer's head. This was no fender bender gone awry. I wrinkle up my nose at the burnt rubber smell of either his brakes or the skidding of his tires.

Dad sticks his head out of the window. "Move out of the way!" He reverses the SUV to our white box trailer next to the shed, and then gets out and begins to affix the trailer to the hitch.

Mother gasps when she sees Dad's arm. Blood streaks across his right forearm and down his fingers. A fresh wound still dribbles blood down the right side of his scalp. "Oh, honey! What happened?"

He is silent as he hurriedly connects the box trailer's wires to the SUV's plug on the bumper. His lips mumble inaudibly, as if praying, or mulling over different scenarios in his mind.

"What in the world happened?" Jimmy inquires.

"Dad, are you okay?" Anna-Lee approaches in jaw-gaping awe.

Dad doesn't answer our questions directly, but shouts, "Everybody come here!"

My jittery heart begins to palpitate with Dad's reluctance to immediately explain what had happened.

Jimmy, the most inquisitive of the boys, steps closer to the vehicle to examine the cracked windshield. Always drawn to controversy and danger, with wonder he examines the shards of glass scattered across the front seats. He opens the side door, reaches in, and pulls out the red brick that must have caused the damage. He takes a look into the backseat. "Who bled in the backseat?"

"What?" I take a step closer to peer over Jimmy's shoulder. "Dad?"

"That was someone I helped rescue from a beating outside of the Gun Depot."

Blood in the backseat?

Dad takes a deep breath. "I learned this morning on the radio that the dollar started plummeting into a major nose dive. It looks like it started in China. Maybe Russia. International markets are abandoning the dollar. Loans are being called. The dollar's crashing. Probably for good."

"The stock market started a correction two days ago," Mom, always the optimist, reminds him. "Big deal. It always comes back up."

"We've never gone through anything like this."

Danny scrunches up his nose like he doesn't understand. "What?"

Dad dabs the blood off his arm with his shirt. "Regardless of the reasons, everybody's panicking. Looting's everywhere and law enforcement's missing in action."

My mind is still fixed on the eerie image in Dad's SUV. The familiar food stains on the gray bucket seat, the children's book on the floor, the candy wrapper in the door, and in the midst, a congealed pool of blood from a stranger. A panic comes over me, causing my heart to speed up and then drop, replicating a dreadful sinking feeling in my chest. My skin breaks out in a sweat. My vision tunnels. I have this haunting feeling that hundreds of armed hoodlums, who bore of playing the "knock-out game" one victim at a time, are heading this way, looking to wreak some major carnage on people and property.

"Riots and looting happens in big cities, Dad," Anna-Lee objects, "not in small town Ohio."

"Well, half our city's on some kind of government handout, and apparently learning their government checks are postponed indefinitely has a lot of folks blaming the government. In addition, there was a prison break at the Eraflew Pen." He's referring to the state prison twenty minutes southwest of here.

Jimmy points into the back seat of the car with a big grin on his face, which seems out of place given the circumstances. "What's in that box?"

Father sighs. "That was going to be your birthday present, if we were going to have your party . . . "

Jimmy takes a long, thin white box out of the backseat, lays it on the ground and opens it. "You didn't!" he exclaims, lifting out a Ruger 10/22 rifle with a wooden stock. The other boys, Danny and Eli, walk up to admire the weapon, though Jimmy doesn't let them touch it.

My rage kindles as I see Jimmy turn the rifle over in his hands to venerate it from every angle.

"I can't believe it!" Jimmy grins ear to ear.

"Happy birthday, son."

"Did you get any ammo?"

Father removes a small box of ammo from his pocket. "Only fifty rounds. I want to work on gun safety first. We'll get more . . . " He bends down to look in the side mirror, and tends to a small gash in his scalp.

I can't believe Father would give Jimmy, of all people, a real gun! I march up to Dad. "How could you do that?"

"I didn't get a chance to talk with her about it beforehand," Mom explains.

I turn to Mom. "You knew about this?"

Dad furrows his brow and stares into my eyes. "Sophia, it's not up to you."

I turn and stomp off toward the house in a rage.

"Sophia?" Mother calls after me.

"Stop, Sophia!" Father orders. "I need your help packing the box trailer. My priority is to keep my family safe—"

"Is that why you bought Jimmy a gun?" I turn and stomp into the house. "On their birthday, no less."

I glance at Jimmy angrily as I march into the garage. Jimmy blushes at my outburst, and, ashamed, slowly puts his rifle back in its box. Dad's impulsive purchase will bring out the worst of my immature, careless brother, I just know it.

I walk through the door and sit on the floor next to the open door, quite beside myself with frustration and disappointment. And fear. I hate guns.

"Would you please tell me what's going on?" Mom's voice is frantic. She reaches down and takes up little one-year-old Joey in her arms.

"Why can't we have Jimmy's party?" Danny wonders.

"Come close." Father takes a deep breath. His words are sharp and unbending. "I'm afraid we have to leave. Just until things settle down . . ."

I overhear him from inside the open door. *Leave?* I grow even more anxious at his caustic tone and drastic remedy. *I'm supposed to get married in 39 days! I can't just leave.*

"Hon, you're over-reacting." Mom draws closer to him, the doubt palpable in her tone and demeanor.

"You don't understand." He takes a knee and speaks more calmly. "There's bloodshed everywhere."

Gracie and Jimmy say the word at the same time: "Bloodshed?" Gracie mutters it with trepidation. Jimmy says it with adventure lust.

Faith Victoria wraps her arms around Mom's waist, a fearful grimace on her round facial features. Six-year-old Faith, by far, has the most sensitive constitution among us. She is easily moved to weeping by fear, grief, or even the mildest of scoldings. Mother gently teases a blonde curl behind her ear. "It's okay, sweetheart." I can hear the quiver in Mom's voice. She hugs little Joey just a little tighter.

"Listen carefully to my instructions." Even Joey, still in Mother's arms, grows still, awaiting Dad's orders. Faith nervously sucks a finger of one hand while clasping Mother's shirt with the other. Jimmy draws near, holding his boxed Ruger. "We need to leave for our hunting cabin as soon as possible. We've prepared for this, but we all need to work together and fill this trailer with everything we'll need to survive . . ."

Survive? Who would have thought just ten minutes ago that we'd be worried about what we'd need to do to survive? My, how fragile everything suddenly appears. The urgency swells within my chest, suddenly making me feel breathless. With my face dripping with tears, I rush upstairs to avoid Dad and Jimmy as they head toward the house, vengeance in my heart. My absence, however, is only temporarily tolerated.

We rush about the home and the shed, following Dad's hasty instructions. Jimmy fetches the ammo. Faith throws the sleeping bags and pillows down the stairs into the foyer, then carries them out to the trailer. Eli and Gracie stack frozen food into coolers. Danny retrieves the five-gallon buckets of stored rice and beans from the basement. I am responsible for getting the tools, the fuel, the candles and lanterns, and the water purification tablets into the trailer. Anna-Lee carefully loads our box trailer with about a hundred quarts of vegetables, canned from our garden over several years.

Dad rushes inside to gather his four guns from the gun safe to put them safely in our box trailer, but he cannot locate the key that's necessary to open the combination safe. As he searches the drawers around his bedroom and bathroom, I hear Mom following on his heels, yapping out questions faster than Dad can answer.

"You're over-reacting," Mom criticizes him. "You always think something bad's gonna happen—"

"Have you heard a word I've said? It *is* happening! Right now!"

Dad comes running out of the garage. "Hey! Kids! Does anyone know where the gun safe key is?"

I step between them, holding two red five-gallon gas canisters, my magazine still rolled up under my left arm. "Dad, I'm supposed to get married in 39 days."

"Just do what I told you to do, Sophia!"

There are tears in my eyes. "But Dad! What about Adam?"

He turns to me. "I'm so sorry, Sophia. Hopefully everything will still work out." He takes the magazine out from under my arm, and points at me with it. "But I need your help right now. Pack this trailer as quickly and efficiently as you can . . ."

Mom grows more critical in her tone. "You always think something bad's going to—"

"Yeah, you said that," Father interrupts. He sighs wearily and hands my magazine to me. I let it drop to the ground. "Now go pack the clothes, Kate! Please."

Mom stomps back into the home, still holding Joey on her hip. Seeing the grimace on Dad's face, I can tell he has accepted the fact that he will have to apologize later for raising his voice. I bend down and rip out a page from the magazine, the page with the dress I picked. I quickly fold it and put it into my pocket as I rush to the shed to grab the last five-gallon can of fuel, and set it in the back of the trailer.

Dad sees me packing in the last of the fuel containers. "Make sure the fuel is in the middle along with the ammo. The food buckets and other supplies should be on the sides of the trailer." He turns toward the home, mumbling, "I've got to find that key. Does anyone know where the bronze key is to the gun safe?"

"Why do you want the fuel in the middle, Dad? Shouldn't we put the fuel containers in the back by the door?"

Dad ignores my inquisitiveness, and heaves a deep breath as children pass him to set their goods in the back of the trailer. "Everybody! Hurry up and get in the car!"

Yep, he'll apologize to all the kids once we're in the car.

On my way into the house, I hear Jimmy ask, "Can I run inside to get my sword and my—?"

"No!"

"But Dad, it'll just take a—"

"No! Finish what I told you to do, then get in the car. Have you seen the key to the safe?"

Mom comes out the side door lugging a large suitcase on wheels. Joey follows close behind.

"Did you find the key?"

She shakes her head. "No. I looked everywhere you would've kept it . . ."

I rush to pack in the last of the garden tools and vegetable seeds. Then I help the younger ones lift two coolers of frozen meat into the box trailer.

Dad puts several more buckets of food into the SUV, plants his hands on his hips and looks around with frustration.

"Be patient." Mom stands in front of him. "Everyone's moving as fast as they can—"

A noise in the distance distracts them. Dad's eyes widen, and he turns southeast, toward the city.

Mother's eyes fix on the horizon. "Is that smoke?"

"From several fires, it looks like." Dad points to several lines of smoke that ascend skyward. "Downtown's burning." He pauses.

"Adam!" I see Adam's Honda puttering over the hill and down our driveway. He's driving faster than expected.

He gets out and walks up to Dad. "I can't make it home. I can't—"

"I know," Father says, setting a hand on his shoulder.

"What's going on?" I ask Adam.

"It's what I said," Dad answers. "Downtown's burning—"

"Shh." Adam quietens us. "Did you hear that?"

"What?"

"Shh. Listen."

Anna-Lee sets a box full of canned vegetables in the box trailer. "There's two more downstairs," she tells me. "Hey, Adam. What are you—?"

"Quiet," I interrupt her, my ears searching for whatever it is that arrested Adam's attention.

A moment's silence reveals what he heard, making my heart pound once again from adrenaline. It sounds like gunfire. I hope the wind is playing tricks on me, but the furrows on Dad's brow make me feel naïve.

Mom fearfully grasps Dad's hand.

"It's nothing we don't deserve." Dad's eyes search the horizon. "Could be our nation's last chapter."

Mom orders the kids to get in the SUV. She buckles little Joey into the backseat.

Upon Father's instructions, Adam fetches an armful of loose tools from some drawers and cabinets.

"That's all the food," Danny says as he and I lift a heavy plastic bin full of rice bags into the rear of the box trailer. His voice is strong and gruffer than normal, as if he is attempting to reassure us with his feigned confidence. With his square jaw and short blond hair, he has the look of an injured Junior Varsity football player who inflates his abilities to the coach to be allowed to stay in the game. "Anything else, Dad?"

"I can't fit this in!" Anna-Lee is unable to find room for the last box of canned goods.

"I'll pack it." Dad trots to the back of the trailer and points to the SUV. "Get everyone in the car."

While Dad gets in the box trailer to move things further back, Jimmy sets two heavy green metallic boxes of ammunition on the ground, turns, and sprints past me back into the house.

"Where are you going?" I ask him. He disappears into the side door.

Dad hears the side door slam shut. "Who went back inside?"

"Jimmy," I answer.

"Get him, Sophia. We're leaving!" Mom cranks the SUV while Dad recruits Anna-Lee to help him better situate the boxes and buckets in the trailer.

I head toward the side door to fetch Jimmy when I hear something that instantly chills my blood. It sounds like gunfire coming from just over the hill of our cul-de-sac!

I run back into the driveway and look toward the road, my mind buzzing with panic. *That was close.*

Mother takes a step away from the vehicle, a horrified look on her face as she fixes her gaze toward the end of our driveway. "Honey?"

"I heard it!"

"That was in our subdivision!" she exclaims. "We've got to get out of here."

"But Jimmy's still inside," I object.

"I'll get him." Mom bolts toward the house.

A beat-up car breaks to a stop by the mailbox in our cul-de-sac. Four armed men exit, measuring up our home like hungry wolves checking out an injured deer. Father reaches into his ankle holster and removes his concealed carry 9 mm Kahr handgun. He keeps looking back at us, then at the four men. One of the four is studying us through binoculars.

Mother rushes inside the home yelling, "Jimmy!"

The older kids in the SUV see the threat and come spilling out of the SUV. Anna-Lee commands our blue-eyed mutt, Lucy, to get into the SUV with the little ones. She slams the door shut.

"What do we do, Mr. Johnston?" Adam asks.

"Where's Jimmy's Ruger?" Dad keeps his eyes fixed on the four men.

"I don't know," Danny responds.

"He must have taken it inside with him," Anna-Lee speculates.

Father takes the small box of ammo out of his pocket and hands it to Adam. "Find Jimmy and load this into his Ruger 10/22, please." I wince of the very sight of that box of ammunition. I've never been a fan of weapons and bullets. It always made me nervous to be near something that could explode.

"Yes, sir." Adam takes it and disappears into the side door of the home.

"That's our way out!" Danny motions down our driveway toward the cul-de-sac.

Taking cover behind the corner of the trailer, Dad wonders aloud, "Why are they bypassing every home in our neighborhood to harass *us*?"

Father chambers a round in his 9, raises his handgun, and fires a shot into the air. "There's nothing here worth getting killed over!" he screams at the hoodlums.

Upon hearing the gunshot, I place my hands over my ears. I wasn't prepared for the blast of that bullet. The four men by the road also jolt and fall to the ground. I think I see the reflection of the sun off a scope lens by the mailbox.

"Get down!" Dad says.

The sunny field of green grass and spring-budded trees appear inappropriate for the vast gap that separates us from the indecisive hoodlums. Danny and Anna-Lee duck behind the tire of the trailer, but my feet are stuck in concrete. I can't move. Father reaches into the white box trailer into the ammo box labeled "9 mm" and grabs a fistful of bullets. One of the four armed men bellows out an order to the others. Then a shot whizzes by us. It sounds like it was aimed high.

Dad drops to a knee, aiming his 9 at them. "Get everyone in the car and leave, Sophia."

"Wha—?"

"Now!"

"Leave? Without you?"

Father takes a knee and fires once. He ducks behind the box trailer. He sets his fistful of bullets on the ground.

I look down and see that the page with the picture of my wedding dress has fallen out of my pocket. Several of Dad's dropped bronze bullets appear to frame the picture of the model in my dress. Why does the worst of all my fears seem to be mocking me?

Dad grows impatient with my carelessness. "Quickly, Sophia!"

"What about Mom?"

"Leave—now!"

My efficiency only slightly improves with my father's scolding. My icy limbs don't appear to function properly. Everything moves in slow motion for a few seconds as a simultaneous rush of anxiety and sluggishness handicaps me.

Another gunshot resounds. Closer this time. Then another. Blam! The bullet scrapes the concrete beside me, casting sparks into the backyard. My heart skips a beat, and my head spins.

I look down our driveway and am horrified to see the four armed gunmen begin to creep toward us, crouching low, aiming their weapons at us.

One of the gunmen runs behind the line of spruce trees that separate our ten acres from our neighbor's land. I hear distant shouting, like one of them is yelling at the others. The sharp blast of a gunshot precedes the metallic *smack* of the bullet against the box trailer, right by Dad's head.

Father flashes a furious, violent snarl, such as I have never seen. Out of the corner of his eye, he sees us ducking, trembling for fear. "Don't be afraid!" he shouts in a gravelly voice.

Father quickly fires two shots on the run as he races into the front yard to take refuge behind a large birch tree, I presume, to draw the attacker's gunfire away from us. Bullets whiz past him and strike the ground at his feet, throwing dirt onto his legs.

To my horror, I witness him take a bullet in the upper abdomen— I gasp and scream, long and shrill.

He lands hard on his back. For a second, he is motionless. Then he rolls and claws for the fallen weapon.

"Dad!"

A bullet speeds just over my head. I peek around the box trailer to see Dad crawl for the cover of the tree, gasping for air. He leans with his back to the tree. His face quickly drains of color, turning an ashen gray. A circular patch of red spreads outward from the center of his shirt.

One of the kids opens the side door of the SUV, and our blue-eyed mutt Lucy, who was shut inside, rushes around the SUV toward the attackers, barking aggressively. She quickly takes a bullet that sends her spinning to the ground. Whimpering pitifully, her tumbling comes to a stop beside Father's feet.

One of their bullets hits the concrete right beside Danny's head. He rolls behind the cover of the box trailer wheel, trembling with dread, trying to squint away the concrete dust out of his eyes.

Finally, Mom rushes out of the house with Jimmy. He holds his Ruger box, has a sword in its scabbard under his belt, and wears his camouflage backpack.

Adam has already begun to load the 22 caliber bullets into the Ruger's mag. He drops to a knee in the garage and sets the box down too hard. Bullets scatter across the garage concrete floor. Jimmy takes the Ruger out of the box as Mom begins to fill the second ten round clip.

The SUV's engine is still running, but now smoke emanates from the hood, and I hear a hissing sound coming from under the car. Bullets strike the SUV's windows, sending shards of glass upon the little ones. They squeal for fear and struggle to crawl out of the side door. They huddle around me, ducking behind the SUV.

Mom inserts the magazine into the Ruger and fires at the intruders, halting their progress to the home and forcing them to take cover.

Mom points to the woods. "Run!"

I bend down to pick up Joey when a bullet whistles right past my ear, causing me to fall for fear and for the sharp pain in my ear, and it pierces the rear window of the SUV. Joey tumbles out of my arms to the ground, but leaps quickly to his feet. He climbs onto my back, crying. I struggle to stand. "Hold on, Joey." Carrying Joey and dragging Faith by the hand, I rush for the better cover of the brick wall of our home at the far edge of the driveway. The little ones follow me.

With all the little ones secure behind the corner of the home, I peak around to check on the others. With Mom providing cover, Jimmy grabs our two black and red "bug-out bags" full of emergency supplies and runs to me. He sets both bags down at my feet with the order, "Run to the woods!" He turns and runs back to Mom.

My eyes fix on Dad. With his back to the tree and his life ebbing, he angles his pistol toward the intruders and pulls his trigger several times. Bullets strike beside him, creating long brown divots in the green grass. A red, wet spot in the center of his shirt grows in diameter as his breathing rate increases.

Danny yells something at me as he runs toward me, but I cannot make out his words because of the whistling of the bullets around us.

I see Jimmy arguing with Mom and Adam for a moment. They scream at him, and wave him toward the backyard.

One of the intruders drops to a knee and takes careful aim at Mom, waiting for her to expose herself around the brick corner of the garage to take another shot at them.

I see Father has run out of bullets. The slide on his semi-automatic handgun is in its posterior position. He lowers it with his thumb, and acting like he's got bullets, he exposes himself toward the intruder that's aiming at Mom. Dad points his empty gun at him, and the intruder shifts his aim and shoots Dad in the chest.

"Come on!" Jimmy shouts as he picks up the two bug-out bags at my feet and sprints toward the tree line. The others need no encouragement to follow him.

"We can't leave Mom and Adam!" I object. I see Mom has begun to load a mag while Adam fires at the intruders.

"They will follow us!"

Holding Faith's hand and carrying Joey, I peek around the corner of the home to watch Adam emptying his clip at the approaching assailants.

Anna-Lee practically drags poor Eli by the arm, yelling, "Run!"

Suddenly, I feel Faith's body jerk violently and then go frighteningly limp. I turn to see her head drooping toward the ground. "Faith? Faith!" Her legs lose their strength, and holding her hand, I ease her down to the ground. Her eyes are wide open, yet lifeless. Her mouth is gaping. Blood streaks down the side of her head. As soon as I see the blood, I know I should have left when Mother told me to run. I tarried for fear, frozen with indecision, and now Faith bleeds for it. I see her lips contort into a grimace, and she takes a deep breath and blinks. Then just as quickly, she's unconscious again.

A bullet strikes the corner of the brick wall right beside my head, sending shards of red brick against my face and neck. I turn and rush to follow the others as Jimmy leads the way across the field toward the woods behind our home. Jimmy is carrying the heaviest load but runs faster than all of us. I shuffle along as fast as I can, carrying little Joey on my back and unconscious Faith in my arms, screaming her name. "Faith! Faith!" I feel Joey bouncing as he tries to hold on, and I hope he doesn't fall off. Shots continue to ring out behind me, and I worry that any moment a projectile will pierce my body and snatch the life right out of me. As I gasp with fear and as my legs run as fast as they ever have, the hunger for air suddenly overwhelms me. I begin to hyperventilate, longing desperately for the cover of the trees and the shadows of the forest.

At the tree line a hundred yards away, we are angled away from the commotion in the driveway and unable to see the box trailer. From the cover of the bushes, we discover to our horror that Mom and Adam are not following us. I hear the faint echo of the cruel beasts whooping and cheering their payday.

The children weep pitifully.

"Shh," Jimmy urges us, pulling Gracie from the open field into the bushes. We see smoke blowing across our back yard from what must be the damaged engine of our SUV. Mom and Adam are nowhere to be seen.

"Mommy!" Gracie screams long and shrill. She is so loud that Jimmy puts his hand over her mouth to quiet her. When I see Faith's pale face and half-closed eyes, my fingers tingle, my stomach grows nauseous, and my vision darkens. I breathe deeply to keep myself conscious.

Now is not the time to freak out.

Anna-Lee realizes that Faith is injured. She rushes over to me, but before she can speak, I see a man come around the corner of the home and take three quick shots in our direction. We duck as bullets whistle past our heads.

We turn and run clumsily through the brush down a deer trail toward the narrow creek in the valley of our wooded property. Eli keeps falling, and Jimmy keeps sternly reproving him for it.

Rain begins to fall when we reach the creek, large scattered drops at first, cold and sporadic, and then smaller drops, denser, that smack the skin as if in punishment. The trees bend with the wind's fury.

Weeping, Gracie holds a backpack Jimmy handed her in the chaos. Oblivious, she drags it into the creek.

"Get it out of the water!" Jimmy shouts at her.

We sprint like mad down the shallow limestone creek bed until we are deep in a dense thicket within the hundreds of acres of forest next to our home. Jimmy raises a hand, motioning for the others to stop. Everyone except Jimmy is freaking out, crying and wailing, gasping for air.

"Shh! Quiet!" Jimmy orders.

I put my ear to Faith's lips. She's unconscious, but still breathing. With her eyes involuntarily open, she has the look of death on her.

The gunfire has finally ceased. I think I hear a woman's scream in the distance, but I'm unsure if it's that or the whimpering of the little ones, or maybe the wind playing tricks on me.

My thoughts are distracted by the fiery burn on my shins and ankles. The stinging nettles on the creek bank have peppered me with their poison.

2

OF STINGING NETTLES
AND JEWELWEED

I STARTLE AWAKE WITH A jolt. It is dark, and it takes me a moment to get my bearings. I am just outside the entrance to our crude tepee shelter. My heart races and palms are sweaty, more from my troubling dream than from the nightmarish reality to which I awake. My legs are numb from the way I have been sitting, leaning against our hastily erected shelter. I reposition my rash-covered legs with a grunt. My hand still grasps a sheathed survival knife that was inside one of the two backpacks with which we managed to escape. My dreams are frighteningly vivid, playing the scenes of the horrifying first day over and over again. I search in my mind's eye for something I could have done differently, longing desperately for a reason why.

I recall the horror in the faces of my brothers and sisters as they grabbed what they could from the bullet-ridden box trailer and sprinted for the tree line. I cannot forget the way Faith's body jerked after the blast of the stranger's rifle, and how she flopped limply in my arms as I ran carrying her. Many, many nights I have stayed awake praying for Faith to recover and begging God for Joey to survive the severe diarrhea he endured after drinking dirty creek water. And their constant whimpering and whining – it haunted me for weeks, testing my patience. All of the powerful emotions, made all the more raw from overwork and lack of sleep, flood my senses like one overwhelming nightmarish montage.

I am still in a state of shock at how much we have lost, and how helpless we are in the belly of this damp and dark, pitiless and comfortless forest.

I hear gunfire faintly in the distance, toward the city. It startles me from my dreamy stupor, and I turn to the eastern horizon. The glow of a hundred fires, barely visible through the dense woodland, and the occasional clatter of gunfire are grim reminders that our once thriving city has been destroyed by the very people who once called it home. I don't know if I'll ever fully understand what precipitated the rioting and anarchy, but I suspect the ones who pioneered it regret the aftermath. Even thieves hate theft when they are the ones targeted for plunder.

The quarter moon illuminates the fog, providing an eerie backdrop to a windless forest buzzing with ten thousand insects and the mysterious cracks of twigs and the growls of shadowy beasts all around us. The fog appears alive as it drifts slowly up the tree-covered banks on both sides of our shelter, as if they are warring spirits struggling for control over the eight children who've made a new home out of a leaky, tarp-draped tepee that barely insulates them from the wet and the cold.

We were able to scavenge these tattered old tarps that Dad used to cover the stacks of firewood behind our home. They didn't protect the wood very well; it all rotted from the rain dripping through the leaky old things. However, wrapping them around our triangular frame of tree branches provides us with some protection from the chilly night winds, if not all of the raindrops.

I breathe deeply, reminding myself that I am the oldest of these eight children, and my brothers and sisters need me. I am in charge. I always loved being in charge, but now I feel like I'm the one left holding the car keys after a wreck on the interstate, and I wish someone more capable had the lead.

I crawl inside the shelter to see Joey crying softly in Anna-Lee's arms, struggling to rest. I hang the holstered knife on a branch I've situated within our shelter's frame. Anna-Lee tries in vain to quiet little Joey.

Faith lies beside Anna-Lee, closer to the fire. In the dim light of the fading embers, Anna-Lee's eyes flicker.

I reach into my pocket and pull out the folded page from the magazine of models in wedding dresses. I carefully unfold it and study the now-familiar page of beautiful white dresses. I study the face of the model wearing the dress I picked. I wonder what she was thinking when she flashed that Hollywood smile. This would have been *my* wedding dress. My heart throbs with grief, and I wonder what in the world has become of Adam.

"Stop looking at it." Anna-Lee's whisper takes me by surprise.

"What?"

"You're like Frodo with his ring, always obsessed with staring at that picture when you think no one's looking."

I blush at her criticism.

"And you're always spinning your engagement ring around your finger."

I realize I am doing it, and stop. "Do I really do that a lot?"

She nods. "Shh. Not so loud."

"Sorry."

"Let's focus not on what we lost, but on all that we have to be thankful for," she whispers. "All the kids are still alive. We have some food—"

"Barely."

"And we'll have a good night's sleep if you don't wake anybody up," she whispers. "Please, keep your voice down."

I sigh deeply and lie back down. She's right. I desperately long for how things used to be, and this longing shackles me with discontentment for how things are. I just cannot let go of my dream, however unlikely and elusive it appears. I refold the magazine page and put it back in my pocket.

I snuggle close to Faith, lying on my side with my back to the stone fire pit.

I stroke Faith's hair, careful not to disturb the scab that has formed where the bullet grazed her on the first day. Her fever has broken, and she's damp with sweat. Her calm, steady breathing, backdropped by the crackles of the fading embers, soothes my rattled nerves.

I reach into my pocket again, and by the light of the embers, admire the magazine page of dresses where I had circled my favorite and written, "This is the one" in black marker.

"You don't have to hide it."

It's Anna-Lee.

"What?"

She doesn't answer.

Ashamed, I fold it up and put it back into my pocket. I *am* obsessed. It's all I can think about.

"You can talk to me, you know."

I turn away from the fire. "I know." I take a deep breath. "I can't get out of my head how"—I suck in the smoky air and exhale unsteadily— "how in one minute our lives were so perfect, and in the next minute, everything was gone."

"We took a lot for granted." There is a melancholy tremor in her voice. "Life is fragile."

Joey's whimpering crescendos into a restless cry due to our whispered conversation. Anna-Lee jostles him comfortingly. "It's all right, buddy. Shh."

Jimmy rolls over toward the center of the shelter. "You gotta keep him quiet." The frustration is palpable in his sharp tone. As usual, his grip is firm around his sheathed sword. He is obsessed with always having it with him. That and the handmade bow and arrows he crafted, which Danny has in the lookout.

Anna-Lee responds with a harsh whisper, "Have pity. He misses his mother."

"But they might hear him." Jimmy's raised tone makes Joey cry even more loudly.

Jimmy's unjustified anger revives my offense. "You shouldn't have gone back into the house to get your coin collection—"

"Oh, please, not this again." Jimmy rolls his eyes.

"And that dumb ole' sword. We could've gotten out of there in time."

I hear Anna-Lee sigh heavily at my critical words, and I can sense her predictable reproofs bubbling to the surface. She bites her lip for a moment and then finally speaks, careful to keep her voice down. "Please stop bringing that up."

I turn to Anna-Lee. "Dad and Mom are gone, and for what? So Jimmy could fetch his pawn-shop, Pakistani-made sword? And his little box of trinkets and coins, while we were getting shot at?"

Jimmy grunts animatedly, his fury ebbing to the surface once again as it daily has in the month since the crisis began. "It's a real samurai sword! And it cost a hundred and ten dollars!"

"Shh," Anna-Lee pleads.

"Oh, it costs a lot more than that, Jimmy."

I don't share Anna-Lee's awareness of her volume, and the proximity of sleeping siblings. The little ones stir at my shouting.

I shake my head back and forth, upset at myself for being so impulsively loud with my screeching words.

"Now's not the time, Sophie," Anna-Lee whispers harshly. "Stop arguing. You're thinking only of yourself." I find this criticism unexpected, and from an unexpected source. I sit up and look at her, offended.

"Sophie doesn't have a mirror, only a magnifying glass," Jimmy comments. He struggles to his feet, making as much ruckus as he can, bumping into the wall of the tepee and stepping on Gracie's foot.

"Hey!" Gracie grabs her painful foot.

Jimmy snatches up his sword. He levels an index finger at me. "I told you, Dad said I could go back inside." He tightly grips his weapon, staring at me with murder in his eyes.

I am too hungry and tired to be intimidated. "Oh, did I forget to mention your shark's tooth and your fake arrowhead? All your little worthless treasures in that stupid ole' box."

The toddler's cries grow more troubled. "Shh!" Anna-Lee begs, her eyes darting back and forth from Jimmy to me. "Please."

All the little ones are either crying half asleep or awake and turning toward us. The strife threatens to awaken even Faith, who usually sleeps like a rock. Jimmy is completely oblivious to the welfare of his restless younger siblings, and it stimulates my guilt for starting the argument in the middle of the night.

Jimmy ducks underneath the flapping door of the torn and dilapidated brown tarp that covers our entrance. "I'm relieving Danny on watch. It's not like I'm gonna sleep anyway."

"Walk in the creek bed," Anna-Lee whispers to him.

"Footprints in the mud are easier to follow," I add, reaching to hold Faith's hand to try to settle her.

"Whatever you say, boss."

I listen carefully to his footsteps as he avoids the creek to take the far too thoroughly trodden trail up the steep hill toward our lookout, where the older boys take turns keeping watch for intruders. I hear him slide in the mud and catch himself on a fallen branch with a grunt.

I glance at Anna-Lee, a fire in my eyes and a snarl on my lips. "That boy!"

She flutters her long eyelashes thoughtfully, unintentionally informing me that she is frustrated with me.

I turn toward the dying embers, studying their orange glow. The little ones gradually begin to settle.

Momentarily, Anna-Lee breaks the silence. "A house divided against itself will not stand, Sophie."

"He lied, Anna-Lee. What he did cost Dad his life. Probably Mom and Adam, too."

"Sophie, if you would have left when Dad said to leave, instead of standing there in the driveway like a mannequin, then we'd be at the hunting cabin with all our supplies and full stomachs right now. So stop blaming Jimmy for what's partially your fault."

Her words pierce all my defenses and impale my heart like a sharp arrow. "*My* fault?"

"Some humility's in order. It's easier to give forgiveness when you realize how badly you need it."

My heart throbs painfully, snatching my breath away. I swallow hard. My mouth is dry as a desert.

If she only knew . . .

"You need to smooth things over with him, and stop being so critical."

I nod. She's right.

Eli stirs, crawls close to Anna-Lee, and snuggles up next to her. She sighs contentedly. He stretches and rests a hand on my leg, as if unconsciously wanting to let me know that he loves me too. In spite of all that has happened, I am pleased that he finds comfort in knowing I am here.

"We're still a family, Sophie."

I lie down and look up to see the thin wisp of smoke escape through the smoke hole in the top of our tarp tepee. I catch a glimpse of the pale moon through the foggy night air. I imagine God sits on the edge of His throne, looking down on us, watching us, studying us. Does He grieve with us over yesterday's loss? Is He repulsed by tomorrow's lack? Is He pleased with our living nightmare? Does He plot our pain, or does the devil—and who's in charge anyway? I know we have a loving heavenly Father; I just wonder what in the world He must be thinking.

I listen to Jimmy's trek up the muddy slope toward our camouflaged lookout on the hill. In a moment, I can make out his birdlike whistle through the cacophonous chirps, flutters, and pitter-patters of the forest night. With my adrenaline levels still high from the argument, I quietly exit the shelter and follow him.

Danny whistles back to Jimmy, and then Jimmy scoots up to where Danny is keeping watch.

I climb the slope on all fours and soon get close enough to overhear Danny say, "It's not Joey being too loud, it's you."

I approach quietly, thinking to spend the early dawn with the boys in the lookout. In spite of my suspicions of Jimmy's honesty, I long to smooth things over with him. The fog-covered horse field behind our house is only barely discernible through the oaks, maples, and blackberry bushes. The trees are still on this windless night, making the boys' conversation easy to overhear.

Jimmy asks, "See anything?"

"Several coyotes came running past me about an hour ago, yapping away. I was about to try to shoot them with the bow, but my aim stinks. I can barely pull it back. Can you loosen the tension?"

"No. It won't be powerful enough to kill a man if you loosen it. You just need to practice." He takes the bow in his hands and pulls it back several times. "We should trap the coyotes."

"If you leave them alone, they'll leave you alone."

"I don't want to leave them alone. I want to eat them. Do the math, Danny. We're gonna run out of food."

They are silent for a moment until Jimmy asks, "Hear any gunshots since you came on?"

"Not from our neighborhood."

"Maybe they're gone," Jimmy says optimistically. "We should go back to the house."

"Did you ask Sophie?"

Jimmy harrumphs with unconcealed spite. I am about to whistle to the boys to alert them of my approach when I hear Jimmy's harsh words: "Why does *she* suddenly become the master of the family?"

I freeze, feeling the quickened pulse in my temple as my bitterness rouses. I can barely make out their silhouettes in the foggy moonlight. I bite my lip in the shadows, tempted to upbraid Jimmy for his foolish criticism, but too curious to break my concealment.

"Mom and Dad always said that when they're gone, she is in charge. She's the oldest."

"Mom and Dad are gone, Danny."

"Exactly. And that's why Sophie's in charge." I hear Danny's noisy sigh, raspy and coarse since leaving the house without his asthma inhaler.

Jimmy motions toward the shelter. "You go get some sleep, bud. I'll take the rest of your night watch."

I quietly head back to the tepee, not wanting to be anywhere near my intolerable brother right now.

*   *   *   *   *

I awake to Anna-Lee's voice and the gentle sound of rain sprinkling against the tepee. She sings so pretty when she thinks no one is listening. It is a song I don't think I have ever heard.

You have been a shelter, Lord,
To every generation.

A sanctuary from the storm.

You have been a shelter, Lord.

I watch her through the entrance slit as she binds some branches to the shelter, trying to better camouflage our refuge from unwanted attention. The humid air accentuates her reddish-blonde curls so well. Mine looks like I've stuck my finger in a light socket—all frizz. Oh, I miss my bathroom, my coconut-scented shampoo, and my Paul Mitchell hair gel. What I wouldn't give for a hot bath, a bag of chips, and an hour of nothing to do.

Danny, since he spent most of the night in the lookout, is due a couple more hours' sleep. I exit the tepee quietly to see the girls gather around the small fire kindled in the stone circle about eight feet from the shelter, waiting for the boiled stream water to cool so they can drink it.

"Where are the boys?" I inquire.

"Hunting crawdaddies," Gracie informs me.

The cold drizzle is sporadic, and has not yet driven the kids back into the relative dryness of our shelter. With the temperatures dropping, I worry that the raindrops will soon harden to snow. The children would be entertained with the transition, but I know the whining it would elicit once their clothes were wet and muddy. Without the dependable comforts of home, a great deal of the cheer or misery of our mood depends on the unpredictable fluctuations characteristic of Ohio's spring season.

"Hey, guys, come here!"

It's Jimmy on the other side of the creek. Gracie stands. "What is it?"

"Come here. I want to show you something." Jimmy turns and heads back up to the lookout. We cross the creek by walking on the large tree that traverses it like a bridge, and we follow him up the steep, muddy trail. At the top, he leads us to where the deer trail spills out onto our horse field. He stops and points at the ground.

I gasp. Footprints.

"So close!" I exclaim.

He nods. "Three sets of foot prints. I'm telling ya, Sophie. This is the closest they've ever come to finding us. We've got to stop kindling a fire when the sky's blue. Only at night, and only when it's cloudy."

Our shelter is well hidden, embedded in a small wooded valley in the middle of a huge conglomeration of dead branches and thorn-bushes beside no easily traversable trail. But it's hard to camouflage eight kids. We leave footprints everywhere we go, we make quite a bit of noise, and, oh, do we love our campfires.

The wind is stronger on top of the hill, and the kids grow chilly in their damp clothes, so we head back down to the fire pit.

"Summer is coming." Eli flashes a predictable grin, showing his chattering teeth. He acts as if there's still something special about the summer season. I can think only of the steamy hot nights made more unbearable by the fire the little ones will demand in our small fire pit inside the tepee. With the batteries in the flashlight long since drained, they will doubtless beg for the light of the flames to provide security from the pitch blackness—and for protection from the hordes of mosquitoes we are certain to face. In the first few weeks when the night temperatures dropped into the fifties and even the forties, as happens in the early Ohio spring, talking and singing around the heat and light of the fire was one of the best parts of our day, but in the summer, the sweaty heat may eclipse any joy we get from the light.

Faith pulls a strip of worn tarp more tightly over her shoulders as she nudges closer to the fire. "At least in the summer, it won't rain as much, and we don't have to do school."

"We don't have to do school anyway." Gracie stacks flat pieces of rock on a fallen log nearby, while Joey playfully knocks them down.

"That's gonna change." Anna-Lee stirs the embers beneath the pan of cloudy creek water, which is propped up on two red bricks. "We will start school before long."

It has become a morning ritual for all of us to warm our hands over the fire after breakfast and talk about Mom and Dad and sweeter days until the water's boiled and cooled. Then I assign them their daily chores.

The first ray of the morning's sunshine breaks through the damp, gloomy gray and brings a smile to the little ones' faces. But the sunshine is only a blip in a sky full of increasingly gray clouds. It looks like it's going to be another chilly, windy day.

Jimmy plops down beside the fire and unties his muddy shoes. "It's rained for the last two hours," he gripes. "It would be my luck that Danny gets the dryness of the night, and out of the goodness of my heart, I cover his last three hours and God sprinkles ice water from the sky upon me constantly." He cackles disrespectfully.

He leans against the fallen tree beside our shelter and sets his rain-wrinkled feet up on a warm stone. He removes his hat and runs his fingers through his reddish-blond hair.

Gracie moves closer to the fire, holding little Joey. With Joey watching carefully, she points at one of the large round rocks that surround the fire pit. "Hot! Hot!" She touches the rock and pulls her hand back as if in pain. "No. Don't touch."

Joey shirks away from the rock. "Hot, hot," he says with his characteristic head bobbing. "Hot" was the first word he had ever said many months ago, and it never ceases to make the children cheer. They clap for him. He smiles, points to the fire, and repeats, "Hot, hot." Then he speaks his next favorite word. "Da da."

Eli grins and leans closer to him. "Da da?"

"Don't, Eli!" I blurt out, frustrated with his forgetfulness. "I've told you over and over. It makes Joey restless, and he looks around as if expecting you-know-who to show up any minute. Don't repeat that word when he says it."

Eli nods. "I forgot."

Anna-Lee unscrews a canteen and asks Gracie to hold it tightly. Eli holds the strip of hard plastic she had found, positioning it to act as a funnel. She wraps a strip of tarp around the pan's handle and then pours the warm water into the canteen. "Hold it still."

"Don't burn me," Gracie pleads.

"I won't. It's cooled off a little."

"I'm starving!" Jimmy exclaims. "What do we get this morning?"

"We each get six berries," I respond, "and one piece of deer jerky."

"I think the people that find the most berries should get a larger share," Jimmy suggests.

I ignore his self-serving comment and divvy out his portion of six berries. Counting two extra berries, I give them to him as a gesture of peace.

Jimmy winks and clucks his tongue in his cheek, acting like he deserved them. He shoves his berries into his mouth.

"Jimmy?"

He pauses to look at me as if he were observing a fly he considered swatting.

"Let's pray." Without waiting for Jimmy's typical smart-aleck comment, I begin, "Lord, bless this meal. Help us find some more food today. Thank you for the clouds this morning, allowing us to enjoy a good fire. In Jesus' name, amen."

Jimmy impales his strip of jerky on a stick and props it up with rocks so it hangs over the flame.

Danny crawls out of the tepee, squinting from the morning light.

"G'morning, Danny," Anna-Lee greets him lightheartedly as she gives little Joey some water carefully from the canteen. "Isn't it a little early for you to wake up?"

He takes a seat next to the fire and feigns a weary smile. "I smelt something good."

Jimmy repositions his jerky over the fire. "A little flame and smoke does wonders to a strip of stale meat, don't it?"

"Yep," Gracie agrees.

I hand Danny his portion of food. He devours his berries and tries to heat his strip of meat over the fire like Jimmy.

Anna-Lee notices that Eli still has not eaten his strip of jerky. "Eat it, Eli. You can't count on between-meal snacks to hold you over."

"It's rotten." He shakes his head with a frown on his face. "I don't like it."

"It's not rotten," I correct him. "Dad prepared it so it won't rot."

"Germs wouldn't touch it with a ten-foot pole," Jimmy comments.

Eli winces. "If it's so bad that germs won't eat it, then how can it be safe for us?"

Anna-Lee hands the canteen to Gracie, to begin its trek around the circle. "Eli, you've got to eat it."

"What kind of meat is it, anyway?" Gracie wonders.

Anna-Lee responds with cheer in her voice. "It's venison."

"Deer meat," Jimmy explains.

Eli frowns and offers his meat to Danny. "I don't like deer."

Danny reaches for it and, returning from the creek with another pot of water, I stop him. "No, Danny. He's the thinnest of us. He needs it more than anybody."

"Certainly more than you do." Jimmy ogles Danny's protuberant mid-section.

Danny grins and wiggles his stomach. "Slowly dissolving, isn't it?"

"Take a hundred years before anybody would notice." Jimmy clucks his tongue in his cheek.

"Hey, be nice," Anna-Lee scolds Jimmy.

"It's alright," Danny responds with a grin. "Jimmy would starve long before me, so I get the last laugh."

Danny and Jimmy chuckle at the joke, but I don't find it funny at all.

"Deer's yummy." Faith raises her eyebrows at Eli and nods enthusiastically. "You've gotta just chew it up good."

"It's not yummy to me," Eli insists.

"A deer was probably the first animal ever killed, when God made Adam and Eve's clothes," I say.

"I don't mind killin' 'em. It's eatin' 'em that makes me sick."

"But when God created the very first deer," I rebut, "He said it was good."

"That was before Adam and Eve sinned. Now it's disgusting. I'll wear a deer, but I ain't eatin' one."

"Look at me, Eli." Our eyes meet. "Adam's sin messed everything up, but I don't think it ruined the taste of deer meat. Now eat it."

"The Bible says, in everything give thanks," Anna-Lee says. "Take a bite and thank Him for it."

Eli cautiously takes a bite, and then scrunches up his nose. "Ew."

I see him gag and tell him, "Don't spit it out, don't spit—"

Too late. He has spit it out.

Tears come to his eyes. "It's yucky."

"Nowadays, I like to thank God even more for food that tastes bad," says Faith, "like those sour red blackberries. Then they don't taste quite so bad."

"I thank God all right." Eli nods. "I thank God He let me spit it out, 'cause it's really yucky. It's vulture food, not kid food."

Amidst the chuckles of the others, Jimmy says, "Don't worry, Eli. We'll catch some more crawdaddies today."

"Yeah." Gracie's countenance, like Eli's, is bright with anticipation.

Jimmy pats Eli on the shoulder. "I'll teach you how to catch 'em yourself. How's that?"

Eli smiles ear to ear. "Okay."

Danny lifts his pants leg to scratch a rash on his calf. "So, Sophie, how can we give thanks for stinging nettles?"

I take a deep breath. Answering questions about the suffering of others is easy, but when it's personal and painful, all my unsatisfying answers fall flat on their face.

"Quit doing that." Anna-Lee instructs Danny to stop scratching his rash. "It'll only make it worse."

"Jewelweed," I say. "That'll help keep the itching tolerable. My rash was horrible the first week."

"I'll get some jewelweed for you." Gracie leaps up and takes off toward the creek.

"That'll make it better." Faith follows her big sister toward the bubbling waters.

"Danny," Anna-Lee says, "it's not '*for* everything give thanks,' but '*in* everything give thanks.' Thank him *in* any circumstance, however bad."

"I found some!" Gracie and Faith return with exaggerated excitement. They act as if they had just discovered buried treasure, but truthfully, this stuff is more valuable than gold when you have a smattering of stinging nettle blisters on your legs. Faith has crushed the lush green vegetation in her palms. "Here you go, Danny."

Danny takes a clump of the moist plant flesh and rubs it against his rash. Momentarily, he smiles. "Ah, thanks."

"You're welcome."

Danny turns his eyes to heaven. "Thank you, God, for jewelweed."

Gracie sits on the ground next to Eli. "You always find the remedy for stinging nettles right near the stinging nettles. Cool, huh?"

Faith nods. "Yep. They grow together."

Danny looks down at the soft substance between his fingers, emanating from the crushed stems. "That's better."

Jimmy begins to rhythmically cock and release the bolt of the AR-15. In a moment, it begins to irritate me, and he earns my laser stare.

He winks at me to spite me. "I love the sound of the bolt release shoving a bullet into the chamber, don't you?" Jimmy says, his eyes all sparkly. "Danny, ain't that the most beautiful sound in the world?"

"Yeah." Danny grins and extends a fist toward Jimmy, and they tap fists amiably.

"The ding of a microwave oven," Gracie says, "when the popcorn's done."

"Or a long burp after drinking down a root beer float." Eli licks his lips.

Anna-Lee steps around a tree carrying several small sticks. "Amazing Grace in four-part harmony at our family reunion. That's the most beautiful sound in the world." She's always careful to be respectful when discussing sacred topics, providing a nice balance to Jimmy's increasingly careless irreverence.

"Sophie," Jimmy says, "we haven't had looters at our house in two days. Danny and I believe we should go back. There's stuff we need that we might find there. We might find the gun safe key Dad lost. Then we can get some guns to defend ourselves."

"Yeah," Danny agrees. "A handmade bow and arrow in the lookout is a joke if you see a couple guys approaching with guns."

I shake my head vigorously. "No. The fires are still raging in town, Jimmy, and there's constant gunfire. We can't go back."

Danny wipes his hands onto his pants legs. "We haven't heard a gunshot or seen a looter in our neighborhood for two days and nights."

Anna-Lee nods. "We need a bigger pan to boil water in. Maybe we'll find some water purification tablets in the garage."

"We've been boiling water just fine," I object.

"But it takes a fire to do that, and with the weather warming up, the sky will get clearer more often. And—"

"I know," I interrupt her. "I know."

I cannot bear the thought of going back to the house. The memory of that first day is still so painful.

"Maybe we will find a leftover antibiotic for Faith?" Anna-Lee's point is the best one so far.

Joey walks over and plops down into Gracie's lap. "If we can find some diapers," she says, "then maybe poopie-pants here won't stink so badly."

"And we need a new Bible with big letters," Eli adds.

"For devotions," Faith chimes in.

The little New Testament that was in the bug-out backpack has such tiny print that it is difficult to read by firelight.

I study Jimmy, trying to discern the motive behind his prickly sneer. Why do I get the impression he's scheming something?

Halfway through a heavy sigh, I say, "Diapers and a large print Bible. Things we've always taken for granted, huh?"

"Along with toothbrushes, toilet paper, and a thousand other things." Gracie sighs.

"And we need to bury Mom and Dad," Danny adds gloomily.

A moment's uneasy silence follows.

Jimmy reads my mind. "Don't worry, Sophie." He briefly raises the bow. "If there are any bad guys around, we'll be ready for them."

All eyes fix on me as if waiting for me to make a decision.

Why would God give a seventeen-year-old girl such responsibility?

3

SHADOWS OF HOME

WE TIPTOE UP THE WINDING trail back to the house. Danny carries the bow, Jimmy, his sword, and I have our survival knife affixed to the end of a carved staff. Anna-Lee stayed with the little ones at the shelter.

When we arrive at the five-trunk tree, I stop. My head is spinning with memories at this spot. The beautiful maple tree spits its five thick trunks out of the ground toward the sky. Dad loved this tree. It grows right at the fork where one trail divides into two—"the Y," we called it. The wide, straight trail to the left leads to a vast cornfield on a gently sloping hill. Beyond that, the city. The right path of the Y is curvy and bordered by thorny-branched trees and blackberry bushes. That trail meanders north to the field behind our home.

"Are you all right?" Danny asks me kindly.

Before I can answer, Jimmy prods us on anxiously. "We've gotta keep going."

I nod. He is right. No time to reminisce. Our mission is to fetch what necessities we can scavenge and get back to the others as quickly as possible without attracting unwanted attention.

A stirring in the woods behind us frightens me. Danny pulls back his bow and turns it toward the noise until he realizes it is Anna-Lee approaching with the little kids.

"What are you doing?" Danny blurts out. "I could have shot you."

"We'll stay at the tree line." Anna-Lee's eyes well with tears. "We won't go into the house."

Gracie's tears summon my pity. "We want to see our home at least."

Why do her tears appear to be twice the size of any other tears I have ever seen? With her full lips, thin figure, long strawberry blonde hair, and bright blue eyes, doubtless she's going to be the most attractive of all of us.

"But it's not home anymore," Danny reminds her.

Anna-Lee blinks away the dampness in her eyes, visibly shaken. "I want to help bury Mom and Dad."

I nod sympathetically. "Okay. Stay out of view of the house when we get to the field, okay? And keep the little ones quiet."

Anna-Lee nods. I put an arm around her, searching futilely for the right words to assuage her fear and grief.

"Thanks," she says, finding comfort in my gentle touch. She wipes her damp eyes. "I'll be okay."

I'm thankful my friendly touch is all she needs, because my mind is void of consoling words.

I take off toward home on the narrow trail at the Y. Jimmy, not wanting to follow, runs up the left path, bypasses the five-trunk tree, and darts through the brush to take the lead.

When we arrive at the tree line in view of our home, we wait for half an hour, watching for any movement through our binoculars.

Our neighbor's home has burned to white ash, the smoke long since dissipated. Only the red brick chimney remains standing.

Several windows are broken out of the rear of our home. The curtains are still and lifeless on this windless morning. We can't see well into the darkness of the unlit rooms.

A chilling fear sweeps over me that we will find Mom dead in one of those dark rooms, or where we last saw her in the garage, bravely firing at our attackers, giving us time to make our breathless getaway. I imagine how the others will react if we find her body, and I pray a silent prayer for peace in the midst of this storm.

Jimmy tiptoes into the open field. Danny and I follow closely.

I look back at Anna-Lee to see her eyes wide with dread as she watches from behind a bush. She appears embarrassed that I witness her emotion, so she turns away and tends to a thorn in her hand. "Keep praying, and stay out of sight," I instruct them. "If Joey cries, head back to the shelter." Without looking at me, Anna-Lee nods dutifully, biting her trembling lip.

We walk slowly to the house, studying our surroundings very carefully. A gusty wind begins to pick up, and everything seems to move, providing unnerving distractions. An unlatched barn door alternatively creaks and slams in the distance, making me feel like someone's watching us. An empty bird feeder thumps against the trunk of the tree on which it hangs. The weather-worn swings on our playhouse rock and sway eerily. The occasional gust causes the large tree in our back yard to groan like an old man getting out of bed. The leaves left over from winter on our unkempt lawn awake from their slumber and roll creepily toward the house, as if they want to see our reaction to whatever horrible things we will discover. The horizon is gray and dark. It looks like a storm is coming in.

Our feet take us toward the home in the direction we left. When we bank the corner where Faith got shot, the smell of something dead makes me fearful we'll find Mother in the garage. But she's not there. I am relieved to find the source of the stench to be the entrails of some of our chickens. I take a deep breath to calm myself.

We walk to where we last saw Mom at the lip of the garage shooting at our attackers. To my horror, I see a rectangular-shaped blood stain about the size of the "Welcome" mat on our front porch. The bullet-ridden box trailer has been looted of everything except a few grains of rice, chunks of broken glass, and dehydrated apple slices from the bullet-pierced mason jar, remnants left over from the chaos of the first day's gunfight. The two rear tires of the SUV are flat, and a large oil stain has puddled beneath the engine.

Without a word, I wave Danny toward the front door and Jimmy toward the garage door. Jimmy moves immediately, but Danny is frozen, staring at the brown-colored splatter on the concrete. I nudge him in the right direction, and he inches toward the front porch. I force my eyes away from the bloodstain, fearful of the image being impressed too deeply upon my mind.

I walk around to the back deck, peeking through the broken kitchen window. When I see how everything has been wrecked by our attackers, my heart twists painfully. My thoughts return to the bloodstains in the driveway. The unsatisfied longing to grieve over the loss of Mom is like a pebble in my shoe I cannot ignore and do not have the time to remove. This is not getting any easier.

The back door is locked, but the door's glass has been shattered. I reach in and unlock it. All the glass plates and cups have been dumped out of the kitchen cabinets and broken. I wonder what possible circumstance could have provoked the looters to simply destroy things. The cabinets and drawers are empty of food and silverware.

I pass through the kitchen and find Jimmy in the homeschool room. Books are scattered across the floor. A dining room chair had been thrown against the wall, and one of its legs has impaled the sheetrock. There is a bloodstain on the floor beneath it and on the wall, evidence of a fight between degenerates. I turn my head toward a waft of stench that seems to be reaching for me from the corner of the dining room, and I catch a glimpse of something rotting in a plastic grocery bag. I wonder what it is.

Jimmy nudges me. "Let's get this over with."

"Hey." Danny calls out to us from the foyer. "See anything?"

"No." Jimmy leads me into the living room, which has been rendered unrecognizable. Our family Bibles and hymnals have been strewn across the floor, the criminals obviously having found no use for them. I pick up a large print Bible that is relatively undamaged. Danny finds Dad's red Gideon Bible—one of his favorite Bibles from which to read during family devotions. Jimmy's eyes are fixed upon the clothes in the foyer—Dad's mostly—that are scattered haphazardly. The couch sags in the middle and the cushions have been ripped up—who knows why. Music CDs are strewn over the floor.

Rage bubbles just under the surface of my skin, making my cheeks feel flush, but I keep my words caged.

"At least they left," Danny spits.

As if in explanation, Jimmy nonchalantly says, "No electricity." He flips the light switch.

Danny is still looking up the stairwell in the foyer. "There's a rotten—"

"There are nasty smells coming from every corner of this house," I interrupt. He shakes his head, his eyes angled up toward the top of the stairs in the foyer.

I distract Danny from what he must be thinking. "You guys check out the basement first. I'm gonna go look upstairs."

Without another word, I bolt up the stairs two at a time. I cannot wait another minute.

"Wait," Danny says. "Let's stick together." Danny and Jimmy follow me up the stairs to my room. I reach under my mattress and am horrified to discover it's not there.

"Oh no, oh no . . . " I frantically begin to search the room. Jimmy enters.

"What in the world are you looking for?"

"I can't find it," I mumble as I overturn books, clothes, and pieces of paper, looking for it.

"Find what?"

Finally, as I reach further under the bed, I feel the cold metal object. I clench my fist around it and whisper thanks to God.

"What is it?" Jimmy, then Danny, step closer and look over my shoulder.

Reluctantly, I open my fist to reveal what I have found. It is the bronze key to the gun safe.

"Yes!" Danny exclaims. "You found it."

"What was it doing there?" Jimmy comes around to look into my eyes. "You didn't! You took it? You hid it from Dad?"

"I was mad." Tears begin to flow down my eyes. "I was mad he bought you that gun. I was going to give it back—"

"A little late, don't you think?"

"I'm sorry, all right? At least we have it now."

"Oh, Sophie." Danny shakes his head back and forth, ashamed of me.

"I'm sorry." I stand and head downstairs. "Let's go see if those thieves have cracked into the gun safe."

I rush down the flights of stairs into the darkened basement. When I open the door, a disgusting rotten fish scent rises to my nostrils, causing me to gag. Danny winces, and then descends a few steps into the eerie basement, lit only by the few open windows in the guest bedroom and the windows in the door that leads to the garage. Danny's hand-pumped flashlight illuminates the way. We can see well enough to discover that the basement has been utterly destroyed. Even the sheetrock and closet doors weren't spared. Our aquarium is cloudy from the rotting fish.

I hand Jimmy the key and then fetch a green light stick out of my backpack. Jimmy and Danny head to the gun safe in the corner of the room. They find the gun safe on its side, warped from what must have been a hundred blows from a sledgehammer, which lies on the ground next to it with a broken handle.

"It looks like they didn't crack it," Jimmy says as he inserts the key. He pushes the six-digit combination. Then he twists the handle. To our amazement, the door falls open.

"Ha! We got it!" Jimmy checks the two AR-15s, and Danny grabs the 9s. "The ARs look good."

"So do the handguns!"

"Thankfully, Dad kept some ammunition in the gun safe," Jimmy says, opening a box of .223 ammunition and beginning to fill a magazine. "Here, Danny, load a 9 mag."

I cannot bear the sight of the weapons, so I take a look around the basement, searching for anything worth keeping.

I pick up two empty mason jars that lay on the stained carpet. The towels in the basement bathroom are all soiled and foul beyond use. I rip down a curtain, thinking it might be useful.

As Jimmy and I ascend the stairs, Danny sees something that catches his attention—a favorite blue Transformer toy. He picks it up and sits with his back to the wall, rubbing his eyes with the back of his hands, grieving quietly in the shadows of his playroom. His sobs seem to be to the cadence of the squeaking sound of his hand-pumped flashlight. I pause at the top of the stairs, giving Danny a moment alone, searching in vain for any words that might ease his pain.

Recently, silence appears to be my only response to the suffering of my brothers and sisters. How can I comfort them? How can I give them what I don't have?

"Why not stay here?" Jimmy proposes. "We'll clean it up."

"With what? There's no running water."

"At least we have locks on the doors and a dry place to sleep. We'll board up the broken windows."

"The people that shot Dad'll be back."

Jimmy briefly raises his rifle. "We'll defend ourselves."

Nausea rises up in my gut at the sight of Jimmy holding the AR-15. "They'd surround us and burn the house down, Jimmy. Better to be camouflaged in the woods. Inconspicuous."

At the top of the stairs I call down to Danny. "Come on, Danny."

He clears his throat. "I'm gathering some toys for the little ones." Poor kid, trying so hard to sound brave to impress his hard-to-please big brother and sister.

Stepping into the kitchen again, the warmth of a memory floods into my mind. It was just a few weeks ago, a memory as fresh as Mom's sugary friendship bread.

* * * * *

I was sitting at the dining room table pouring through dozens of magazines and catalogs and every website I could find, looking for the perfect silky white wedding dress to wear down the aisle. I had my heart set on one that was within our budget, but I wanted to wait and see what Adam picked.

"Hey, did you hear me?"

It was mother. She was staring at me from the kitchen with her fists pressed into her hips like I'd forgotten something important.

"No. What?"

"I told you, tell the kids to come upstairs."

"Oh, I'm sorry. I didn't hear you. Can you look at this first? I think I've got the one."

Mother set down her stirring spoon and came around to look at the pic. She admired it with me and then bent down to kiss me on the cheek. "I'm proud of you, honey." She headed back into the kitchen to take out the bowls and cups. "Now fetch the kids."

"Yes, ma'am."

I opened the basement door and descended a few steps when I heard Danny ask Jimmy, "Do you ever think we'll have to really fight a real war one day?" Danny threw his toy car at Jimmy's meticulously erected plastic soldiers, knocking over several of them.

Jimmy shrugged. "Maybe."

"My turn." Eli raised a plastic dinosaur to throw at the others' armies arrayed in battle formation.

Little Joey hobbled over next to them, threatening to obliterate all their armies.

"No, no, no!" Jimmy prevented him.

I smiled at them from the top of the basement stairs. "Time to eat, boys."

They turned their heads and Joey, in one fell swoop, destroyed their armies, sending pieces flying.

"Joey!" Jimmy griped.

Eli imitated Joey, knocking around their forces, army men, toy cars, and robotic figurines. Joey and Eli laughed, each trying to outdo the other with their destructive capacity.

Jimmy accepted the premature conclusion to their game and turned to follow me up the stairs. "All right, y'all have to clean it up."

"If we ever do have to go to war," Danny said, "we'll just sic Joey on 'em." We laughed as we entered the kitchen.

Dad and Adam were just entering from the back door. Dad was carrying his Glock handgun in a hip holster. Adam carried his handgun in a carrying case. They smelled of gunpowder.

"Whooped him again," Adam boasted to me.

I furrowed my brow and helped Mom set the table. For a man of his quality, Adam was still so slow to pick up on my cues.

In a moment, we were all holding hands around the dinner table as Dad prayed for God's blessings on the best-smelling, steaming turkey, mashed potatoes, gravy, green beans, and garlic bread you've ever smelled. I peeked, looking at Adam beside me, only to find he was peeking at me. I closed my eyes shut with a bashful grin, and he squeezed my hand a little firmer, rubbing his thumb gently across the diamond of my engagement ring.

* * * * *

I can almost smell it. I lick my lips and try to imagine what Adam looked like around that dinner table.

Danny finally reaches the top of the stairs with a backpack half full of toys. There's no joy in his countenance today—only sadness. No flicker in his eyes from the warmth of a fond memory—only an all-encompassing grief that appears to eclipse everything good about life.

"Go." Jimmy nudges me impatiently into the kitchen and into the erratic wafts of the putrid stench of our present crisis.

Upstairs in our parent's bedroom, the chaos is even more catastrophic. The criminals were clearly searching for any hidden weapons or valuables. Clothes and blankets are strewn across the bedroom. The mattress and chairs have been cut up and disemboweled. I can see into the bathroom, which has towels and toiletries scattered across the floor.

Danny enters. "The smell up here is a dead criminal in the boys' room, shot by a bullet. Mom and Adam are not here."

"Thank God," I mumble.

"Maybe she's still alive." Danny has a glimmer of hope in his eyes. I shrug. "I pray so."

"Maybe we shouldn't pray so." Jimmy speaks what I am thinking, but I'm still not happy with the way he says it. "There are some things worse than death."

I think to reprove him. I'm so frightened the little ones will hear him talk like that. But I know Jimmy would just dig his trenches and defend himself all the more forcefully, so I let the comment pass unchallenged.

Jimmy walks to the window, his eyes fixed on something outside. From his frigid frame and pale, frozen stare, and the way his hands are grasped tightly around his rifle, I discern something traumatic outside holds his attention.

"Jimmy?"

I walk to the window to stand beside him, where his eyes are fastened on Dad's decomposing body in the front yard. I gasp, my heart throbs painfully, and tears begin to swim their way down my cheeks.

Jimmy's breathing grows rapid. He shoulders his rifle as he scours the front yard and the horizon, as if preparing to shoot the one responsible. I feel so sorry for him. He's just a kid.

So soft, barely audible, Jimmy utters, "Why, God, why did you let this happen?"

Danny walks up beside us and suddenly spits out, "Somebody's coming!" Several men crest the hill over our cul-de-sac and bank right at our mailbox, coming right down our driveway.

Danny and I duck, but not Jimmy. He fixes his crosshairs on one of the men.

"That's Robby and Chris." Jimmy lowers his rifle.

"Are you sure? Who are the others?"

Jimmy bolts out the room and down the stairs, with Danny right behind.

Robby, an older boy in the homeschool co-op, appears a dozen pounds of muscle heavier, with the edges of his facial features sharp and inflexible. He looks like he's grown up a decade in the last month. Robby has a pistol on his hip and a shotgun on a shoulder sling. Chris, wearing a red cap, walks behind Robby, carrying a heavy duffle bag. A cowboy hat obscures the facial features of the third, and a sweat-shirt with a drawn hoodie obscures the countenance of the fourth, though I can make out what appears to be a bloody, swollen lower lip. He has a limp, and appears to be in pain.

Jimmy puts his bag full of ammo and one of the AR-15s on the kitchen island. Danny inserts his pistol in a holster, and tucks it under his belt. Danny opens the front door. "Robby! Sup?"

"Is that your Dad?" Robby looks over his left shoulder at the dead body in the front yard.

I nod. "Come in, guys, and keep your voices down." Jimmy and Danny give Robby and Chris a friendly handshake and hug. I prod them inside so I can shut the door. "Come in. Those looters have been staying here, and they may come . . ."

"Is Sophie here?"

I freeze when the man with the drawn hoodie enters, limping, my name on his lips.

"Adam?"

Our eyes fasten.

"Adam!"

I run into his arms, my face awash with tears of joy. "Oh my! I hardly recognized you. What happened?" His lower lip is twice the size of his upper lip. His face is unshaven, and there are dark circles under his blue eyes.

"Oh, Sophie, I'm so glad you made it."

"What happened, Adam?"

He sits with his back against the wall. I stoop to check on his leg wound.

In spite of his obvious pain, he raises his palm and rests it against my cheek. "You're okay. What a relief."

I give him another hug, then roll up his pants leg to inspect his wound.

"Here." Robby stretches his hand, palm down, to Adam. Adam puts out a palm and Robby drops an oval blue pill into it. Adam pops it into his mouth and swallows it dry.

"What's that?"

"Relief," Robby replies.

"For an infected leg?" I study his six-inch long infected, open wound. It is deep into the lateral side of the calf muscle, and has cut a vein, causing a tremendous amount of bruising. His right shoe and sock are soaked with blood. "I don't think a pain pill's going to heal it. It may do the opposite, because the pain pill keeps you walking on it when you shouldn't."

"I don't have a choice." Adam's gaze darts back and forth between me and Robby.

"What happened after we left, Adam?"

Adam is silent. He lays down flat against the ground. His eyes droop with fatigue.

"Why won't you answer?"

Robby's eyes keep glancing over his shoulder through the window beside the door. "Um, this morning, Adam got whacked with a long-knife by this . . . uh . . . "

"Have you seen our Mom?" Danny's eyes are full of hope.

Robby shakes his head side to side.

The fellow with the cowboy hat carrying the heavy plastic bag sets it down at his feet with a grunt.

"Can you stitch the wound, Sophie?" Robby asks.

"No. Not a dirty wound like this."

I inspect it for debris, and with Betadine and saline from the first aid pack, I clean it thoroughly. I place some non-stick bandages over the wound, then begin wrapping it with an Ace wrap.

As Jimmy begins to tell Robby and Chris our story, Danny bends down to check out what's in their black plastic bag.

The fellow with the cowboy hat wraps his fist around Danny's wrist. "Hands off!" He pushes Danny away.

I glance at Robby, who rests his right hand on his pistol.

Jimmy takes a step back. "Take it easy, man. He's just checking what you got."

"Is it food?" Danny asks. "Where'd you get it?"

The cowboy's eyes meet Robby's. Robby shakes his head back and forth. "Deep breath, Cowboy," Robby says.

Cowboy turns to Danny. "Don't ask. And no, you can't have any."

Their exchange confuses me. "Robby, are you stealing?" I stand and take a step closer to him, wanting to search his eyes for the honesty in his answer.

Robby refuses to make eye contact with me. I look down at Adam. "Adam?"

Adam lowers his eyes, embarrassed. "Adam, are you looting?"

Chris pushes his red cap further down on his brow, and breaks the uneasiness of their silence. "Where are y'all staying?"

Danny points in the direction of the woods behind our house, as if he's going to tell them. "We are—"

I gently knock his hand down. "We're a good distance away. Safe."

Adam must sense the wall I have erected. I hear him sigh heavily.

"How'd you get that cut, Adam? Someone trying to defend themselves from you?"

Chris raises his voice, "Don't you even try to judge us, Sophie! Our parents were killed just like yours, and we gotta do what we gotta do to survive. We've got a grandma to feed."

I ignore Chris, keeping my eyes fixed on Adam. "Whose blood is that on the handle of your knife, Adam? Hmm?" I look closely at the white wooden handle of his Bowie knife. It is streaked with blood. "Is that your blood?"

Jimmy sees the bloody handprint on Robby's thigh, and takes a step backward. I slowly reach down for the Bowie knife on Adam's hip, and unsheathe it. I raise it to examine the smeared blood on the blade.

Robby, with his hand on his pistol, barks, "Give it back to him, Sophie."

A long moment passes as we all measure each other up.

"Or what, Robby? You gonna shoot me? Steal our stuff?"

Cowboy bends down to wrap his fists around the top of his knotted black plastic bag. "Let's get their stuff and get outta—"

Jimmy clicks the AR-15 off safety. "What makes you think we're gonna let you take our stuff?" They stare each other down for a heart-pounding moment.

I give the knife back to Adam, who reinserts it in his sheath with a painful grunt.

Chris taps Cowboy on the shoulder. "Come on, Robby, Jimmy, and Danny are ole' friends. Lemme give 'em some food. They look hungry."

Danny's "Thanks" is premature.

"We don't want your food," I bark. "Not if it's got innocent blood on it."

"So you'd rather starve?" Adam asks. I look down at him. He licks the blood off his swollen lip.

"Than murder and steal? Of course. Are you serious?"

"Dead serious." Robby chuckles insincerely. "You'd rather your brothers and sisters starve? Eli? Faith? What about them? You've gotta adapt to the new world if you want to survive."

"You adapt by trusting in God, not by violence and . . . and stealing. What if someone treated you that way?"

"They did!" Robby answers.

"And was it right or wrong?"

"That's beside the point." Robby turns to Danny and Jimmy and grins mischievously. "Is that 'trusting God' getting you fed?"

Jimmy shakes his head side to side.

"Jimmy, we're not starving." He fixes his eyes on mine, but I can see his doubt.

"Yet." Jimmy turns back to Adam. "We're not starving yet."

I furrow my brow at him. "And even if we were, we wouldn't murder and steal if our life depended on it."

"You boys got some nice guns." Robby gawks at Jimmy's's AR-15 and Danny's hip-holstered 9 mm. Cowboy takes a long look at the AR-15 on the kitchen island.

"That one,"—he points at the island—"is that bad boy equipped with EOTECH?" he asks, referring to the optic on the gun.

Robby clucks his tongue in his cheek. "Why don't you come with us and eat well for a change?"

"Yeah, no one's going hungry with Robby." Chris takes a step back till he's by Robby's side.

"You've come a long way from Sunday school, haven't you?" I look down at Adam.

Robby taps his boot against Adam's good leg. "Get up, Adam. We've grown up, Sophie. If you wanna exchange your gavel for a fork, you might live long enough to grow up too."

Adam tries to stand, but he appears to have lost his strength.

Robby opens the door, and Chris tries to help Adam to his feet. Adam grunts in pain and falls. "Stop. I'm dizzy." Chris helps him to the floor slowly. Adam collapses to his back.

"Robby, I'm afraid Adam's going to have to stay here." Chris kneels beside him. "He's lost a lot of blood."

I put my foot down. "No way."

"Look, your bandage is already blood-soaked." Chris lifts Adam's pants leg a few inches to show the bloody bandage.

Adam sits up on his elbows. "Sophie? Are you giving up on me?"

Tears come to my eyes as I study Adam for a moment. He has changed so much. I can't believe he would resort to looting and killing. "Just leave. Now."

Chris tries to help Adam up, but Adam swats away his hand. "Leave me alone," Adam begs. "I just need a minute."

"I'm afraid it's gonna take more than a minute." Chris turns to Robby. "I don't think Adam can travel now. I mean, look how pale he is. And he's breathing real fast."

"He can't stay here," I insist.

Jimmy takes a step toward me. "But Sophie, we can take care of—"

"No!"

Chris looks at me. "Whatchu gonna do? Shoot your fiancé?"

I bite my lip. Jimmy appears more than willing to help care for Adam, and not once since the crisis have I seen Jimmy express any tenderness toward anyone. "Will you help me care for him, Jimmy?"

Jimmy nods. "Well, Robby, if you give me some food for him, we've got some medical supplies so we'll tend to him and try to get him on his feet. Then send him off."

Robby consents, and Cowboy reaches into his plastic bag and tosses us five boxes of macaroni and cheese, a can of tuna fish, and a box of cake snacks.

"I'll try to leave some more food in your mailbox in two or three weeks," Chris proposes. "If it's okay with Robby."

Robby nods. "Sure." He turns to Danny and Jimmy. "Plenty more where that came from. You're welcome to join us at Grandma's, boys. Anytime."

* * * * *

We dig a shallow grave for Dad in the garden, while Adam sleeps on a tarp beside us. We work fast and hard, motivated by the fear of returning criminals.

When Jimmy and Danny drag Dad's body, wrapped in a curtain, toward the grave, I can't handle it. It feels unnatural, almost wrong to see him like this.

I go fetch the others as they bury Dad and our dog Lucy in the same hole.

I take my time leading the others back, giving the boys space to do the hard work. I carry Joey, and Anna-Lee hoists Faith on her back. Gracie and Eli stay close behind us.

On the way to the house, Anna-Lee sees the open gate to the horse field, and freezes.

I rest a hand on her shoulder. How she loved those horses. "Maybe Taffy and Pockets got loose."

For a long moment, she just stands there staring at our maroon, tin-roof barn and the horse field, overgrown with grass and weeds. With resignation, she sniffs, and clears her throat. "Maybe."

When we arrive at the garden, I sigh with relief to discover Dad's body has already been covered with dirt. The boys have worked fast. When the initial trauma of seeing the shallow grave resolves, we all help put dirt on the body, tears dripping down our red cheeks.

An eerie stillness comes over us as we surround the grave, speechless. The boys are drenched with sweat from their work. Jimmy pushes his shovel into the ground and, as though not wanting to waste a moment on impractical sentiment, begins to wrap duct tape around his two AR-15 magazines to fasten them together facing opposite directions, making his second loaded magazine more accessible for any possible upcoming firefight.

At the head of the grave, Danny grasps a shovel in one hand and Dad's red Gideon Bible in the other. Plastic grocery bags of stuff like used toiletries, two hair brushes, three soiled towels, a few pieces of clothing and books scavenged from the home are on the ground beside us. At the foot of the grave, I hold Joey, who appears fearful with all of our emotions, yet oblivious to our loss. He must be unaware that the dirt piled in the hole in the ground in front of us covers his father. He keeps pointing at the horse field and calling out, as if expecting a horse to come galloping to the edge of the fence any moment. Oh, for the euphoria of a toddler's innocent ignorance. I pray he forgets the images that will haunt the rest of us.

Faith sits back against a pile of goods, tears falling pitifully. Anna-Lee reaches down to hold her hand. Faith rises to hug Anna-Lee's leg, wiping her tears on her shirt. Eli is on his knees looking at Danny's bag full of toy figurines, finding a much-needed distraction in his superhero fantasies. Gracie ties two sticks together in the form of a cross with some wire she found in the garden. She sticks it into the ground at the head of the grave, her contribution to the solemn ceremony.

With his foot, Danny forces the shovel into the ground so it remains upright. He flips through the Bible, as if looking for something to read. Momentarily, he gives up, and closes it. After a moment of silence, he rubs his eyes with the back of his hands, characteristic for him when he's sad or whining about something. "I wish somebody would say something. Something nice."

"Jimmy," I ask, "do you want to play something on your guitar?"

He shakes his head. "It's only got four strings left."

"Aw, you can still pick a tune."

He shakes his head side to side, his eyes fixed on the pile of dirt. A long moment of silence follows.

Anna-Lee finally speaks. "Do you remember when the old go-cart caught on fire?" We stare at her for a moment, unsure where she is going with this out-of-place question.

"I remember," I respond.

"Were you sad?"

Danny's gaze turns to Jimmy. If I remember correctly, Jimmy was the only one who actually got mad. Danny fiddles with the shovel, taking it out of the ground and stomping it back in. "I wasn't mad or sad."

"Why?" Anna-Lee asks.

"Because I knew Dad was going to buy a new one." Danny chuckles unexpectedly. "That burned-out thing was an eyesore beside the driveway for a month before Mom finally made him take it to the dump and replace it."

Anna-Lee smiles. "We all knew Dad was going to buy a brand new go-cart, so we weren't sad."

Puzzled, I gaze at Anna-Lee and shake my head. "What's your point?"

"Dad's not here." She points at the shallow grave. "This is that burned-out go-cart on the side of the driveway."

After a moment's silence, Eli cocks his head to the side and squints. With a confused frown, he asks, "So Dad's got a new go-cart in heaven?"

I chuckle, but halt. It feels out of place to laugh at Dad's graveside, and I worry Eli is offended. He scrunches up his nose, wondering what he's not quite comprehending about Anna-Lee's metaphor.

"No, Eli." I pat him gently on the shoulder. "Dad's got a new *body* in heaven."

Eli's blue eyes widen. "Oh, yeah."

Anna-Lee nods. "So we don't have to mourn the loss of the old one. Dad certainly doesn't." Anna-Lee flashes a bright grin. "What's that crazy song he wanted us to sing at his funeral? It always irritated Mom. It was an old song from that Christian rock group Audio Adrenaline."

"Dad was kidding about that," I say.

"No, he wasn't." Danny's fingers flip through the red Gideon Bible. "He was serious."

"Really?" I glance critically at Danny and point at the grave. "He said he wanted the leader of the band to stand on his casket—"

"Which we were supposed to make ourselves," Danny adds.

"And sing a grungy rock song called 'I Will Not Fade.' Mom would've boycotted the funeral!"

Everybody laughs except Jimmy. Though I do think I see one corner of his mouth rise a little. I always thought it would feel sacrilegious to laugh during the burial of a loved one, but it doesn't feel that way at all.

"The Bible says to rejoice with those who rejoice, and I know Dad's rejoicing in heaven." I kneel to be eye level with Faith. Joey comes around and tries to playfully climb onto my back. "He is with Jesus, and it doesn't get any better than that. They're waiting for us at the finish line with big smiles on their faces, rooting us on."

"They?" Eli's voice is soft. "You think Mom's with him?"

"I was referring to Dad and Jesus, but Mom might be there too."

After a moment of silence, Faith breaks the stillness with a whispered comment. "Heaven's gonna be nice."

I push a blonde curl out of her eyes. "Yeah."

Anna-Lee kneels to put a consoling hand on Eli's shoulder. "We'll dance to 'I Will Not Fade' with Dad."

"It's kinda rocky though," says Faith, as if wondering if such music will be allowed in heaven.

Eli's and Gracie's giggle box get turned on something fierce. Gracie proposes, "Maybe the angels will perform a Top-40 version that wouldn't offend the mainstream believers." Her voice teeters between crying and chuckling.

"Yeah." Danny wipes his tears with the backs of his hands even as he flashes a smile.

Momentarily, the giddiness calms, and Anna-Lee sings the song our parents often sang *a cappella* in church.

When peace like a river attendeth my way . . .

I clear my throat and join with the others.

When sorrows like sea billows roll,
Whatever my lot, Thou hast taught me to say,
It is well, it is well with my soul.

Jimmy doesn't so much as hum a note, but by the end of the chorus, his crystal blue eyes, finally, have dripped their first tear. I wrap my arms around him and wet his shoulders with my own. "It's okay to cry, Jimmy. Dad would want us to cry."

He grasps me tightly, and we cry our grief to heaven together.

Ah, jewelweed.

4

FACING SNAKES

SITTING AROUND THE SMALL FIRE inside the tepee, with Adam and the little ones asleep, we quietly sift through the details of our visit to the home.

"I love the AR, but I still wish I had my birthday present." Jimmy's eyes light up with passion as he reflects, his hands gripping the AR-15 he has claimed as his own.

"Mom needed the Ruger more, I'm sure," Anna-Lee says.

"Personally, I'm glad we don't have your gun, Jimmy," I respond. "I'd prefer to not have the ones we do have."

"Your preference got us into this mess. Hiding that key." Jimmy clicks his tongue in his cheek and wags his head, disappointed.

"Lighten up, Jimmy." Anna-Lee leans in toward him.

"It's true!"

"I told you I was sorry," I say. "Why won't you drop it?"

Jimmy leans forward with his elbows on his knees. "What do you have against having the means of defending ourselves, Sophie?"

"Guns are for killing people, and I am against killing people. Remember the Sixth Commandment?"

"Killing someone in self-defense," Danny asserts, "or in defense of another, is not wrong."

"He's right," Anna-Lee says. "Not according to God's law, and not according to American law."

"The very fact that guns kill people," Jimmy adds, "is the best reason the good people should have them. Murderers are less likely to murder good people if they are more likely to suffer for it."

I'm beginning to feel like they're ganging up on me. "Thou shalt not kill," I respond, irritated. "Seems like a no-brainer to me."

"And in the next chapter," Anna-Lee rebuts, "it says what should be done to those who commit murder." She sets two small pieces of wood on the fire. "Do you know what the Bible says a homeowner can do to someone he finds breaking in to his house?"

"Let me guess." Jimmy smirks. "It says they can dial 9-1-1 and lock themselves in a room and pray the armed criminal can't find them."

"No," Danny chimes in. "They can kill 'em."

"Doesn't it also say they should be put in prison and given food, medicine, education, and entertainment for life?"

Anna-Lee and Danny chuckle at Jimmy's sarcasm.

I take a deep breath and lay back. Anna-Lee taps me on the shoulder. "What about Luke 22, Sophie?"

"What about it?"

"Jesus told His disciples to sell something to buy a sword. What do you say to that?"

I take a deep breath. "I just don't feel right about it."

"Well, your feelings are irrelevant. I feel better about having the means to defend myself," Anna-Lee says, "than I do about being defenseless."

"Amen," Danny and Jimmy exclaim.

"I'm sorry for taking the key. All right?"

I lay down and turn away from the fire. All is quiet for a moment.

"I'm sorry," I repeat. Anna-Lee reaches over and grabs my hand. She doesn't say anything, but I can sense she's forgiving me.

"Thank you," I mumble.

I'm not tired, but I feign like I'm going to sleep, listening to their conversations. They talk about Robby and Chris and the dilapidated state of our home. My thoughts are on Adam. Soon, the fire dies down, and everybody sleeps peacefully, yet I'm still wide awake.

I'm careful not to be next to Adam around the fire pit or in the tepee. I do not want to give him any hint that I'm still interested in him. Not after what he's done. Do I miss him? Absolutely. I just can't let him know.

Thanks to my growling stomach, I'm teetering in and out of sleep, dreaming of Thanksgiving dinners and birthday parties and wedding cake when I get a nudge on the head. I sit up, alert. I sense the absence of Anna-Lee. Oh, she's in the lookout.

Adam reaches over Gracie, trying to get my attention. By the light of the dimming embers, I see his teeth are chattering, and his face glistens with sweat. Once he sees I'm awake, he flops back to his back with a grunt. "I think I'm dying."

I scoot up beside Gracie and place my hand on his head. "You're burning up."

"My leg is killing me. Can you give me another pill?"

I shake my head. "No. You're not due another couple ibuprofen till morning. It'll hurt you more than help you if you take too much."

He grunts uncomfortably. "Oh, Sophie."

I lie down and reach for his hand. "You'll heal. The wound is looking good." I sound more confident than I feel, but it does him no good to suspect the worst—tetanus, or overwhelming sepsis, that'd be the end of him quick.

"I think it's infection. Can I have some of that antibiotic?"

"No. I told you, we only have enough for Faith. And I don't think you have infection—"

"What's causing the cold chills then?"

I shrug. "Maybe you've got narcotic withdrawal. I saw Robby give you a pain pill. Had he been doing that?"

He looks away and nods. "Robby was giving me a lot the past week, since I sprained my ankle pretty bad. I can see why that stuff's so addicting." He grasps my hand. "I think he preferred me stoned so I would shut up. I joined him to try to keep an eye on your Mom, and when we separated from the guys who took her, he wouldn't tell me where she was."

"Oh." I swallow hard. "Why didn't you tell me that?"

"I'm not going to tell you things that'll hurt you just to satisfy your curiosity."

"But I want honesty, Adam."

"Well, you'll have to settle for the lack of dishonesty. You'll have nightmares if I tell you everything. And for what?" He shakes his head as he stares into the fires. "It's hell on earth out there. Everyone alive's a demon." He clears his throat. "You, in contrast, are my angel. Thanks for taking care of me." His fingers find my ring, and he gently runs his index finger across the jewel. "I'm holding out hope."

I clear my throat. "Try to go back to sleep." I lie back down, but I can't get his words out of my mind. He reaches to rest his hand on top of mine, but I jerk mine out of reach.

Moments later, Jimmy nudges me. "It's time."

"What?"

"You know, what we talked about last night. Time to go murder some deer."

* * * * *

In the moonless pitch blackness of the pre-dawn night, Jimmy carefully walks the large fallen branch of a tree to where it broke off the thick trunk in the valley. You could barely see your hand in front of your face.

Lightning had struck the tree at the second story level, and the fallen branch had come to rest on a hill beside it. Thus, James steps out onto the branch at the top of the hill, but by the time he makes it to the part of the tree that is still standing, he is 20 feet above the ground.

"I can't see you. Are you up there?" Danny beckons with a whisper. "Don't fall."

"It's not the falling that frightens me," Jimmy responds, finally making it to the safety of the standing trunk. I hear one of the branches above my head sag as Jimmy grips it to steady himself on his precarious perch. "It's falling with this in my hand." He shakes his staff, which has his camouflage survival knife affixed to it. He has camouflaged his clothes, face, and hair with moss, small branches, and mud. He has obscured his smell by rubbing his whole body with ashes and wild onion. "Now y'all go quietly up to that ridge," he whispers, "and slowly make your way toward me through that heavy brush. Maybe you'll drive the deer down toward this trail."

"I don't see why we're going to all this trouble," Danny says in a harsh whisper. "Just wait 'em out and shoot 'em with your gun."

"We don't want to use ammo unless we have to," I respond. "And we can't take a chance of letting bad guys know that we're in these woods." Jimmy stills himself on the branch. "Now go. Quietly."

Dawn is just pushing back the chilly night as Danny and I tiptoe up a wide deer trail to the ridge in the starlit woods. We circle around and come down different, smaller deer trails as Jimmy recommended. When I draw to within view of Jimmy's position, I see he has his spear raised. His concentration is fixed on an approaching beast I cannot see. I quietly tiptoe further down until I see two deer—a buck and a doe—slowly making their way down a trail that leads right under his tree.

* * * * *

An uninvited memory arrests my attention.

I recall being in a camo blind with Dad and Jimmy the first day of deer season two years ago.

A thin layer of snow covered the ground, making it easy to spy the whitetail. I took a crossbow shot at a doe and missed. It was Jimmy's turn.

The eight-point buck was sniffing our bait pile of rotten apples, set up twenty-five yards in front of us with the wind in our face. Jimmy quietly lined up his bow sights and released the arrow.

A moment later, Dad and Jimmy slapped high-fives. "Kill shot!" Jimmy is as excited as I've ever seen him. He's impaled his first buck! He turned and high-fived me with a wide grin on his face, smacking my gloved palm so hard it hurt, as is always his fashion.

He reached for the zipper to exit the blind, but Dad stopped him. "Patience," he said. "If you pursue too quickly, the deer will get an adrenaline rush and run and run and you may never find it."

After waiting for about ten minutes, Dad led the way through the woods, easily following the blood trail in the snow. Our breath was white in the twenty-degree air. My thick camouflage bibs and hunting jacket kept me cozier than I thought they would when I first inhaled the chilly night air two hours earlier.

Father placed a hand on Jimmy's shoulder as we walked. "I'm proud of you, son."

Jimmy smiled at him. "Thanks, Dad. Can we mount his head on our wall next to your ten-pointer?"

"Sure. Unless it's bigger, then we'll put yours in the basement."

"You wouldn't!"

Dad laughed. "Just kidding."

"That's a lot of blood, Dad. Do you think the buck is suffering?"

Father nodded. "Possibly. That's why we should eat what we kill. No wasted suffering. Suffering is for a greater purpose."

"Is suffering always for a greater purpose?" I asked. "Or is there needless suffering?"

Dad thought for a moment. "All things work together for the good of those who love God. Even suffering."

"I thought Jesus suffered so we wouldn't have to." Jimmy looked up at Father. "So we could be happy."

"No, Jimmy. Happiness comes from being right with God, not from the absence of suffering. Jesus is our example, and He calls us to take up our cross and follow Him."

Jimmy tossed up his arms. "Well, why did He die on the cross then?"

"He died for our forgiveness, not for our comfort. Jesus calls us to walk in His footsteps, which sometimes lead through the valley of the shadow of death. Yet even there, the Lord is my shepherd."

"Is it true," I asked, "that all the apostles were martyred?"

"No, Sophia." The blood trail gets thicker.

"We're getting close," Jimmy said excitedly. "There's no way that buck could survive that much blood loss."

Father looked back at me. "One of the twelve denied Jesus."

I corrected him. "No, two, right? Peter?"

Father nodded. "But only Peter repented and was forgiven. Like the buck nipping away at our apples, Judas took the bait and wound up mounted on the devil's wall. He thought God was withholding something good from him, and that he had to betray the Lord to get it—"

"There it is!" Jimmy pointed and sprinted to the large eight-point buck down by the creek. Father removed his gloves and took out his cell phone for a picture. Jimmy and I posed behind it with the crossbow.

"Good job, Jimmy." Father snapped the picture.

* * * * *

I freeze as the two deer walk directly under Jimmy. He lets the doe pass, and silently drops out of the tree, plunging his spear right through the shoulder blades of the big buck.

Danny applauds like mad as the buck collapses, his back legs limp and motionless from his severed spinal cord. The terrified doe leaps frantically into the shadows.

Jimmy presses the buck's neck against the ground with his foot and thrusts his fists into the air triumphantly. "Steak tonight!"

The buck throws his rack toward Jimmy, trying to gore his leg, but he leaps out of the way with a shrill victory shout.

Jimmy lets Danny finish him off by cutting his throat.

* * * * *

We celebrate the grand opening of Jimmy's All-You-Can-Eat Venison Restaurant with much drama. The cost for entrance is five acorns. Strips of venison brown on a flap of rabbit fencing over the flame. They smell so tasty! Gracie makes Jimmy a bow tie out of leaves and twine, and with a mud mustache, he's playing the last four strings on that guitar like a pro. He acts like he's a performer on stage, and the others occasionally tip him by tossing an acorn into the bowl at his feet.

Everyone's lips and teeth are red from the "kid-wine" cooling in the pan beside the fire pit. I discovered some use for the red food coloring scavenged from the home after all.

"But I have only four acorns," Danny complains.

Gracie, the "bouncer" at the restaurant entrance, is adamant against bending the rules. "This is a respectable establishment. Five's the price of admission."

Danny extends a begging hand toward me, and I'm prepared to give him an extra acorn. Gracie suddenly knocks his hand away. "No loitering on the premises. Go find another acorn, bozo. Or I'll call security"—she glances at Eli—"and have you forcibly removed from the premises. And banned for life."

Eli sticks out his chest, removes a carved wood handgun from under his belt, and aims it at Danny, squinting down the wooden sights. "Back off, punk!"

Anna-Lee and I practically laugh our heads off. Danny walks off a few feet, and I kindly toss him an acorn when Gracie isn't looking.

Eli, still hungry after enjoying his meager harvest of six small crawdaddies, eats some tenderloin to much fanfare.

Faith pauses her stirring of the pan of red liquid so that Anna-Lee can lower a cup into it for another drink. Anna-Lee takes a drink and then bears her red teeth to the others, prompting them to laugh. "That's the best kid-wine I ever had!"

I smile so much that my jaw muscles begin to ache. "Sure beats plain old creek water."

This has become one of our most enjoyable days since the crisis began.

At least until Adam's unshaven face pokes through the tepee door, where he's spent most of the last ten days resting and healing.

"Something smells good," he says. I can almost hear the smile on his face—his first smile, I think, since he joined us.

He has his color back. I am taken aback by how handsome he looks with his thin beard and his straight brown hair that is several inches longer than he would normally tolerate it.

I try to sound unimpressed. "There he is, back from the dead." I fake a smile, just as my heart's frown begins to hurt.

He hobbles out, rebuffs Danny's offer of assistance, and manages to stand on his own with the help of a crutch the boys created for him. That's a first.

Anna-Lee begins to pour him some water from the pot over the fire. "Thirsty?"

He waves off Anna-Lee's kindness. "In a minute." He turns to me. "Sophie? Can we talk alone? For a moment?"

I nod and follow him down the trail about twenty feet. He sits on a fallen log, and raises his wrapped leg up on the log with a grunt.

Be strong, I tell myself. *Be strong.*

"I'm scared, Sophie."

I stand across from him, holding my forearms tightly over my chest like a barbed wire fence. "Tell me why."

"I'm scared because I'm getting better, thanks to you. And soon I'm gonna have to leave. Thanks to you."

"Since we're being so honest, tell me, Adam, how many people did you kill?"

He takes a deep breath and turns his eyes to the dirt.

"Don't go crawling into your shell again, like the last time I asked you. Tell me."

He raises his eyes to mine. "Personally, one. But it was a life or death situation."

"How about, not personally? Tell me about all the deaths in which you were an accomplice."

He shakes his head from side to side. "It's all a blur."

"Because of drugs? Booze? Or just a convenient amnesia to help you live with yourself?"

He scratches his ear and keeps his shifty eyes focused on the dirt. "I guess it was a combination of all the above. Robby was a bad influence on me, but it's what I thought we had to do to survive. We were starving. My family was out of town when the crisis began, and I had no way of figuring out where they were or how to get there. Robby's grandpa had been killed, and his grandma was hungry. She needed us. Plus, I wanted to keep an eye on your Mom—"

"As if any of that justifies the unthinkable crime of murdering an innocent person—"

"Aw, he wasn't innocent—"

"Even murderers have a right to a fair and speedy trial! There's no excuse for what you've done, Adam."

He nods. "You're right."

"Not for Robby, not for his grandma, not for Mom, not to prevent your own starvation. That you're still giving excuses means you aren't really sorry."

"It's not an excuse. It's an explanation. But I am sorry, Sophie, I am."

"Tell me about the one you personally murdered."

He twiddles his thumbs and takes a deep breath.

"That one, that was necessary to save my own life. I certainly would have been dead if I didn't kill that guy that was reaching for a pistol to shoot me."

"Why was he reaching for a pistol?"

"Well, Robby had shot his dad, and—"

"Why'd Robby shoot his dad?"

Adam refuses to answer. Tears come to his eyes.

"Was it because you were trying to steal from them?"

He nods.

"So Robby shot his dad to steal from them, and when this man's son reached for his dad's fallen weapon to defend himself from some lawless looters, you did what, Adam?"

A sob rises in his chest, and his breathing becomes erratic, summoning my pity. But I give him none. "Answer the question, Adam. You're gonna have to be real honest with God on Judgment Day, so you might as well get a less painful taste of it now."

"I killed him," he says with shame. "With my knife. We let his mother be."

"Oh, his mother was there? Did she see y'all kill her family? Her son?"

He nods.

"We left her with some food. Some of the boxed cake snacks they had stashed. Robby didn't want to."

"You took almost all her food, probably her means of defending herself, and left her alone to starve. To bury her husband and son all by herself. How virtuous of you to leave her a snack."

He hangs his head in shame. "I hate myself for what I have done."

"Join the club!" At these words, tears flood down his face, dripping down his nose and beard.

A mixture of pity and rage fills me. I am so angry for what Adam has done, but simultaneously I pity him for how sin has ravaged his life and shattered his dreams.

"Yes, shame on me, Sophie. But didn't Jesus bear our shame as much as He bore our sins? Should I wallow in my shame to pay penance to you? Or is His free gift enough?"

I stare into his eyes. Is he sincere? Has he really repented?

"Sophie, I want you to know I still love you."

I shake my head in frustration, more at my own divided heart than at him. I am so torn, so violently torn.

He reaches for my hand. "You're still wearing the ring, which means you haven't completely given up on our dream."

"My dream, Adam, was to marry a godly man." I snatch my hand out of his. "A man who's proven himself faithful, who'll be a good father and husband—"

"I know, I know—"

"Not a thief. Not a murderer. Not a man who will betray His Lord for some Little Debbie cakes."

"I am sorry. What else can I do, Sophie?" He spreads his hands wide. "What can I do to prove myself to you?"

I turn toward my siblings, whom I can barely see through the greenery of the bushes. "You were justifying the unspeakable just seconds ago, and now you want to know what you can do to make things right between us? I don't know, Adam. Not now."

"Maybe? In time?"

I shrug, fighting off a tear that threatens my proud composure.

He reaches for something in his pocket. "I found this." I look down at him as he unfolds the picture of my wedding dress. I dig my hand into my pocket. It's not there. It must have fallen out.

"I found it in the tepee. It has made me realize just how much I've lost." He studies the marker-circled picture, and tears flood his eyes afresh. For a long minute, he just stares at it.

"I picked that one when I first laid my eyes on it, but I didn't tell you because I wanted it to be a surprise. On our wedding day."

"Our wedding day." He whispers the words, as if they hold some distant meaning he's trying to recall. "I think we would have been married by now."

As I think about it, I realize that today would have been our wedding day. The thought sends a crop of goosebumps all over my body, but I restrain my urge to embrace him. I clear my throat. "Do you want the ring back, Adam?"

"No, but I want it to mean something." Our eyes meet. I take off the ring, and hand it to him.

"It's not right for me to keep it."

He takes it reluctantly. I don't know what to say. I rest my ringless hand gently on his shoulder and fix my eyes on the pale, smooth streak of skin where the ring used to be. I wonder if it will ever go away.

"The only reason you lost me, Adam, was because you lost your faith."

"But I've found it again."

"Which makes you my brother but not my fiancé, and . . ." I pause and remove my hand from his shoulder. "Never my husband."

He looks up at me longingly. "Never?" His lip trembles and his eyes well with tears.

I turn my gaze toward the shelter and clear my throat, trying to be strong.

He lowers his face to the glossy, worn magazine page, and begins to cry his tears into it.

Finally, my pity begins to win the tug of war raging inside me. When I think I can hold back no longer, and I'm about to fall to my knees in front of him, wrap my arms around him, and cry with him, Joey falls and gets hurt by the fire pit. I rush to check on him, leaving Adam by himself.

Inwardly, I'm thankful for the distraction. I just don't know if I can ever trust him again. I feel I've grown stronger in my resistance to his predictable advances, but now, I feel guilty for it.

* * * * *

Anna-Lee, Gracie, Eli, and I scour the "tire graveyard" for anything that may be of use. Jimmy sets up a groundhog trap in front of a burrow. Faith digs a little further down, closer to the creek.

This was our neighbor's junk yard in a valley between their two hundred acres and our ten acres. It is filled with old rusty appliances, hundreds of tires, and groundhog holes in a wooded valley.

Anna-Lee stands with the 9 mm in hand, guarding the little ones, watching for approaching hoodlums.

Gracie digs with the shovel and clanks something metallic. She grabs what looks like a pole sticking out of the ground and pulls. With a grunt, she lifts a frying pan with a warped handle out of the dirt. "Look at this, Anna-Lee." The handle appears to be rubberized.

"Good job, Gracie." Anna-Lee pats her on the shoulder. "We'll be able to cook over the fire with that, and the handle won't burn us."

Gracie tries to dig the mud out of the inside edges of the pan with her fingers. "This reminds me when we used to dig cookie dough out of Mom's mixing bowl."

I smile broadly as I recall the details of the memory. I can almost hear Eli and Faith arguing over who gets to hold the bowl. I can almost smell the chocolate chip cookies fresh out of the oven. I see Gracie's distant gaze, and I wonder if she has been enraptured by the same delicious recollection.

Anna-Lee seems similarly reminiscent. "Yeah."

"I hope Jimmy and Danny catch some more crawdaddies we can cook in this pan." Gracie raises the pan proudly. "I'm plum sick of deer meat."

"What is it with you guys and crawdaddies?" My gaze darts back and forth between Eli and Gracie. "They smell like dirty feet."

"It's my favorite." Gracie hands her pan to Anna-Lee and returns to digging. "Even without the Cajun spice."

"Venison's my favorite," says Eli. "As long as it's fresh and ain't been jerkified—squished and rotten and dried up, like a possum that's been run over in the hot road a hundred times."

He overturns an old rimless tire and sees a snake. "Woohoo!" he squeals, while Gracie shirks away.

Anna-Lee immediately recognizes the markings. "Oh, that's non-poisonous."

Without a moment's pause, Eli tries to pick it up, pressing the snake's head into the mud with both hands.

I hold the tire rim up so it doesn't fall on him. "Hold it by the neck, buddy, or it might bite you."

"I got it." He lifts the snake out of the mud and it writhes around his forearm, releasing a potent, foul-smelling odor from its tail.

Gracie shrinks further away in protest. "Yuck."

Anna-Lee agrees, wrinkling up her nose in disgust. "Yeah, that's nasty, but that's the defense mechanism God gave it."

"Obviously," I interject, "it only works with girls."

Eli hoists the snake into the air proudly. "Can we eat it?"

Anna-Lee and I laugh. "You have a strange appetite, little buddy."

"Hey, Sophie," Faith calls out to me. "I found something."

As I head down to her, Anna-Lee says, "I'm tired. I'm going to return to the camp."

"Okay."

"I'll take Eli and Gracie back."

"Be careful."

Joey is next to Jimmy, happily banging a stick against a tree, accented by all of the diverse squish and splat sounds a toddler's lips can invent. He's starting to create a bare, barkless spot. Faith lifts a thin, rusty necklace out of the dirt. "Check it out."

"Wow." I set the handgun in my hip holster and take a knee. She hands me the necklace proudly. It is a pendant on a rusty chain. "Wonder who belonged to this." I try to rub the mud off the pendant. "We can loosen this chain with the grease from the deer Jimmy killed. I—I think it's got a word on the pendant. But it's chipped. I can't read it." I hand it back to her. "You can keep it. It'll make a nice toy."

Faith takes it gently, studying it carefully. "What do you think it says?"

"It's got some word on it that starts with a Y."

She stares at it for a moment and then hands it back to me. "You."

"You can read that?"

"No. I'm giving it to you. I had a dream Mommy was in heaven, and she told me that you are my new Mommy now."

She smiles at me warmly. I'm her new Mommy? The thought moistens my eyes. I love her so much right now, I feel like my heart could simply burst for joy. Here it is, in the midst of so much grief and fear, here's this tsunami of heaven in my heart.

"Thank you, sweet Faith." I take the necklace in my hand, and think I have never received such a precious gift. "It's so pretty."

She grins wider than I think she should. "It's for your birf-day."

"It's junk," Jimmy coldly announces.

I am furious that Jimmy would dare to ruin what was otherwise such a tender, memorable moment. "Maybe so, Jimmy, but junk with love is better than something useful without it."

He doesn't appear moved by my maternal reproof. "Luxuries that don't keep you alive are a waste of time and energy, Sophie."

"Like your little coin and trinket collection?"

He ignores me. I watch his ears redden. "Better than your key collection," he quips.

Faith begins digging again. "I'm gonna find something for your birf-day too, Jimmy."

"That's thoughtful, Faith. Don't let Mr. Party-Pooper here spoil your kind spirit."

Faith's screwdriver clangs against something metallic and hard. "Wonder what this is. I'm going to find something for Anna-Lee's birf-day too. I wish we had some wrapping paper. And helium balloons. And cake. And ice cream." She licks her lips. "Do you think we'll ever taste ice cream again?"

I pity my little sister Faith. We had so much excess, followed by so much lack. In some ways it would be better to never know such wealth and luxuries than to have them snatched away so violently. If we had always been impoverished, then she wouldn't know what she was missing, and contentment perhaps would not be so elusive.

"I wonder if Mom and Dad will still celebrate our birf-days in heaven."

Suddenly, we hear gunfire across the field, much closer this time. Geese, which must be bedding in the farm field, take off, flying over us. There are several more gunshots.

"Let's get outta here." Jimmy snatches up his AR-15 and runs down the hill. He stops thirty yards away when he realizes that we are not following. There's no way I can flee with Faith and Joey, not without risking making too much noise and attracting attention. I shake my head at him and my lips mouth the word, "No!" I grasp my handgun and quietly chamber a round. I take cover with Faith behind a fallen tree. I fix my gaze on the horizontal line between the pale brown cornfield and the evergreen trees in the distance, searching for the fearsome images of approaching hoodlums. Four armed men crest the hill in the midst of the cornfield, heading toward us. Sweat beads on my face. I hear Faith's respiratory rate quicken, and see the fear in her flushed cheeks and fidgeting fingers.

Joey whacks his stick against the tree trunk several more times.

"Joey," I whisper. I place my index finger over my lips. "Shh."

He reciprocates. "Shh."

"God, keep us safe," I pray under my breath. My worst fear is suffering at the hands of evil criminals. No—my worst fear is seeing my brothers and sisters suffer at the hands of evil criminals.

The four men continue to walk straight toward us, and my mind buzzes with adrenaline. I see that the one in front holds what looks like a short-barreled assault rifle with several long clips affixed to a bandoleer that crisscrosses his chest. I duck low. "Faith," I tell her in a harsh whisper, "stay close to the ground."

I glance at Joey. He has raised his stick, and acts as if he's about to strike the tree again.

"No, Joey. No."

He turns to look back at me, confused. The four armed men are about forty yards away, heading straight for the deer trail that separates me and little Joey. If I reach for him or take his stick, he may cry, and they may hear him. If I let him be, he may swing his stick against the tree and they will hear him.

They are twenty yards away now, and their pace appears to increase. I lower my head to the ground, sprinkle some leaves on my hair, then raise my head and steady my handgun arm against the fallen log to tighten my aim. I set my sights on the largest of the four men, who's in the lead. One of them has a cowboy hat on his head. Could be Robby's friend, the tall, mean one they call Cowboy. They slither toward me like poisonous snakes. There's no way I can retreat safely with the little ones.

"Faith," I whisper as forcefully as I can, "if those men fire at me, I want you to pick up Joey and run as fast as you can back to the shelter, okay?"

Faith takes a deep, tremulous breath. Out of the corner of my eye, I see her shake her head. "I don't want to leave you," she responds in a high-pitched voice.

"Shh."

Joey grunts playfully. He's looking at me, holding his stick out to me as if expecting to clash toy-swords.

The four armed men are close enough they could probably see Joey, if only they were to look down the deer trail.

Faith draws closer to me, resting her head against my arm. It's sweet, but not appropriate while I'm aiming a weapon.

I sigh with relief when the hoodlums turn left at the tree line and walk parallel to it, away from us.

I can overhear one of them. I recognize the voice. It's Robby.

"We need to check these woods for those hold-outs . . . " Robby is glancing into the woods past me. "I know for a fact there are some kids in there with ARs."

I rest my finger on the trigger with my sights lined up on Robby's chest.

"There's nothing in there," one of them says. "We've looked."

Cowboy chimes in, "Robby's right. There are a half dozen kids in there, with food, guns, and ammo. Adam's with 'em. Or was. He probably died from his leg injury . . . "

I watch them walk away until I can no longer hear them. I never thought I could actually kill a person, but now, I'm beginning to wonder. I quietly remove the bullet from the chamber and insert it back in the mag. I hate that Glocks don't have a safety, and so for peace of mind I always keep the chamber empty.

I holster my handgun and look over my shoulder to see Jimmy has left us.

As soon as we arrive back at the shelter, I stomp up to Jimmy, fuming, longing to give him a piece of my mind. Jimmy is sitting by the fire with his back to me, entertaining the little ones with a funny song on his four-string guitar.

Adam, who sits against the tepee reading our red Gideon Bible, sees me.

"Sophie? Are you all right?"

I walk over to him. "It's Jimmy. He just left us when these four armed crooks came past us. One of them was Robby. He spoke of us like we were a target. Like he wanted to attack us."

"You?"

I nod.

Adam winces. "As bad as he's become, I can't believe he would turn against you guys."

"I smelled the alcohol on them from twenty feet away."

Jimmy pauses his guitar playing and turns to me. "You talking about me?" He acts like he doesn't know why I'm so offended.

"We should have laid low until they passed, Jimmy. You just took the AR and left me to defend Faith and Joey all by myself with a handgun."

"I said we needed to make a run for it, and you just sat there. If you remember, I was against bringing the little ones that far out for this exact reason. You're the one that put us in danger. I'm not going to risk my life to save your neck if you do something foolish."

"How about Faith? Would you risk your life to save *her* neck? Or little Joey? I couldn't make a run for it, Jimmy, and just leave Faith and Joey sitting there, now could I? And how was I supposed to carry them running, all by myself?"

"You were thinking only about yourself, Jimmy." I love it when Adam reproves Jimmy.

I can see on Jimmy's face that his selfish heart has been exposed. He puffs out his chest, angrily sets his guitar down, and acts like he's going to get up.

Adam reads his mind and aims at him with his crutch. "No, you don't. No getting up and running this time. You're gonna sit there like a man and deal with this."

Jimmy studies Faith and Joey for a moment as Faith helps Joey pile small rocks into a pyramid. He takes a deep breath.

"Before you'll ever be a good leader," Adam continues, "you need to be a good follower. You may disagree with your sister, but following her leadership in the wrong direction is better than rebelling against her leadership and doing your own thing. We are only as strong as our care for the least among us. By that standard, you are weak indeed, Jimmy, all your bravado and gifted instincts notwithstanding." Jimmy is silent. Introspective. I know he is at a crossroads between humility and pride. He stands with a sigh, picks his backpack up beside him, and heads into the tepee without a word.

"Jimmy?" He ignores Adam. "Jimmy, God gives grace to the humble, but resists the proud."

I hear Jimmy unzip his backpack. I know what he's doing. He's admiring his little box of trinkets and treasures, his drug of choice to shield his pricked conscience from the painful truth.

I turn my gaze to Adam, appreciative of his wisdom. He sits down beside the little ones around the fire with his Bible and begins to tell them the story about the Good Samaritan, how we are always to care for those smaller and weaker than we are. My heart begins to thump wildly.

Anna-Lee clears her throat. I glance at her. She smiles at me, her eyes wide with concern. I know my face is as red as a beet. She glances at my hand. I didn't even realize it, but I'm running my thumb like mad along the pale, recessed band of skin the engagement ring once covered.

Having Adam here is killing me.

* * * * *

Gracie holds the handgun, staring down a "frowning face" and upper torso carved with Jimmy's knife into a tree. There's an X in the center of the chest. Jimmy does the instructing while the others listen. "Aim for the chest, not the face, Gracie. Pull the trigger very slowly, while keeping your sights aimed at the center of the chest."

Gracie nods and squints her right eye to line up the sights.

"And never point it at someone unless you want to kill them," Adam adds.

"And always pay attention to where it's pointing." Danny's volume, as usual, is much louder than necessary.

Gracie glances at Jimmy. "Don't I need to put a bullet in the chamber first?"

"No, hold on." Jimmy lowers her weapon. "Look at me. If you need to shoot this gun, we always keep a bullet in the chamber and it'll always be on safety. This one has a safety. The Glock Sophie carries doesn't. We'll train you on that one later. This is the Hi-Point. Show me its safety button again."

Gracie points to the safety.

"Good. Now, you gotta take it off safety before it'll shoot."

"I know."

Jimmy takes the gun from Gracie.

"All right, there aren't any bullets in it now, but let's pretend there are. A bad guy comes and threatens—"

"Don't scare her, Jimmy." Anna-Lee has taken a break from her wood chopping and leans against a tree nearby, her hatchet in hand.

Jimmy grins mischievously. "Okay, the bad guy threatens to steal your, uh, pet goldfish."

Danny laughs. "Yeah, while armed and dangerous."

"An armed and dangerous goldfish thief?" Gracie flashes her characteristic wide smile.

"Stop being silly while holding a gun," Adam scolds them.

Anna-Lee leans close to Adam and says, "I'm so glad you said that. I hate always being the one to scold them for doing dumb stuff."

"I don't want her to be scared, Adam." Jimmy glares at Adam for a moment, then shoots his gaze back to Gracie. "Fear will make you shake. It'll tunnel your vision and race your heart." He points to Gracie, lecturing her. She hangs on his every word. "Whatever you do, do not be afraid. Stay calm. Fear is your greatest enemy in a fight."

"That's true," Adam admits.

Jimmy sets the handgun on a stump in front of Gracie, and points at the target. "All right, Gracie, there he is—the bad guy. Now get the gun and shoot him."

Gracie reaches for the weapon.

"Hold it tightly," Danny interjects, "like we showed you, 'cause it's gonna kick you hard."

Gracie glances at Danny cockeyed. "How can it kick me when it doesn't have any legs?"

Danny laughs until he catches the smirk on Anna-Lee's face. She shakes her head, frustrated with the boys' attempt at humor while training Gracie. Pointing at the frowning face carved into the tree, Jimmy says, "Anna-Lee's right. No goofing off with guns. Now, shoot the bad guy."

Gracie raises the weapon, squints, and lines the sights up with her right eye. She tries to pull the trigger, but she is unable.

"You forgot to take it off safety," Danny informs her.

Gracie purses her lips, disappointed in herself. "Whoops." She takes it off safety and aims again.

"You can't forget." Jimmy stretches out a hand, palm up. "Put it on safety and hand it to me safely."

Gracie flips the safety switch and hands the gun to him, being careful to keep it pointed at the ground. Jimmy takes the gun and sets it on the stump.

"Let's do it again . . ."

"Guns," I mumble with a shudder. "I can't take this." I turn and walk away down the trail.

Adam calls out to me. "Where are you going?"

"For a walk."

"Hey."

I stop and turn to him. "At least take an assault rifle with you." He extends a rifle toward me. I smirk at his invitation. "You might hate seat belts, but they can still save your life."

* * * * *

After finishing an evening meal of grilled tulip buds with some squirrel meat and beetle grubs mixed in, Adam and Anna-Lee join me around the outside fire pit. The others are playing a game inside the tepee, trying to be the first to get a fire going with nothing but a stick, a strip of twine, and a piece of flint. Joey, bored, hobbles over and plops into Anna-Lee's lap.

Joey gets up and switches to my lap. Anna-Lee pretends to be offended, so he switches again. Anna-Lee and I take turns appearing offended that he switched to the other. He laughs, continuing the game for fifteen minutes until we're sick of it. He enjoys the attention, and we tolerate his obsession with the game to give him some much-needed pleasure.

Anna-Lee rummages through the backpack. I can tell by the look on her face, she's worried.

"How much?" I ask.

"Huh?"

"How much emergency food do we have left?"

She sniffs, fighting a cold today. Or allergies. She opens her mouth to answer and then widens her eyes at Eli and Gracie, who come bolting toward her out of the tepee. Anna-Lee and I agreed not to discuss such issues in front of the others. We don't want to create unnecessary fear in our younger siblings.

"Well?" Eli draws near in anticipation of Anna-Lee's answer.

"How much?" Gracie wonders aloud.

"Y'all go back inside the tepee for a bit. We're having a private conversation." Eli and Gracie reluctantly shrink back into the tepee as Anna-Lee peeks into the satchel. She draws close to me to prevent the others from overhearing. "We've got to catch or pick what we eat every day. We have only two days of emergency rations left. We need to not touch that except in emergencies—"

"What?" Gracie stomps out of the tepee.

"Only two days of food left?" Eli's right behind her, his brow furrowed.

Anna-Lee apparently didn't whisper quietly enough, thanks to her plugged up sinuses. Faith crawls out of the tepee, then Jimmy and Danny, all joining in the complaint.

"But I'm hungry now." Gracie looks like she's about to cry.

"Me, too." Eli's poor appetite in a home overflowing with food has suddenly blossomed in a forest strikingly devoid of edible calories.

"Jimmy," Anna-Lee asks, "is there anything we can do to try to improve our catches in your traps?"

He sighs. "Going farther away is risky."

Anna-Lee turns to me and mumbles, "Gives new meaning to the prayer, 'Give us this day our daily bread.'"

Danny throws up his hands. "Maybe we should just let the little kids eat for now. We got more stored up."

"You do!" Jimmy objects.

"No, I'm serious. Let me finish. The little kids'll starve first. I'm not going to survive on a starvation diet while they die off one by one. No way. I think we four oldest should fast and pray, and let the little ones eat what's left of the food. We can last until the corn in the field"—he points eastward—"is edible in about five to six weeks."

"*If* it's edible," Jimmy comments.

Danny turns to him. "What do you mean?"

"They didn't get to plant before the crisis. What's growing is probably hybrid leftovers from last year. That's why it looks so bad. There might not be much in the way of ears on all that greenery."

"He's right," Adam says. "We can't count on it. Besides, in five or six weeks, that field of corn will be so raked over there'll be nothing left."

I study the little ones for a moment. They don't appear as traumatized by this conversation as I expected. They know full well what's at stake. "Danny, it's easy to speak of fasting after you've eaten, and abandon the notion once the hunger pains begin."

Danny shakes his head side to side. "I haven't had a full stomach since we devoured that buck."

Jimmy stares at him with a disbelieving smirk. "You fast when you have food in your fridge, not when you're starving. I need to keep up my strength. We all do. We might have to defend ourselves at any time, and I guarantee you, all the maniacs out there are not fasting." "Everyone in the city is not a maniac." I turn to Jimmy. "There are still good people out there."

Anna-Lee nods. "Right. It's just that there's too many bad people to risk going out there to find them."

Jimmy shakes his head in disbelief. "Did any of our neighbors come to our help when we were attacked? No. We're on our own."

"Well, did we go help any of our neighbors?" I ask. "No. Let's not judge others by a standard we aren't following. It was every family for themselves on the first day."

Adam's eyes appear glossed over as he recalls those desperate first days.

Eli is troubled. "Are we gonna starve?" His voice is high-pitched, as is characteristic for him when he is anxious or in trouble for something.

"We're gonna fast and pray until God meets our needs," Danny asserts confidently. "Fasting is just prayer with more power. He will answer our prayers. You'll see."

I jostle Joey in my arms as he falls asleep. The thought of running completely out of food has never been as disconcerting to me as it seems right now. "I'll fast with you for a miracle, Danny."

"Me, too." Anna-Lee reaches for Danny's shoulder. "I'm proud of you for proposing it."

"You're being unrealistic!" Jimmy grows angry. "Crazy!"

"Realistically," Anna-Lee quips, "manna shouldn't have fallen from the sky. Realistically, the Jordan River should have never parted, and five loaves and two fishes should have never—"

Jimmy interrupts, "You don't think we should look for food, Anna-Lee? That's insane!"

Anna-Lee keeps her calm. "I think if we seek first the kingdom of God and His righteousness, then all these things will be added unto us."

"Fine, you fast." Jimmy turns to Eli. "We could use some extra heapings on our plates, huh, bud?"

Eli nods at Jimmy, and then, sensing my disapproval, turns his gaze to the dirt disgracefully.

Anna-Lee, Danny, Adam, and I spurn Jimmy's mocking to skip a day of meals. It is harder than I thought it would be. The night is fitful as our stomachs growl with hunger. Every twist of my gut reminds me just how close the little ones are to feeling this pain for lack of food, our stores are dwindling so low. I make a deal with my whining body, that every time I think of food, I will call upon Jesus' name. The more delicious the food I'm imagining, the more passionate will be my prayer.

I cry myself to sleep over and over all night long, whispering Jesus' name. I know the Bible says He loves us, and He knows what we need before we even ask. If we ask anything in His name, we will receive it. If He spared not His own Son upon the tree, how will He not freely give us all things? Why then do I feel like I need to beg a reluctant God to do what a loving God would have already done?

5

A THIRST FOR VENGEANCE

THANKS TO ADAM'S GIFT OF making tasty meals from insects, frogs, and edible plants, and spurts of increased harvests in Jimmy's traps—definite answers to prayer—the following weeks provide periods of relative plenty interspersed with times of desperate need. The presence of Adam has made tolerating Jimmy much more palatable. Adam's still limping, and he can't run; deep down inside, I'm glad he has to stay longer. The most significant contentions with Jimmy appear to occur when Adam is gathering food or taking his turn in the lookout. Adam's very good at concealing our footprints and camouflaging the trails we often take, making our presence more inconspicuous and those trails less passable. I still struggle with forgiving him, though I cannot deny he has changed for the better. When we are inadvertently alone, my heart still beats wildly and my palms get sweaty. I try to avoid those situations, even as he appears to covet them. He knows the kind of discussions that make me uncomfortable—about marriage, child-bearing and rearing, home-making, etc.—and so, deferring to me, he tries to engage in conversation with me on subjects that do not threaten our unstated truce. However, whenever he's engaging in conversation with Anna-Lee, especially on those sensitive subjects, I cannot deny that I fight the urge to get jealous. Sometimes I feel so, so torn about Adam, so fickle.

Gathered around the small fire in the early evening of the hottest day of the year so far, Jimmy opens his coin set to admire his collection and his other cherished treasures, with Danny and Eli looking over his shoulders. He fingers through the gold and silver coins. He pulls out his shark's tooth, his Indian arrowhead, and precious gold nuggets and polished agate stones one by one, appreciating the color, the luster, and the diversity. Occasionally he hands a coin or a strange rock or a shard of old pottery to one of his siblings to enjoy—with stern warnings to be careful and return it unharmed, of course.

In spite of the smiles on everyone's thin faces, I can tell Jimmy's treasures have lost much of their luster in his own eyes. When you're hungry, the few clothes you have are wearing down to threads, your shoes barely fit, and you're fearful of thieving criminals roaming the shadowy woods around you, the attraction of trinkets diminishes considerably.

Anna-Lee entertains little Joey by tickling his belly, making him roar with laughter. When she lifts his white shirt, soiled brown and black from overuse and the lack of soap, I am taken aback by how thin he is. I can see his ribs. He has always been skinny, but now he looks unhealthy. However, as the youngest of the eight of us, Joey already appears to have forgotten the luxuries of our well-to-do lifestyle and is clearly the easiest to please.

Jimmy puts away his coin collection in his backpack, and then he and Danny meticulously clean the guns with strips of sheet salvaged from our home. If we go two weeks without cleaning the guns in the hot humidity of these woods, rust begins to develop in the corners and crevices of the metallic parts. Jimmy and Adam agree that gun cleaning is one practice they wish they could have mastered more thoroughly before the crisis, since our livelihood depends so much upon the functionality of these weapons. It does little good to have perfect aim if the weapon were to malfunction, should we ever need to use it to defend ourselves. In spite of my hatred of guns, I cannot deny that having them gives me some security. Thankfully, Jimmy managed to salvage some motor oil from the raided garage, which has been helpful to protect the weapons from the unkind elements.

Adam motions for Gracie to hand him his crutch by the tepee.

"It's my night in the lookout."

"Are you sure?" Anna-Lee doubts he can do it. "You're still limping."

"I've got to try to push my limits, or I'll never get better." He takes a deep breath. "Mind bringing the AR-15 up for me, and light the way?"

"Sure."

"We'll keep you in our prayers." I keep my eyes fixed on him as he hobbles into the shadows to the scraping cadence of the hand-pumped flashlight.

Jimmy finishes up cleaning the guns, and asks me, "Sophie, what do you think's gonna happen?"

I decide I should speak what I hope, not necessarily what I feel. "Maybe things will turn out better than we fear. The Bible says our prayers will be answered if we believe they will be answered. Doubt does nothing productive. Let's pray for America to be great again, with godly leaders. Freedom. Justice. We know it's God's will. Let's pray for it and believe it."

Jimmy doesn't interrupt. I consider that a breakthrough, especially considering the impracticality of my hopeful, yet naïve words. By the time the last syllable has left my tongue, it seems that my faith in those words is gone. I feel a hypocrite for simply uttering them.

Like a child who puts a tooth under her pillow hoping the tooth fairy visits but knowing that it won't. My hunger pains after our pathetic meal of grubs, grasshoppers, and wild onions seem to mock my fleeting, optimistic hope for a children's storybook ending.

"Faith in crisis always comes before great promotions," Danny says. "Daniel's lions' den adventure preceded him being elevated to second-in-command." He widens his eyes. "Of the whole pagan nation!"

Anna-Lee pauses her wrestling match with Joey. "Same with Shadrach, Meshach, and Abednego. Same with Joseph. From slave, to dungeon, to V.P. of Egypt." She raises her eyebrows and glances at me, as if expecting me to affirm her words. I just turn my gaze to the fading fire, hoping she cannot see through my veneer.

They speak with as much confidence as I have feigned, but I can tell from their demeanor that they are more steadfast than I am.

Jimmy harrumphs, as if he's less optimistic. He grabs a stick by the fire pit and stokes the fire.

Danny asks Jimmy, "What do you think's gonna happen, Jimmy?"

Jimmy raises his eyebrows and sneers, as if he was upset it took so long for someone to ask him that question. "Realistically"—he slings a rascally simper my way—"nothing good if we stay here, counting our blackberries and grubs, waiting for bad guys to find us." He leans forward and aims his index finger at me. "You said so yourself, Sophie: their footsteps are getting closer and closer to our pathetic shelter. It's just a matter of time before there will be a confrontation."

His gaze shifts from sibling to sibling, as if he were a politician making a case and they were the voters. "When winter comes, if we stay here, we're going to slowly starve to death. Especially when Adam leaves, which he's sure to do when the bone-cold nights begin to set in."

"Why are you doing this?" Anna-Lee blurts out. Jimmy's gaze darts to her, and he shrugs in wonder, pretending he doesn't understand what upset her so. "That kind of negativity, it—it just makes things worse." "It's a mathematical equation. Pretending two plus two equals something other than four doesn't alter the facts. We simply don't have enough food here to survive. We need a change of plans."

"I don't think WalMart's in business." Anna-Lee clucks her tongue in her cheek.

"And I don't think they'd take your old coins," Danny says with a smirk.

"I know we're going to have to fetch food from somewhere else besides these woods." Jimmy turns to Danny.

As if on cue, Danny says, "It's true. I remember reading that hunter-gatherers have to keep moving, or they run out of food in one place. Unless they're farming or growing grazers."

"We can set more traps farther away." Anna-Lee holds little Joey on her lap, who has grown solemn with our contentious conversation. "We've got more wire. We need to put it to use."

Jimmy rolls his eyes. "It's just a matter of time before the looters who occasionally hunt these woods find one of my snares. What then? They'll wait me out and kill me for food, or worse, they'll follow me back here for the mother-load." He motions to his siblings. "And when all the crooks in town run out of homes to loot, and the town's starving, or when they need wood to keep warm, then these woods will be crawling with criminals."

My pulse is suddenly pounding painfully in my temples. I stand and pace thoughtfully in front of Jimmy and Anna-Lee. "Well, until we run out of food, Jimmy, I say we shelve plans that involve a bunch of kids sacrificing themselves to satisfy your restless desire to look for food roaming a countryside crawling with criminals."

"Will there be fewer criminals when winter comes?" We are all silent as we contemplate Jimmy's valid point. "How do you know God won't give us the ability to take back what is ours, Sophie? To punish those who killed our parents?"

I am stunned at the foolhardy implications in Jimmy's question. "Is that what this is about, Jimmy? Vengeance?"

Jimmy leaps to his feet and raises his rifle eastward toward the city. "Our parents were murdered. Murdered! In cold blood! And the murderers are still out there!"

I stand toe to toe with him, matching his passion and volume with my own. "And they should be caught, tried, and punished, but that's not our job, Jimmy! The sword of vengeance belongs to civil authorities." I tap the scabbard of the sword in his belt. "Not you!"

"Try to make it your job," Anna-Lee says, "and it might be you getting cut by that sword."

He rolls his eyes and plops back to his seat. "We're gonna die anyway," he grumbles. "Might as well take a few of 'em with us."

"No, we're not going to die," I respond. "God's gonna come through for us. We're going to stay right here and trust Him to meet our needs."

"Let's vote on it," Jimmy calmly proposes.

That proposal rouses my anger even more. "No, we're not voting on it." I turn to Anna-Lee and Danny. "See how he always starts this junk when Adam's away?"

Jimmy raises his arms in an exaggerated shrug. "Why not just vote on it?"

"Because this isn't a democracy!" Anna-Lee exclaims. "And you're not in charge. Sophie is."

"Thank you." I nod and smile at my sister.

"Why does a vote threaten you so?" Jimmy asks.

"Democracy got the Israelites wanting to go back to Egypt." Anna-Lee gives a nod my direction. "Sophie's in charge. End of debate." Joey grows irritable with our raised voices, and Anna-Lee hands him to me. I take him in my arms and sit down against the fallen log beside us.

"Mom puts Sophie in charge over us when she's running to the mailbox to fetch the mail—" Jimmy rebuts.

"I'm not going to let you lead us into doing something suicidal!" I shout.

"That doesn't mean that you can set yourself over us forever like a little tyrant!" He overpowers me with the sheer force of his intimidating, burgeoning masculinity, all the more threatening when it has been pressure-cooked in the brutal, unforgiving setting of our wild and impoverished existence.

I am absolutely speechless. This isn't a disagreement over the rules of a game—this disagreement has life or death implications for all of us.

Jimmy glances around at the others. "Who else wants to go eat at Robby's place with me?"

Danny raises his hand. "I do."

"Robby's place?" Anna-Lee acts like she can't believe her ears. "You can't be serious."

"Robby's a murderer," I remind him.

"Who eats real food!"

"Laced with innocent blood and drunk down with a mug full of guilt and wrath. Tasty going down, but poisonous."

"What you're doing is wrong, Jimmy." Anna-Lee stands beside me. "We're not splitting up. We need to stick together. You boys should be helping us instead of conspiring to abandon us."

At those words, Eli is brought to tears. He moves closer to Anna-Lee and embraces her.

Anna-Lee leans in toward Jimmy. "What you're conspiring could kill us all!" With the darkening, cloudy sky overhead, the fire casts an eerie, shadowy glow on Anna-Lee's facial features.

"Thank you, Anna-Lee." I nod at her. "We are going to stay here and keep doing what we're doing." I sigh deeply, feeling like I finally have the upper hand with my assertive little brother. "Wait on the Lord, and He will renew our strength."

Jimmy harrumphs, tosses his stick into the fire, and grabs his rifle. Without a word, he disappears into the thicket.

"You got the lookout tonight," Danny bellows as Jimmy walks away.

Adam walks up from the opposite direction. "Y'all need to lower your voices."

"Find anything?" I ask Adam, wide-eyed with hope, as the little ones come look inside his bucket.

"What happened to Jimmy?" The little ones begin to dig through the greenery in his bucket. "Don't touch. We've got to divvy it out so everyone gets a little." He looks at me. "Found some small carrots in your garden . . ."

"You went all the way to the house?"

"On my hands and knees. I think the house is empty right now, but—"

"Please be careful."

"I was." He shakes his head side to side. "It looks like your looters have been back to the house. More windows are busted out." Adam looks at the trail down which Jimmy stomped away. "What happened to Jimmy? Another temper tantrum?"

I take a deep breath and place my forearms on my knees and drop my head onto my forearms. My headful of frizzy red hair drapes over my arms, concealing the vexation in my countenance from the others. I feel like there's a splinter in my brain, like there's something I need to do, but I don't know what it is. I glance at Adam. I'm so glad he's here. I know what I need to do. I need to forgive him. Fully and completely. But if I do that, how can I resist the love we have for each other?

Anna-Lee distracts me as she drapes her arm over my shoulders. "Days like this make me look forward to heaven."

"Which makes it a good day." Adam takes a drink from the canteen. "Got to see the glass as half full, right. A bad day with a good God is a good day indeed."

"I don't think it's very good. Remember . . . " Eli's squeaky voice breaks the silence, but he doesn't finish his sentence.

"What?" Gracie asks.

"I remember Mom reading a book to us about heaven." He glances at Faith and Gracie. "Remember that book about heaven with all the colors?"

"I remember," Faith says with a faint grin.

I recall the picture book to which he refers. The pictures were vivid, the angels were strong and gentle, and all the children were happy. No one argued, no one went hungry, and no one you loved died.

Only the popping of the bark on the burning wood and the gentle breeze through the trees interrupts our quiet introspection.

Eli leans over and whispers something to Anna-Lee.

"What'd you say, buddy?"

"I want to go to heaven to be with Mommy and Daddy."

I wish I could say something to comfort him, but if I let out a word, I know it will quickly evolve into a sob that may be difficult to suppress. So I scoot closer and embrace them both tightly, biting my lip. It's not easy to hold back the swelling tide of emotions that entice me to despair and resort to measures I may regret. Grief over what *may* happen tomorrow isn't grief at all—it's unbelief. That is never a good foundation from which to speak or act. So I keep my mouth shut, and just embrace them lovingly.

Gracie and Faith come close too, longing for the comfort of an affectionate touch.

"I miss them so much," Eli whispers, his face buried in Anna-Lee's long, increasingly knotted hair.

"Me too," Faith says, crying openly, with tears drifting steadily down her chubby cheeks.

I cradle Joey closely, who's falling asleep. "It's going to be all right, Joey. Everything's going to be all right." I feel my heart's anguish ease with the peaceful look on his little face and the love we share with each other.

I look off in the distance to where Jimmy has fled, wishing he could be here for this.

Adam painfully lowers himself to a seated position beside the fading embers, and raises his swollen leg up on a rock. Our eyes meet, and he gives me a thumbs-up. "Love never fails, Sophie," he whispers. "You're doing well." I can tell that, in spite of my inadequacy, Adam's proud of my leadership.

My heart pounds wildly with his confident wink.

* * * * *

Anna-Lee and I are up before dawn. We sit on the fallen tree that bridges the stream by our shelter, out of earshot of the little ones. She allows me to vent some frustration.

"Doesn't God promise not to give us more than we can handle," she says, trying to comfort me. "Doesn't His grace match the need? *When* we need it, not before?"

"So God thinks I can handle being a parent to so many kids in the woods? Drinking muddy creek water. Running out of food. With chaos and anarchy in the city—and everywhere, as far as we know. And arms' length from a fiancé who's broken my heart, with blood on his hands, whom I desperately love but can't bring myself to trust? Are you serious?"

Anna-Lee listens more than she talks. That's one thing I love about her. When I hear someone share their problem, I always want to fix it and move on, but Anna-Lee is willing to be quiet and just listen. Even if she has the right answer on the tip of her tongue, she knows that a prayerful, listening ear is often all the remedy that is necessary. More often than not, rather than just give the answer needed, she asks the right questions to bring me to the answer on my own.

When she does assert herself, she's always urging me to praise the Lord and be grateful for something. It goes down like castor oil, but boy, does it help. When I turn my eyes from my circumstances to the Savior, my burden is lifted, and I feel light again.

We quietly enjoy the singing of the birds and the rippling of the creek as the dawn pushes away the night. It seems we are a continent away from the brutality and suffering just a few miles away.

When the little ones begin to stir from their slumber, Anna-Lee's voice lifts spontaneously in a song, sweet and clear.

Through the change of the season, the turn of the tide,
Through the storm and the quake, the laugh and the cry,
Across oceans and desert, in mountain caves deep,
The center of God's will's the best place to be.
Wherever God leads, whether near or so far,
My home is where You are.
Home is where You are.

Our eyes meet, and I wrap an arm over her shoulder. She smiles sheepishly.

I take a deep breath of the sweet smell of morning as the first rays of the sun find their way through the dense canopy of the forest.

We watch the sun rise together in silence. As the sun warms the humid air, Gracie and Faith awake and join us, one on each side. At their request, we sing the song again, then take turns recalling happy memories from happier days.

Adam returns from his morning gathering with bad news. Nothing but two edible mushrooms and a half dozen beetle grubs. And his leg started bleeding again. His limping has worsened with the pain.

Danny comes down from the lookout just as Eli announces he's brought the water to a boil. Joey exits the tepee anticipating breakfast. He and Faith gaze longingly into the bowl of boiling brown water, hoping that something edible could be cooking at the bottom of the pan.

I am lured back to despair at the thought of having so little food to give them, but I fight the urge to be melancholy. We grasp hands around the fire pit and thank God for our morning meal, in spite of the fact there isn't much food for which to be thankful. It looks like we're going to have to dig into our emergency supply for today's meals. The harvests of grubs and edible plants are increasingly scarce. I refuse to fear tomorrow's lack, focusing instead on today's sustenance and God's boundless provision.

Before Adam can even get his harvest in the pan, and before Anna-Lee can even reach into the bug-out backpack for what is probably the last of our rice, Jimmy arrives from checking his traps with a dramatic announcement. He has set a new record! Spirits are high as he displays his trophies – three squirrels, a groundhog, and the biggest raccoon I ever laid my eyes on. We share the squirrels for breakfast and half the raccoon for dinner. We skin the groundhog and let it soak in salt water overnight to try to take some of the toughness and gaminess out of the meat.

We tell jokes until the daylight dissolves into a bright Milky Way overhead, and the forest shadows dance into the night to the rhythm of the insects' symphony. This was a unique, one-of-a-kind day, like the colorful sunset in the west, so diverse and strange you just know unusual weather must be approaching, but its prelude is too refreshing not to enjoy. The buzzing and chirping all around us and the crackling of the fire, the clapping of the leaves and groaning of the trees, the bubbling of the creek water and the swoosh of the breeze on the hilltops— all creation, including us, praise the Lord this night. As I rest my head to sleep tonight in the tepee, I have a hard time wiping the smile off my face. If we only have grace for today's problems, my cup has truly overflowed this day. I feel like a beloved daughter. I feel like I have nothing to worry about. Thank God, I started the day with praise and gratitude. It appears to have made all the difference.

6

THE Y

AT THE CRACK OF DAWN, I immediately discern something is wrong. I can't quite figure out what it is at first, but something's definitely out of place. I count the kids, as Mom and Dad frequently asked me to do when we piled into the van after a grocery store trip—we all are there, minus Jimmy who I presume is in the lookout.

Is it the heartburn from last night's raccoon? What I wouldn't give for a Tums right now.

Then, it hits me. Adam is missing. Maybe he's outside using the bathroom. Then I notice that the two bug-out bags, which are usually situated between Anna-Lee and me in the shelter, are missing.

I shake Anna-Lee. "Anna-Lee, where are the backpacks?"

She looks at me blankly and then rubs her eyes. "What?"

"The bug-out bags with food and ammo and supplies? Did you move them or see them?"

She sits up wearily. "No—where are they?"

"I don't know. Adam's missing too."

I wake up the others. They all deny taking it.

"I remember they were here when we went to sleep." Anna-Lee points at the spot where they set between us in the night. My mouth turns dry and a sweat breaks out on my skin.

Suddenly, a surge of rage courses through my veins. "Adam took 'em!" I am immediately grateful I did not pull him aside last night, as I was sorely tempted to do, and express to him my renewed desire to be with him. "I'm so naïve!"

Anna-Lee's eyes dart around the tepee. "Maybe he's with Jimmy in the lookout."

I crawl to the tarp door and raise it to exit. "Not likely. I told you we couldn't trust him."

I exit the shelter and call out to Jimmy more loudly than I would have under normal circumstances. "Jimmy!" He doesn't answer, so I climb the hill. When I arrive at the top, he jolts and rubs his eyes.

"Were you asleep?"

"No. What do you want?"

"Where's our bug-out bags? The red and black ones?"

"How am I supposed to know?"

"And where's Adam?"

He shrugs.

"The black and red backpacks are gone, Jimmy. And so is Adam."

Jimmy looks past me. "Well, there's half of what's missing, right there."

I see Adam slinking down the trail back toward our tepee. "Hey!" I shout at him.

He flinches and turns to me.

Marching right up to him, I say, "Where've you been?"

He takes a step back. "Do you mind telling me why you look so mad at me right now?"

"You know." He furrows his brow at me like I'm crazy. "Where'd they go, Adam?"

"I don't even know what you're talking about—"

"Where were you then?"

"Why's it so important to you? Do I need your permission to scout the area?"

"No, I just find it quite a coincidence that you would disappear the same time our bug-out bags disappear."

"What?"

"Don't act like you don't know!"

"Sophie." He smiles and takes my hands warmly, and I snatch them out of his grasp. His smile fades to a frown. "I didn't steal anything, Sophie." His cheeks blush.

"If he took it," Anna-Lee says, walking up, "he wouldn't have come back."

"Unless he wanted to come back to steal something else." I keep my eyes fixed on the thief. "Is everything else accounted for, Anna-Lee? The weapons and ammo?"

She nods. "Yes. But half our ammo was in those bags."

"Why won't you trust me, Sophie?"

I stare at Adam coldly. He closes his eyes and shakes his head. "Never mind. Don't answer that." He bypasses me to go to the tepee. "We'll find them. They'll turn up . . . "

The next fifteen minutes make me sympathetic toward Dad. He would have freaked out, blamed everybody, and ordered everyone to scour the house whenever he lost something of value, like his keys when he was on the way to work or an appointment. We search everywhere for those bug-out bags—twice. I act like a drill sergeant screaming at limping privates who dare to arrive at the end of the line after a long hike.

Adam joins me in my quest, except he is more patient than I. I suspect he's feigning like he's really looking for the backpacks, because he has stolen them and wants to cover his tracks. As far as believability, he'd win an Oscar. I'm more concerned about proving him a liar than I am in finding something I know we will never find. Losing that backpacks was quite a trauma, but having a Judas Iscariot living with us is an unending litany of disasters in the making.

"I didn't steal anything, Sophie." Adam shrugs. "What else can I do to prove myself to you?"

"Where'd you go then?"

"I went to check the mailbox. Remember? Chris promised to bring us some food."

"Oh," Anna-Lee says. "Why didn't you say so? Did you find anything?"

He shakes his head, disappointed.

"Is that where you took our bags, Adam? Hmm?"

He turns his gaze to me, and his eyes well with tears.

Gracie calls out to us from down by the creek. "Hey, I found something. Sophie! Come see this."

We head over and find a set of large boot prints leading to the shelter and then away. The stranger apparently walked along the creek, and from there on the fallen log to the shelter, which is why his footprints were so difficult to discover. It confirms my worst fears: it has been stolen, and a thief knows we are here.

Adam sighs. "Thank God," he says, feeling vindicated. He walks over to the fire pit, plops down beside it, and begins to play with sticks with Joey.

Red-faced and soaked with sweat, I sit by the creek staring at the boot prints, my conscience intolerably pricked. "I can't believe it. Someone stole it." My guilt for being so quick to falsely blame an innocent person is only slightly assuaged by pointing my finger at the guilty person.

Anna-Lee takes a deep breath, probably more perturbed with my barking out orders and dishing out blame prematurely than in the missing food, utensils, Benadryl, bandages, duct tape, wire, water purification tablets, razor blades, about two hundred rounds of .223 and 9 millimeter ammo, and other useful goods that were thoughtfully packed into those bags.

"What are we going to do?" I ask no one in particular.

Anna-Lee remains somewhat hopeful. "It's not a death sentence. We didn't lose everything."

My heart throbs with remorse. "Sorry for being such a jerk."

She smiles. "There's nothing to forgive."

Gracie apparently disagrees. "I forgive you for being a jerk."

I chuckle at her innocent frankness. "Thanks, Gracie."

Gracie glances at Adam by the fire. "Hey, Adam?"

"What?" he says without looking.

"Sophie is apologizing for being a jerk. Do you forgive her for being a jerk?"

I laugh at her innocent yet irritating way of playing peacemaker.

My eyes shift to him apprehensively. I feel guiltier for accusing Adam more than anything. I am about to open my lips and apologize when he speaks first. "Of course, I forgive you, Sophie." The smile on his face is so refreshing. I can see he doesn't hold it against me. I blink hard, finding the mercy quite unbelievable. "I may have done the same thing if our roles were reversed, Sophie."

If only I could be so kind to him.

Several minutes later, Jimmy walks up to me and plops down beside me. "We found another couple boot prints, up on the deer trail." Jimmy's eyes dart up the hill above our shelter toward the city, opposite the lookout. "Same boot size and make as this one."

Danny adds, "The back of the left heel has a chunk chipped out of it. Plus, there's one other set of footprints up there too. Looks like tennis shoes."

"Yeah." Jimmy nods. "Man's size. Not belonging to any of—" Suddenly, as if a light bulb goes off in Jimmy's head, he freezes for a moment. Then he leaps up and rushes into the shelter.

"What is it, Jimmy?" I ask as he tosses things around inside the tepee.

"Jimmy! Don't make a mess." Anna-Lee comes to the entrance to see what he is doing.

"Has anyone seen my box?" he shouts. When no one answers, he bursts out the shelter's entrance, trembling with rage, colliding with Anna-Lee. "Has anybody seen my box? Eli! Danny!"

"Not today." Danny shakes his head, fearful of being a recipient of Jimmy's sudden, strange rage.

"Eli?" He looks down his nose at Eli and Faith angrily. "Faith?"

"Don't go blaming people, Jimmy, like I was just doing." I wink at him. "Ain't worth it making everybody miserable."

"I've got to find it!" Jimmy's face reddens. "Who moved it?"

"You had it in your lap when I went to sleep," Eli remembers. "Before you went to the lookout."

Faith, who's holding Joey beside the stone circle, nods. "Yep. I remember."

"I saw it by the entrance to the tepee," Danny says. "I didn't touch it, though."

"Oh, no." Jimmy drops his head in his hands and begins to pace. "It's gone. Gone!"

I feel a sense of pleasure that Jimmy is distressed about losing that stupid coin collection. Every time he opened it to admire his treasures with the younger ones looking over his shoulder, it reinvigorated my sense of fierce distrust in him.

I open my mouth, but Adam speaks first. "We lost our ammo, food, and medicine, and you're whining about your box of old coins?" I am glad Adam spoke first, because that's exactly what I was going to say.

"You don't know what you're talking about!" he screams. "It was important to me."

I fix my gaze on Jimmy. "It was stolen on *your* watch, Jimmy. You were supposed to stay awake and keep watch last night."

Jimmy winces. "I did!"

Danny rests a gentle hand on my shoulder, as if to calm me.

Jimmy is perturbed by the way we all stare at him. "I do more nights in the lookout than any of you. I didn't see anything, but there was no moon. It was very dark."

"If it was so dark, the thief had to have had a flashlight, Jimmy," Anna-Lee responds. "How could you not see that?"

"Maybe he had night vision technology."

I glare at him like that was the most idiotic proposal he had ever made, but keep my mouth shut.

"Not likely." Anna-Lee sits Joey in her lap. His eyes fasten curiously on his big brother, having rarely seen him quite this flustered. "We've still got some food." Anna-Lee glances into her personal backpack and pulls out a quarter-filled jar of blackberries. "A little."

"You don't get it, Anna-Lee!" I walk to the door of the shelter. "Whoever reached through this tarp door and grabbed our stuff knows we are here. Probably all his buddies too. We're going to have to move."

Adam nods. "That's right."

"Move?" Danny and Jimmy suddenly comprehend the gravity of the situation.

"Whoever stole from us last night will be back, you can be sure of it. There are more valuable things in this shelter than food, ammo, and medical supplies." I glance at the little ones, hoping I don't have to elaborate. "We're gonna have to relocate."

"But where?" Tears come to Gracie's big blue eyes.

Adam reaches over and puts a comforting hand on her shoulder.

"We'll have to scout out a new place, more secretive, more camouflaged," Adam proposes, his hand still on Gracie's shoulder. He reaches over and squeezes Anna-Lee's shoulder as well. She reaches up to touch his hand, and smiles at him. "Far enough away that when the thief returns and finds us missing, he won't discover us even if he searches the area very carefully."

Finally, he removes his hand from Anna-Lee's shoulder. She smiles at him, then her gaze darts to me. I frown.

Anna-Lee stays with the little ones while Adam volunteers to keep watch in the lookout all day. Danny tries to take a nap, since he plans to take the night shift. Jimmy and I begin to search the woods for new campsites.

We find some places to come for food, and that brightens our spirits. We discover several large patches of blackberries, and several groundhog holes among some thorns.

After a few hours, his mood lightens. Jimmy teases his spear down what must be an entrance to a coyote or a fox den, judging from the paw prints and the feathers in the bushes around it. With half his spear shoved down the hole, it appears as if something grabs the end of it and pulls him violently toward the hole. I jump back, gasping for fear as he screams for help. He stumbles and falls with his hand at the mouth of the hole, and something jerks his hand down the hole! He reaches for my hand!

"Sophie!"

I grab him by his belt and try to pull him away. He gets one look at the fear in my face and about laughs his head off.

"You goofball!" I hit him playfully on the shoulder.

"You should've seen your face!" He flashes a wide grin as he plucks some thorns out of his arm.

My bitterness melts with his playful sense of humor.

After about four hours of walking and searching, I realize that the spot where we have our shelter is clearly the best location—close to water, well-camouflaged, out of the way of potential hunters and passersby, with an excellent lookout spot and several routes of escape. It's a bummer we will have to abandon it.

"Let's separate," I propose. "You circle around the top of that ridge, and I'll go this way. We'll meet up at the Y in about an hour."

I am the first to arrive at the five-trunk tree in the crook of the Y. The five limbs of this maple tree look like five fingers protruding from the shallow base of a massive tree trunk about ten feet in diameter. While waiting for Jimmy, I spend several minutes praying. I feel much like this five-trunk tree appears, reaching heavenward with every fiber of my being, but never touching. What does God want out of me? Why is this all happening? I know He is sovereign—that He's in control—but what's His plan? Is He just spinning me like a top, waiting for me to fall? My future looks as bleak as this huge, empty wooden hand. I feel like my faith is a tightrope I walk over a deadly ravine to a fog-concealed peak on the other side, and the rope is stretched to a breaking point. To make matters worse, my seven younger siblings follow me across it. I don't think it can bear the weight.

I wonder whether this is all a big gamble between God and the devil, similar to the trial that tested Job thousands of years ago. I can see it in my mind's eye. The devil bets that grief and hardship will make us stop trusting God, while God expresses hope that we will be true. Then He lets the devil at us to test us. All of heaven and hell watches the contest earnestly, cheering and hoping their side wins. Will it be faith with the victory, or will doubt take another victim? Both God and the devil want to press me into their respective mold, God aiming for my good, and the devil for my demise. A frigid chill creeps over my body at the thought of what they have up their sleeve next.

Or, maybe this is like a final exam on a difficult school subject. If I pass, then I move on to the next trial, the next grade level. If I fail, though, the consequences are more devastating than having to take a re-test. If I fail, my brothers and sisters die—or worse, are captured. I shudder at the thought.

Maybe passing the test would include the worst thing I could envision. The prophet Daniel, after all, was carried away as a child into captivity with the remnants of his decimated nation. How must he have felt on the first day he was bound in chains and separated from his family? Was his father killed right before his eyes, like ours? Was his mother kidnapped? Did he lay awake at night, wondering? Hoping? We have it easy compared to young Daniel, I'm sure, but our trial isn't over yet. Would God require us to go into captivity? Would I be separated from my brothers and sisters? Would I have to bury them? How could a loving God be pleased with that outcome?

Even the prophet Daniel, with all his childhood suffering, was found faithful before he was appointed to a position of leadership over the whole kingdom. The testing and trials come before the triumph. The pain precedes the promotion. Is this all just a test?

Jimmy sees me before I see him, and his first words startle me. "If Dad was alive and—"

I gasp. "Jimmy!"

He snickers as he steps inside the circle of the five-trunk tree with me. "Didn't mean to sneak up on you."

He repeats, "If Dad was alive and could prevent all this from happening, do you think he would?"

That seems like a dumb question. I readily nod. "Well, yeah."

He looks upward at the vertical limbs of the five-trunk tree for a moment, admiring this wonder of nature.

"What's your point?" I ask.

"*Why* do you suppose Dad would stop all this from happening?"

I roll my eyes, finding the question silly. "Because he loves us. Duh." "Exactly." Our eyes fasten. He smirks, like he knows something I don't know, some fact or piece of information he plans to lord condescendingly over me. "Now, Sophie, who is more loving, our earthly father or our heavenly Father?"

"Our, uh, our heavenly Father," I respond haltingly, trying to figure out where Jimmy is going with this. It feels like forbidden territory, like clicking a questionable hyperlink when you know it might be something bad and you shouldn't risk it.

"If God is such a loving Father, why would He let things like this happen? Things our loving earthly father wouldn't?"

I don't know how to answer the question. I feel a twinge of guilt for just entertaining it. This is not just a question. It is more than a question. This is Jimmy's charge against God. "Either God is not as loving as Dad, or God wants to prevent this from happening to us, but can't, because He's weak."

"Jimmy!" I rebuke him with a disapproving snarl. "Don't you dare!"

Jimmy doesn't flinch. He points heavenward. "Isn't God big enough to not be intimidated by a teenage boy's questions?" He pauses, and I see his bottom lip tremble. He is looking way too grown up to me right now. "If God gave us a functioning mind and conscience, why should He be offended at a kid's innocent questions?"

"You're dishonoring God with such questions. You're doubting His goodness."

Jimmy shrugs. "I'm just thinking through the evidence, Sophie. Help me. Help me see it differently. Why would God take Becca?"

Becca. I haven't heard that name in a long time. Jimmy's twin hadn't crossed my mind since the crisis began. She died of an accident in the home when they were four years of age. Jimmy and Becca were inseparable. Even as babies, they couldn't be placed in separate cribs without instigating strong cries and irritability in them, even as they inched to the side of the crib nearest the other.

"She's in heaven." I force a smile. "With Dad."

His eyes are distant. "Her death left such a big hole, Sophie." He pauses. "Maybe you didn't grieve over her, but I did."

"We all did, Jimmy. I loved her too."

"Would you have saved her if you could?"

I chuckle at his question, but the way his eyes fasten firmly onto mine, searching me, makes me feel like I'm on stage with a spotlight on me. The seriousness of his charge alarms me.

"Even if you knew she was going to heaven when she died," he asks, "would you have saved her?"

"Of course, but—"

"Well, why didn't God? Who's more loving, you or—?"

"Jimmy!" I take a deep breath. "God is love even if we can't figure Him out."

"Saying it doesn't prove it, Sophie. I want to know how a loving God could let Becca die. How could He let us lose our parents and face cold and rain and starvation in the woods? Was it something bad we did? Or our parents? Is that it? Maybe our suffering is because of God's justice, and our family is just collateral damage in God's divine wrath against our whole nation for forsaking Him?"

"No, Jimmy." I shake my head. "Ezekiel said God doesn't punish the children for the sins of the fathers. He doesn't punish the innocent for the sins of the guilty."

"Well, what was Becca's sin then?"

"No, it wasn't Becca's sin."

"Well, then why?!" The valley echoes his interrogation of God. "Tell me!"

After a moment's contemplation, I answer, "Remember what the people asked Jesus in Luke 13?"

He looks at me cockeyed.

"You remember. Someone asked about a tower that fell on some people and killed them. They asked if the victims were worse sinners than others. Do you remember how Jesus responded?"

He shrugs.

"Unless you repent," I quote the passage, "you will all likewise perish."

Jimmy chuckles disrespectfully as he wipes his brow sweat on his dirty sleeves. "That doesn't answer the question, Sophie."

"Yet that's *His* answer to their question. When you ask why bad things happen to good people, you're asking the wrong question. The right question is, why do good things happen to bad people? We all deserve judgment."

He is quiet for a moment. I add, "There is a devil in this world who comes to steal, kill, and destroy. Jesus comes to save, deliver, and heal."

"Sophie, you can't blame the devil—as if he can do anything to us without God's permission. Who is in charge? I mean, if you watched Becca die while you held the cure for her injury in the palms of your hands"—he stretches out his palms toward me—"how could you *not* be at fault? Hmm?" I feel a thick lump grow in my throat at his inquiry. "You blamed me for our stuff getting stolen while I was in the lookout, accusing me of not paying attention. Well, was God paying attention? Did He fall asleep? Is the stick to blame for clobbering the little kids, or the hand that holds it?"

I am reluctant to venture where his troubling line of reasoning leads. I tremble trying to balance on this tightrope over a chasm so deep and dark I can't see the bottom. I don't think my faith will survive these kinds of questions.

He raises his voice, pointing heavenward. "The hand that holds the stick!" The indignation in Jimmy's voice and grimace makes me shudder.

"I don't understand it, Jimmy, but I still believe . . . " I pause, measuring my sincerity. I don't want to lie, but I don't want to succumb to a lie either. "I choose to believe that God is good."

"In spite of evidence to the contrary?"

"Yes. In spite of evidence to the contrary. God is good. He is loving. He answers prayer."

Jimmy presses his hands against two trunks of the tree, blind to his own blindness. Not unlike sightless Sampson, reduced to a slave when his shackled hands first rested on the pagan pillars of doubt and depravity in that Philistine temple. "You know, Sophie, having to simply accept a lack of understanding or the lack of any meaningful explanation for what we're going through, it can cover up a lot of incompet—"

"Careful!" I interrupt him. "I fear to tread where your thoughts are slithering."

He raises his hands heavenward. "I can't ask God why?"

A haunting silence follows. I don't know how to answer, and Jimmy waits as if expecting God's voice to bellow out of heaven, making perfect sense of it all. A rare tear swells in his eye. I am beginning to understand what's been going on in this boy's head. What may have started out as innocent grief over Becca's death, the loss of our parents, and our way of life is now overshadowed by a seductive anger and bitterness that promises relief, but doesn't deliver. Just as the Israelites ended up worshiping the bronze serpent on the staff that brought healing from their painful snake bites, so God's blessings can be the means of our fall if we cling too tightly to them. I am admonished by Jimmy's bad example. Even if I lose everything, even if my prayers go unanswered and every day brings more and more suffering and grief, I must still cling to Jesus. Grasping more tightly to God's blessings than to God is idolatry, and God is a jealous God.

"There's a reason why bad things happen to good people, Jimmy."

"Yeah, yeah. You take your leap of faith, blind as a bat," he says mockingly. "Maybe I've opened my eyes. That's why I don't jump so quickly."

I am getting really frustrated with him, but I find myself without objection. My conscience dares to take sides with Him against God. Why does my faith seem so fragile? I want to wrestle these poisonous doubts out of both our heads. I just don't know how. Perhaps if I can help Jimmy trust God, I can banish my own wavering.

"Do you remember when Jesus' disciples asked why a man was born blind? Do you remember what Jesus said?"

Jimmy thought for a moment. "I think He said that it was for the glory of God . . ."

"Right."

"Then He healed him . . ."

"Yep."

"But where's the miracle, Sophie?"

"It's coming."

He raises his voice. "Like it came to Becca?" I clear my throat roughly. "You talk about some future miracle because you think it's the right thing to say, but you know the truth." He leans into me, letting me look deeply into his cold blue eyes. "We're all alone!" Spit flies out of the corners of his mouth as he screams. "What happens to us is up to us, not God! There is no loving Father out there to answer our prayers, because if there was, He wouldn't have let this happen to us!" His face reddens as he fumes. "You feel it down in your gut just like me!"

I keep my voice calm. "We walk by faith, not by sight, not by feelings and circumstances that fluctuate like the weather."

"Do you really believe a miracle's coming? Don't lie to me, Sophie."

My heart echoes with his implied accusation. Am I lying? Do I really believe that everything will turn out well? Am I being naïve to believe that God really cares about what we're going through and that He really will intervene to protect us because He loves us, because He answers prayers? People He's surely loved more—martyrs, apostles, and missionaries—people who certainly prayed with more faith than we have, they suffered much worse things.

"You'll only see the miracle," I say, "if you believe. If there is no miracle coming, God will give us the strength to endure." Tears fill my eyes at the thought of it. "And He rewards us in accordance to our sacrifice. But if you disbelieve, Jimmy, what do you have then?"

Jimmy removes the magazine from his AR-15, and reinserts it, keeping silent.

"God's judgment. That's what."

I see Jimmy's brow furrow, and he opens his mouth to speak but stops himself. I try to imagine what impudent comeback he has withheld. It's hard to resist the sway of Jimmy's doubt. If God were restrained by the limitations of man, I'd have to side with Jimmy against Him. But God is beyond us. His holiness is set forth as our example, and His Spirit is given to help us be holy, but His power and wisdom are far beyond us. When I cannot reconcile reality with the description of God's character as found in His Word, I must rest content with trusting Him. Jimmy—I cannot deny it—has reality on his side, but only because He can't see the future. I only have a hope in a good outcome, which lingers suspended by a storm-tattered and sun-beaten thread of children's stories and bedtime prayers.

Jimmy turns his gaze away from me, biting his lip. Sensing a foreboding threat to his soul and a seductive temptation to my own, I swing the two-edged sword again: "Believe in the Lord Jesus Christ and you will be saved, Jimmy. To disbelieve God is to insult God, to spit on His sacrifice."

Those words appear to enrage him. His face reddens and he unexpectedly heaves a mocking laugh. "Well, I feel better already, knowing He's coming to squish all the unbelievers and—"

"Jimmy!" I am aghast at the extent of his fearless mockery.

He leans closer to me and wags his finger in my face. "Listen! We loved God. Now our parents are dead, and we are racing toward starvation and winter. With hordes of godless criminals roaming the city just a few miles away"—he points east— "on their way here now for all we know. And we have to believe God cares about us even when

He doesn't answer our prayers, and we're threatened with hell if the hard evidence dissuades us at all."

"Sometimes the only good answer to the question 'Why' is 'Believe.'"

He sneers at my comment. "That's a cop out. Another red herring to distract from the bankruptcy of obvious, self-evident facts."

I take a deep breath, wondering what words could possibly shake my brother out of his stupor. I wish I could just scare faith into him. Like God did, freaking out Job with a face-to-face confrontation, telling and showing him how great and powerful He was. That made even righteous Job put his hand over his mouth, regretting his questioning of God's justice.

"Do you remember what God told Job at the end of his trial?"

Jimmy shakes his head and turns away.

"He reminded Job how great He was, and how small Job was in the grand scheme of things. We are so puny, Jimmy, compared to God. This short moment of misery is so tiny compared to all eternity. The fear of the Almighty'll keep you from uttering foolish things that may come back to haunt you on Judgment Day."

Jimmy sighs and turns his gaze down to fiddle with the action of his AR-15. He wipes his eye, and I wonder if he is about to cry. For a moment, I think he's starting to break. "I just don't understand, Sophie," he utters under his breath. He steps outside the circle of the five-trunk tree and begins to walk slowly down the trail.

"We are told to pursue understanding, Jimmy, but also . . ." I walk toward him and catch up to him. "Also we're told to trust in the Lord with all our hearts, and lean *not* on our own understanding." I rest a gentle hand on his shoulder, and he stops. "In all your ways acknowledge Him, and He shall direct—"

He suddenly turns and shakes my hand violently from his shoulder, forcing me to take a step back. With a surge of fury in his voice, he exclaims, "Those are just words, Sophie! You can't save precious four-year-old girls with them! You can't cure cancer with them! You can't eat them! You can't kill your enemies with them! I need . . . " He thumps his chest with his fist. "We need *real* help!" He lowers his right fist hard into his palm with each exclamation: "Defense! Provision! Food! Good water! What does the Bible say about telling a needy person you love him without meeting his need?"

I don't answer his question. Jimmy must discern in my facial features that I am troubled by the answer my lips will not speak.

"You know, Sophie. Answer it!" He sneers at me scornfully. "Let's examine God in the mirror of His own Word. Does God demand more love from us than He has Himself? What is love that doesn't meet basic needs when it is in your power to meet them? It's a lie, and you know it!" He takes a step closer to me, balls a hand into a fist, and loudly screams, "I need cold, hard reality, Sophie!"

"God's promises *are* reality . . . "

He overpowers me with his volume, smacking his chest with each syllable. "Not! Empty! Words!"

Though I am tempted to back away from his aggressive posture, I hold my ground and look into his eyes, careful to keep my voice calm. "Faith is the substance of things hoped for, the evidence—the cold, hard reality—of things not seen. Do you really want evidence for the love of God you can't see? Then believe."

Jimmy turns his fiery gaze away from me, clearly struggling not to cry. Suddenly, the limbs and branches of the trees overhead feel like they reach lower for me, trying to smother me with their weight.

The shadows seem to inch their way toward me, threatening me. The air seems heavy, and my breathing rate quickens. I know what's happening. My panic is coming back. I feel as claustrophobic as if I'm locked in a coffin under fifty feet of dried concrete. I dig my toes into the ground, trying to resist the fear that rises to the surface just under my skin, tempting me to flee, to hide. No! I will not abandon Jimmy. I will not be intimidated by his idiotic interrogation of God, or of my own fears and doubts.

Jimmy tries to walk away, but I reach for him and grab his shirt to stop him. I want to give him a hug. What words cannot communicate, sometimes a touch can. But he jerks his shirt out of my grasp and picks up his pace.

"I'm scared too, Jimmy." My voice trembles with fear. "But what's the victory that overcomes the world?"

He keeps walking away. "Stop!" I cry out. "Look at me!" He stops, reluctantly turns, and our eyes fasten. "What's the victory that overcomes the world?"

His eyes lighten. I know he knows the answer, taken from 1 John 5. "Tell me, Jimmy."

He shrugs as I walk up to him. I try to hug him before he can protest. He lets me, and even wraps one of his arms around me briefly, but I sense him more tightly embracing the doubt deep in his heart.

After a moment, he pushes me away and, without a word, heads down the trail.

The sun is setting. We haven't found a good spot. We'll have to look again tomorrow.

7

VIOLENT COLLISION

AS THE SETTING SUN BEGINS to fill the sky with orange and pink, Faith comes up with a grand idea. We put our names in a jar, and decide that on every full moon we will have a birthday party for whoever's name is drawn.

Faith pulls Danny's name first, and I'm so glad. As the fourth of eight kids, I always felt like Danny got left out of things. We sing "Happy Birthday" to him around the dying fire. We give him gifts of art work, paintings the kids spent hours on, using different shades of mud meticulously scraped on slippery elm or chestnut bark. Adam gave him a necklace of different sized acorn caps, and taught him how to press them between his thumbs and against his lips to whistle a different tone with each cap. With a little practice, he catches on nicely. Backdropped by the kids' creative percussion, Danny has quite a symphony going there for a while. He is all smiles and cackles as we tell funny stories about him for an hour. His willingness to engage in self-deprecating humor for our entertainment always makes him a hoot when the little ones' giggle-boxes are turned on. Though we do have to continually remind him to keep his voice down.

Jimmy, unfortunately, missed the party. He wanted to take advantage of the remaining sunlight to try and set new traps farther away. I don't miss him, and it seems to me the others do not miss him much either. There's always contention when he's around, though I do start to worry about him as the sky darkens.

With the warmer weather, the mosquito activity picks up exponentially. Adam's anti-bug gourmet recipes involve quite a bit of wild onion and wild garlic, which makes our breath stink horribly but is quite protective against insect bites. The smoke from the fire is also helpful, and so we keep close to the fire pit on warm evenings in spite of its unwelcomed heat. Mud smeared around our neck, ears, and other exposed parts of our bodies helps keep the bugs away, though it makes our appearance rather frightening.

Under the matching orange glow of the dying embers and the disappearing sun, we softly sing as many songs as we can remember until the little ones' eyes droop with fatigue. I lay back and watch the last rays of the sunlight skim the tops of the trees overhead. The trees gradually darken as the light rises, permitting the night to take over.

Anna-Lee settles Joey down for the night in the tepee, rekindling a small fire inside to drive out the damp humidity that seems to accumulate in our little shelter during the day. Danny fills a canteen with the last of the boiled water in the pan beside the fire and prepares to head up to the lookout for the night.

"Where is he?" Anna-Lee gazes down the trail down which Jimmy disappeared. "He's normally back before dark." Anna-Lee stands with her palm pressed against a tree, searching the deepening shadows of the deer trail. Momentarily, she grabs the guitar and settles down next to the fire to strum one of the tunes she has written.

"He's pouting." Adam is trying to read from the red Gideon Bible by the light of the fire. He turns briefly to me. "He's unpredictable when he pouts. All rules and care for others is shut out of his mind when he's consumed with himself."

"Yep." I nod. "That's Jimmy. At least since the crisis. He was never like that before.'"

"Sometimes, the crisis just reveals what's been there all along." Adam turns his attention back to the Gideon Bible.

I clear my throat, and he turns his eyes up briefly to meet mine. "And sometimes the crisis changes you." My voice is stern, and his countenance drops briefly. He knows I'm referring to his change for the worse after the crisis began.

"Yep," he replies. "But God can always change you back." He turns to me and speaks softly. "Thanks to the help of those who love you most."

We smile at each other, and I feel a warmth flush over me. I turn my gaze toward the last rays of daylight, feigning like I'm unaffected by his kind comment, but I cannot flatten my smile.

"What?" he says, holding his grin firm.

"Adam, thank you for being my friend."

He laughs. "I'll always be your friend, Sophie." He pauses for a moment. "I love you."

Anna-Lee pauses her guitar picking when she hears his proclamation. She catches the embarrassed look on my face and discerns that she should keep playing and not make a big deal of Adam's comment.

I swallow hard and turn my gaze away from him. He quietly adds, "Be it yet unrequited."

Out of the corner of my eye, I see he has turned his attention back to the Bible, so I keep silent. My heart urges me to respond in kind, but the moment has passed, the opportunity neglected.

"I hope he's okay." Anna-Lee pauses her guitar picking to turn toward the darkening east. Faith scoots up close to Anna-Lee, enjoying her musical talent.

"He's fine," Danny assures us. "He took the flashlight."

I motion toward the fire pit, around which Gracie and Eli warm their hands as the night's humid chill settles down on us, dropping dew on our bodies and on the ground. "Stay here. I'll go look for him."

"No, Sophie," Anna-Lee and Adam object simultaneously.

"It's okay. I could use some alone time, and I'll be back before you're asleep. We're going to have to get up early to look for a new location to move."

"Now I'm gonna worry every sound in the woods is Jimmy or you creeping up on me." Danny turns his gaze up the hill toward the lookout, wagging his head fretfully. "Y'all are in danger of getting shot."

"We know you're there, and you know we're out there. We'll whistle at you if we're coming in."

"You better." Danny tosses the AR-15 over his shoulder by the strap. "The full moon will be up for a couple more hours. Be careful."

Danny wishes us good night as he begins to walk on fallen tree over the creek toward the lookout.

With the holstered 9 mm handgun, I take off down the deer trail. There is starlight overhead, but the moon is still too low in the sky to give much light. I hope it will rise soon enough to help illuminate my way back to the shelter. I don't like using the flashlight at night anyway. It makes me nervous to call such attention to myself for every hoodlum and predator within a hundred yards.

At the Y, instead of following the path left toward Jimmy's traps on the outskirts of the forest, I take a right northward toward our home.

It has been my standing rule that we are all to stay out of view of the home in case the looters return, as they are sure to do from time to time. But I have a deep suspicion that Jimmy's wandering would lead him back there. When your faith teeters and the ground beneath your feet feels like quicksand, the temptation to retreat to something familiar, albeit painful, offers a false hope of relief.

Everything looks the same in our backyard except the grass has grown above my knees. I stay behind the cover of the trees for several minutes, carefully watching for any movement through the broken windows. Everything is still. Almost too still.

A crop of sunflowers blooms under the long-empty bird feeder, inviting me to pick a few as I make my way slowly toward the house.

My legs take me where my fearful thoughts have settled. I walk into the garage to the spot where I last saw Mom.

I can barely make out the darker area on the concrete where Mom stood, firing at our attackers with Jimmy's Ruger. It is the angular splatter of blood we saw when we first came back to the house.

My legs are weak. I fall to my knees, and something snaps inside me. I know she's dead. I feel it in my bones. I begin to mourn like I have never mourned before. I have always felt the pressure to be strong for the sake of the others, but here by this splatter of dried blood in our garage, my heart gushes forth tears and sobs.

The raucous sound of my weeping startles me. The night is too quiet to make so loud a noise for the luxury of an honest, long-suppressed cry. I press my hand against my mouth to still my grief.

Why God would ever take you away from us, Mom, I'll never under-stand. If you knew what you left behind, I can't see how you could be happy in heaven. Unless amnesia handicaps you when you cross over to the other side, how could a wave of God's hand remove the tears from your eyes?

I turn my gaze up to the edge of the moon that begins to peek over the shed, shining its reflection down on me. I imagine it is the half-wink of God's eye, staring at me beside the stench-filled, defiled ruins of our beloved home. Is it a wink of doubt? Of mischievous intent? Is it a wink of spite? I imagine the squinted eye is peering down a scope with crosshairs on my chest. I feel so helpless under God's hand, unable to touch Him, unable to move Him.

"Tell her I love her, Lord." The tears flood down my cheeks. "Dad, too. Tell 'em we miss 'em. Tell 'em that we're holding on."

With those words, God's wink takes on a new meaning.

I sense He's proud of me.

I take several deep breaths to try to settle my emotional turbu-lence. Momentarily, I set the flowers on the spot where I last saw her, and bend down low to kiss the stain.

"Oh, Mother," I whisper, as my tears drip onto the blood stain.

I think I hear a noise in the home, and I quickly turn to peer toward the side door. It is closed. At least I think it's closed. I can barely see it, as the other half of the garage is an empty black expanse, leaving room for my imagination to fill in the blanks with monsters. Is that movement I see in the darkness? Is someone there staring back at me? A coyote? A mouse? An escaped convict?

I think to call out for Jimmy, and then reprove myself for such a foolish thought.

I unholster my handgun and chamber a round. Slowly, carefully, I crawl through the garage toward the backyard until I am well into the cover of the thick unmowed grass.

* * * * *

The day is finally here!

I'm in my wedding dress on the platform across from the love of my life, Adam Branson. My dress is exactly what I dreamed it would be. I fasten my eyes on my husband-to-be. Our eyes embrace fully, a prelude to our long-sought oneness. I see the longing in the turned up corners of his lips.

Adam turns and widens his eyes at the preacher, as if to prod him on. Adam and I turn to Pastor John, who grins bashfully, as if he's embarrassed he's lost his place. He glances at the leather folder he's holding, his finger running along his notes, looking for his next line.

The preacher clears his throat. "Adam," he pronounces, "you may, uh, shake your bride's hand."

Everybody laughs. Except me. I turn toward the audience, searching for my parents. Their pew is empty. My brow furrows. Where are they?

The preacher pats Adam's shoulder. "Ah, just kiss her, will you?"

Now Adam's smile is wide and full, baring his teeth. He raises my veil more quickly than we had practiced. I flinch at his careless error. Something's not right.

"My Sophie," he whispers.

The bridesmaids hear his sweet utterance, and giggle. Suddenly, the flower girl drops her flowers. I see it out of the corner of my eye. The preacher fumbles with his leather folder like he's searching for the right page. He coughs. I frown. Something's wrong. I turn back to Adam, who is oblivious. He slowly lowers his lips to mine. His eyes are fastened on my lips. I close my eyes for my first kiss, but only for a moment. I sense the preacher staggering, and someone behind me gasps. I open my eyes and turn to Pastor John. I stretch out a palm to Adam's chest, stopping his lips an inch short of mine. The preacher's mouth is agape, staring behind me into the audience.

I turn to the crowd of friends and family, and before I can focus, everyone jolts with a loud gunshot. It rings my ears. I flinch and clench my eyes and fists. Adam lets go of my veil, and it falls back across my face. When I open my eyes, several blood droplets stain my veil. Adam collapses. There is more gunfire.

The audience screams as one and begins to flee frantically for the exits. Someone is shooting at them from the back of the church . . .

* * * * *

The sound of gunfire startles my heart to a frightening speed in an instant. I feel the pounding pulse in my temples. My fingers tingle, and my limbs feel heavy. Dad falls hard in the front yard. I open my mouth to scream "Dad!" but no sound comes out. Sparks fly up at my feet as the bullets scrape the driveway beneath me. As if through a long tunnel, I hear the echo of Joey's shrill cry of terror, and I feel Faith go limp as I hold her hand.

A cold chill jerks me from my nightmare to the breaking dawn, only to hear the frighteningly close chatter of gunfire. This is no dream. I dart upright with alarm. Joey is crying loudly. I cannot see a thing in the darkness, as the embers have grown dim under a thin layer of white ash.

Anna-Lee stirs the embers, and it provides some light. Her eyes are ablaze with fear. She hands Joey to Gracie and reaches for her Taurus 9 mm hanging in its holster in a crook of the tepee frame.

"Who's in the lookout?" It's Adam's voice. He's alive.

I look around the tepee to see both Jimmy and Danny are missing.

"Danny's in the lookout!" I reach for the Glock. "Where's the other AR? Where's Jimmy?"

Three more gunshots ring out and one of the bullets pierces the shelter, provoking even stronger cries of fear from the children.

"That was from behind us." Anna-Lee pulls Eli closer to the ground, and points to the rear of the shelter.

"Stay low—and pray!" I crawl toward the exit. "Gracie, lower!"

"No, I'll go." Adam tries to crawl to the exit.

"Not with your leg." I chamber a round. "You stay and protect them."

I poke my head out of the shelter's tarp door. The dim light of morning is illuminated by the flashes of Danny's gunfire over a fallen log at the top of the woody hill. He shoots to the left, and then the right of our shelter. A bullet shot from the shadows to my right strikes the rotting tree just a few inches below Danny's flash. Danny disappears below the fallen tree. I worry he's been shot.

Momentarily, I see he has repositioned himself on a fallen tree farther down the hill and is shooting to my right.

I crawl out of the tepee with my handgun and search the shadows to my right, but I can't see a thing.

The echoes of my troubling dream fill me with fright. I'm not ready to tell Adam good-bye . . .

Another blast of gunfire brings me back to the present crisis. There's no time for regrets or hesitation. I duck back inside the shelter, relieved to see Adam is okay. He has moved close to the exit, his knife unsheathed.

"Don't let them capture you," I say. The little ones whimper fearfully, but there's too much at stake to mince words for the sake of their tender feelings. "Fight them! All of you!" Adam grips his knife more tightly. Sweat beads on his brow.

Eli picks up a cool rock on the outer edge of the fire pit, preparing to use it as a weapon. I cannot bear the thought of any of them being captured.

"I'll protect them," Adam assures me.

Anna-Lee checks the action on her handgun. "Sophie, go help Danny."

I step out of the tepee, quietly searching the shadowy woods for the mysterious shooter. There! It brightens the darkness, the gun blast of the perpetrator. Near him on the ground is a fallen flashlight, dimly illuminating the forest behind him. I see some movement, and then he takes another shot at Danny. He doesn't see me. I raise my handgun and aim at him, but can't see the sights. I hear Danny take a shot at him, and then a loud grunt and the thud of a body against the ground. The flashlight on the ground spins and comes to rest beside the bearded face of the shooter. His eyes are frozen open, his mouth agape in death.

I hear two shots behind the shelter, coinciding with an explosion of bark on the fallen tree behind which Danny is stationed. I duck back inside the shelter. Adam and the kids are ducking low. Through the tarp wall of the tepee, I see the flash of the perpetrator's rifle firing at Danny. Anna-Lee turns and shoots six rounds at chest-height through the wall of the tepee toward the attacker.

Someone on the other side of the shelter suddenly screams in pain. She has struck him!

I exit and dart around the shelter as Adam says, "Finish him, Sophie!"

Under the blackness of the low hanging trees, I can barely make out the light-colored shirt of a figure on the ground. He inches away from me until his back is against a small maple. I step closer and feel the pain of thorns digging into my flesh as I become entangled in the long tentacles of a blackberry bush.

He apparently sees me better than I see him. "Don't shoot!" he pleads. His voice is harsh and raspy, and he has a heavy hillbilly accent.

A tense moment passes and my eyes adjust better to the darkness. I can now make out what looks like a dark beard over his light-colored shirt. His right arm is outstretched in surrender. There appears to be a rifle at his feet. I can discern the light-colored wood of its stock.

I can make out the red reflective strip of our bug-out backpack. It lies in the dirt several feet away.

"Sophie?" Anna-Lee cries out with a trembling voice on the other side of our tepee. "Got him?"

"I got our thief! And one of our bug-outs!" I turn toward the lookout. "Danny?" There is no answer. "Danny!"

"I see him, Sophie." Anna-Lee answers as she steps out of the tepee. "He's moving."

"Danny? Are you hurt?" I pause, and all is silent. *Even the insects are quiet.* "Danny?"

"I'm okay," he finally responds, trepidation in his voice. "Someone else is out there. I'm not sure I got him."

I peek over the tepee. I can't see him in the lookout. He doesn't want to make himself a target. He's searching the shadows through the AR with the light-gathering scope. The cloudless sky is black in the west, and barely illuminated in the east, more from Venus and the half-moon than from the oncoming sunrise.

"There were at least three of 'em headin' for the shelter." I hear the click of Danny changing magazines, inserting a fresh one. "They could be injured out there, so keep out of sight until dawn."

I turn back around to see the injured thief reaching for his rifle. "Don't move!"

He freezes and raises his good arm in surrender again. "Don't shoot. I'm—I'm just a hungry fella who wants to live."

Adam limps around the tepee. With my eyes adjusting to the darkness, I can see the moonlight casting the shadow of his Bowie knife over the stolen black and red backpack. "Don't argue with him, Sophie, just shoot him."

"Shoot him?" I'm surprised at Adam's counsel. "You want me to shoot him?"

"No, please don't," the thief begs. "I'm no good. I'm shot."

I take a step closer to improve my aim, but my legs are bound in a knot of thorn bush branches. I see his dark eyes and scraggly beard. He has only one hand raised in the air. His rifle is at his feet. The wooden stock looks like it has been splintered by a bullet. I dare not reach for it. Not at this close distance. His right shoulder is darker than his left and I realize it is probably drenched in blood.

"Put both hands in the air!" I yell, the handgun shaking in my trembling hands.

"I can't!" His voice is raspy and coarse, like it has been scraped raw from a million cigarettes.

"Do it now!"

"I can't! I'm shot!" He coughs a wet, gurgling cough and grunts in pain.

There's more gunfire coming from Danny in the lookout. Adam ducks low. "Shoot him, Sophie!" Adam's words are calm but cold. Almost heartless.

My heart pounds in my chest. My feet feel stuck in concrete. An ocean of fear seems to quickly engulf me. I'm suffocating. My whole body buzzes with anxiety. I am paralyzed with dread.

Oh no. Not a panic attack! Not now!

The nauseating tingling creeps up my arms, up my back and neck, and over my scalp. My skin seems to crawl with ants. I try to squint away the floating white flecks that cloud my vision. I take a deep, sharp breath.

"What else can you do, Sophie? You can't let him go, 'cause he'll be back. You can't call the cops to come get him. And your weapon's needed elsewhere . . . "

I struggle, my finger pressed against the cold trigger. The thief begs. "Please! No!"

"I'm not shooting an unarmed man, Adam! No!"

"How do you know he's disarmed?"

"I am!" the thief responds. "My busted gun's right there—"

"You can't trust him, Sophie—"

I'd toss Adam the gun, but there are several bushes between us, and it's too dark for him to catch it.

"Anna-Lee!" Danny screams.

I hear Anna-Lee gasp and then a backhand collide with her cheek. She grunts in pain, and I hear her fingers scrape the bark of a tree, as if trying to steady herself.

"Look out!" Gracie screeches a blood-curdling cry. The children inside the shelter shriek with frantic urgency.

"I'll help Anna-Lee!" Adam exclaims. "If this crook moves a muscle, promise me you'll shoot him."

I can't see my sights, I don't tell him.

"Coming, Anna-Lee!" Adam turns to head toward the front of the tepee and, right when he rounds the bend, the thief suddenly lunges at me.

Blam!

I take a blind shot. My ears ring from the blast, and the flame that leaps from the barrel momentarily distorts my night vision. Dirt flies up beside the thief's body from where my bullet struck the ground.

When my eyes refocus, I see the thief has fallen short. Adam has tackled him. His arms are wrapped around the thief's legs. I see the thief has a silver blade in his grasp. I fall onto my back in the thorns, dropping the weapon.

"Adam!"

Adam screams in pain. They flip. One of them raises a knife at the other, but I can't tell who's who.

"Help Anna-Lee!" Adam urges me.

I hear Danny charging down the hill through the brush toward the tepee, yelling her name. "Anna-Lee! I don't have a shot! I'm coming!"

I stand, try to free myself from the thorn bush and find the fallen handgun.

The struggle between Anna-Lee and the unseen assailant on the other side of the tepee grows more violent, even as it sounds more distant in my mind, like I'm listening to it over the phone. There is another loud smack, and Anna-Lee groans in pain.

I hear Danny's body tumble down the hill, thumping against rocks, exposed roots, and tree trunks, finally crashing into the shallow limestone creek bed with a splash and a frightful scream.

"Come on!" I shout at myself as I desperately probe the black forest floor for my Glock. "Where is it?!"

A gravelly voice cries out in front of the tepee. "Is that you, Jack? Go get that guy that fell in the creek. I'm gonna scrape the skin off him one inch at a time."

"I'm no good," the injured thief responds, grunting in pain as he struggles with Adam. I hear punches in the darkness, and I wonder who is being struck.

Eli and Gracie shriek again, their voices so shrill it hurts my ears. Faith and Joey's crying in the tepee grows more desperate.

Anna-Lee groans in pain. "No!" she screams. "Get away from us!"

My heart pulsates more strongly at her exclamation, and then seems to take a long pause. I am suddenly so dizzy that I feel I can stand no longer. What an idiot of me to drop the gun in such a moment! I fumble for the weapon, but my panic symptoms worsen. I can barely feel my fingers. My limbs are stiff and unresponsive.

Move! My limbs are impervious to reason. I am hyperventilating. I am so nauseous. My legs are cut up and bleeding. I almost fall over. *God, help me!*

I finally wrap my fist around the coarse handle of the 9 mm. Like coming from a dark tunnel into the bright sunlight, my senses finally become more keenly aware of my surroundings, culminating in a throbbing headache.

"Get off her!" I hear Eli scream. I hear the thud of a rock against a skull, and the giant beast curses loudly in a gravelly voice. Then I hear the thud of a small body against the dirt.

Gracie exclaims, "Eli!"

Breathing rapidly, careful not to fall as I traverse fallen logs and blackberry bushes around the tepee, I soon come in view of a large man with one of his thick arms around Anna-Lee's waist. With his other, he presses the edge of a Bowie knife against her neck. I can see the glow of early dawn reflecting off its stainless steel blade. His eyes search the shadows around me. He can't see me in the shadows.

"Where's your gun?" the giant screams cruelly right into Anna-Lee's ear. She turns away from him, wincing. He momentarily takes the knife away from her throat and jerks her ear back toward him with a violent tug of a lock of her hair. "Tell me!"

"Ahh! I don't know. It fell."

"Hey!" The beast is looking right at me. He has spotted me! "Put down the gun now, missie." His coarse slur is softer now. Seductive. "I won't hurt her. Just put it down . . . "

I set my sights on him. "Drop, Anna-Lee!"

She lifts her legs to drop, but the man is strong enough to hold her up with one arm. He slams her heel against his instep, and he tightens his grip around her waist and drags her backwards until they are obscured by a tree. I see her twist her elbow to strike him in the face.

He grunts, and then strikes her in the scalp with the butt end of his knife. Anna-Lee screams in pain. "Jack! I need your gun!" he bellows to his fellow thief.

The thief locked in mortal combat with Adam exhales an inhuman growl in response.

"Give up your weapon, missie," the giant bellows, "or I'll slit her throat!"

I take aim at the round contour of his scalp, which I can barely see around the tree trunk, but without being able to see my gun's sights, and with my hands trembling so, my confidence is shaken. I don't want to hit my sister, and the brush in which I am standing makes it difficult to reposition easily.

Anna-Lee struggles to pull away from her attacker. I see his head more clearly now. I pull the trigger, but the gun doesn't fire! A jam! I slam the palm of my left hand against the back of the slide to ensure the bullet is all the way in the chamber, and re-aim. Still, the trigger does not fire the weapon. Must be a dud primer. I struggle to eject the round and load another bullet into the chamber, but when I look up, the giant has moved behind the cover of the tepee.

I kick against the briers toward the front of the tepee to get a shot at Anna-Lee's attacker, when suddenly, to my horror, I hear a gunshot in front of the shelter.

"Anna-Lee!"

I stumble around the tepee to see Gracie holding a smoking handgun—the one that got knocked out of Anna-Lee's hands.

Gracie speaks more calmly than I think possible under these circumstances. "I remembered to take it off safety this time."

Eli starts to cry. He's lying on his back next to the fire pit. "What happened to him?" I bend down to check on him.

Gracie informs me that he had the breath knocked out of him when the thief threw him down. Eli begins to hyperventilate, wheezing, gasping for air. I feel the back of his head and spine. No wetness. "Take slow, deep breaths, Eli. You'll be all right."

The motionless thief suddenly begins to writhe and gurgle, struggling to breathe. He is so big, I can't imagine Goliath being a pound heavier or an inch taller.

Still holding the handgun, Gracie takes a step closer, squints her left eye shut, and lines up her right eye down the sights at the man's head, but before she can pull the trigger Jimmy arrives with his AR-15 and puts three hollow-point bullets through his chest. We all startle, jumping back at the unexpected shots from his rifle at such close range.

Jimmy is breathing heavily, branch-scraped, and sweat-drenched from his sprint through the dimly lit woods. Everyone stares disapprovingly at him, wondering where he has been. I'm too angry at him to say anything. Following my lead, no one else does either.

Danny arrives, limping, with scraped elbows and a knot on his forehead. We all stare at him for a second.

"Ow," he says, quite anti-climatically.

Anna-Lee extends a hand for the handgun Gracie's grasping. "Hand it to me safely." Keeping it pointed to the ground, she places it on safety and hands it to her.

Jimmy turns toward the tepee. "Who's back there?"

In the violent conflict where it appears everything I did went wrong, I have forgotten all about Adam. "Adam?" I dart to the side of the tepee, followed by the others. "Are you all right?" Adam's response is so pained, so weak and breathless, it frightens me. "I'm here. I need . . . help."

Jimmy's hand-pumped flashlight illuminates the scene. Adam kneels on the thief's outstretched left arm. They are covered in sweat, swollen with bruises, and blood is all over both of them. There is a bare area in the ground where their struggle has turned over the bed of leaves and exposed the soil. I barely recognize Adam, his face is so bloody and caked with black dirt.

"Adam!" I rush to his side. "Are you okay?"

"No, I'm afraid not . . ."

8

THE CONFESSION

"YOU'VE BEEN STABBED?" I HELP Adam to his feet. "Where?"

He doesn't answer my question but grunts in pain, holding his right arm close to his body.

"So this is the thief?" Jimmy reaches down to grab the thief by the wrist, and Anna-Lee recovers our bug-out bag.

"He's been shot," Adam informs us as we help him around the tepee to the fire pit. "In the shoulder, I think." His words are spoken as if they cause him pain. "He has a knife. We both lost our knives—" Adam takes short gasps of air.

"Found your knife," Danny announces.

"He's unconscious," Jimmy declares. "Man, is he even alive?"

"Be careful . . . "

"Shh," I urge Adam. "Don't talk."

"He's waking up." I hear the thud of Jimmy's boot against the thief's side. "Get up!"

I gently help Adam lie beside the fire pit, providing a backpack as a pillow.

Jimmy prods the thief around the tepee. The thief crawls to the side of the shelter, and grasps the frame with his good hand to try to stand. Jimmy kicks him in the back of the knee, causing him to fall again. "Crawl! Don't walk." The little ones stare at the wounded thief with fear and wonder. Anna-Lee puts the handgun under her belt and bends down to examine Adam's wounds with me.

Adam's face is bloodied and bruised, but nothing too serious. He has a finger out of joint. I reach for his hand and pop it back into place. He grunts and opens his eyes. "What'd you do?"

I rip his shirt to better see the wound. My heart seems to drop into my chest. He's been stabbed in the top of his right thorax, between the shoulder and neck. "Someone get the bug-out bag."

"Here it is." Anna-Lee unzips it.

"Get me a gauze."

Anna-Lee reaches inside and hands me a stack of gauze. I press it against Adam's stab wound. Adam's eyes are closed.

"Adam. Hey, Adam!" I smack his cheek. "No napping."

He blinks several times. "I'm not, I'm just resting. That was exhausting. My shoulder hurts all the way down my arm." He opens his eyes and looks at his arm. "My forearm and my fingers are burning, like they're on fire."

Anna-Lee bends low and whispers, "What's that mean?"

"It means the knife damaged the nerves." I check his wrist pulse. "His circulation's . . . it's—I can't feel a pulse. Wait. I can. It's weak."

As Jimmy prods the thief to crawl toward a tree between our fire pit and the creek, we all get a good look at him. He has a straggly brown beard collecting the blood from a busted lip. His left eye is half swollen shut from the beating Adam gave him. He has a crooked nose, bent to the right with a dip in the ridge. His nose isn't bleeding, so I suppose he was like that before he tussled with Adam. His brow is scarred, and his bottom lip trembles, from fear, pain, or disease, I don't know. Two streaks of blood flow from a bullet entry wound and an exit wound in his left shoulder. The blood oozes onto his dirty white shirt with the sleeves cut off, and trails erratically down his arm.

Jimmy levels his AR-15 at his torso as Danny binds his hands behind the tree, ignoring his cries of pain.

"Let me go. I'm hurt."

Jimmy mocks him. "What do you mean, 'Let me go.' You're a dead man!"

The thief begins to scream as Danny tightens the knot binding his hands. "Let go of me! No! Let me go! Now! I'll kill you all! I'll kill you all—" His temper tantrum quickly abates from the exhaustion of his body and the pain from his wounds.

I keep pressure on Adam's wound while Anna-Lee searches through our bug-out bag. Her cheek is deep red from the criminal's backhand. Her left nostril dribbles blood onto her lip and there is blood and mud smudged on her cheek.

I motion to the blood on her shirt, on the top of her shoulder. "You cut?"

"I'm okay," she assures us. "I think the blood is that guy's, not mine." She glances at the giant dead criminal still lying in front of our shelter. "His arm was grazed by one of Danny's shots."

I turn to Eli. "You okay, buddy?"

"That was scary," Eli says with a quivering voice. "I couldn't breathe. I thought I was dying."

"And you, Danny?"

Danny takes his hands off the back of his head and winces. "We'll find out when the adrenaline wears off."

Eli and Danny appear to be back to themselves within a few minutes, setting my mind at ease.

"Danny," Jimmy asks. "Need a favor. Please drag that dead guy away from our shelter. He stinks."

"They both do." Anna-Lee scrunches up her nose.

The stench that emanates from the men, especially the thief tied up at the tree, has made the air within a ten-foot diameter so unbearable that only Jimmy ventures near him. His scent is a potent mixture of liquor, cat musk, urine, stale tobacco, and unwashed body odor. The children sit on the ground in front of the tepee, looking at him as if he were an injured bear threatening to shake off his bonds and pounce on them.

Jimmy removes the strangled squirrels from his belt, revealing to all of us what he has been doing so early in the morning. He passes them to Anna-Lee.

"We were worried about you, Jimmy," Faith says as she holds Joey on her hip.

Jimmy ignores her, his eyes fixed on the thief.

The hairy thief provokes very little pity from any of us—especially Jimmy, who handles him roughly. Ignoring the man's cries of protest, Jimmy reinforces his wrists-bonds until they are bound so tightly it is painful just to look at him. He also wraps several loops of rope around his waist and neck, thinking that if the thief struggles to free himself, he will be strangled.

There are tears in the thief's eyes as he squeals in pain.

"Don't hurt him," little Faith pleads with Jimmy.

Jimmy pauses his knot-tying and snaps his head critically to Faith, as if her sympathy for the thief offends him deeply. "Hurt him? Are you crazy? This man tried to kill us."

"The 9 mm jammed on me," I inform Jimmy as I glance at the dead giant in front of our tepee, "or I'd have shot that guy long before Gracie. Can you check the Glock?"

"I check it every time I clean it. It's not the gun, it's the shooter." He doesn't even give me the courtesy of looking at me as he spits his smart-alecky comment. I am inclined to respond in kind, but realizing nothing good would come of it, I hold my peace.

"Shut up, you big shot." Adam's rebuke causes Jimmy to blush and clench his teeth. "You don't know what you're talking about. If the gun was clean, it had to have been a bad bullet."

Jimmy ignores him, turning to Danny. "You sure were doing a lot of shooting for just three targets, Danny."

"I couldn't see 'em," Danny responds. "I was trying to guess where their bodies were based on their flashlights. Then when they turned those off, I had to aim for their muzzle blasts while bullets were whizzing around my head."

"You sure wasted a bunch of ammo."

Danny shrugs and keeps silent. He heads over toward the dead giant, asking Eli, Gracie, and Faith to help move him.

"You drawing their fire, Danny, deprived them of ammo by the time they got to the tepee," Anna-Lee speculates. "You saved our lives."

They drag the dead giant to the other dead guy about ten yards away, with Joey following close behind. Faith shovels some dirt over the pool of blood at the entrance of the tepee.

"Please! Untie me! It hurts!" The thief protests. "Please, untie me!"

"Quiet!" Jimmy orders. "We know what you're doing. You're screaming hoping some of your friends can hear you." Jimmy nudges the

thief with his shoe. "What did you do with all the stuff you took out
of our backpack?"

The thief vigorously shakes his head back and forth. His eyes dart
over to where we have piled up the carcasses of his two partners in
crime. "I didn't take it. It was Dillon. Or Big Rig. One of them took it."

"Don't lie to me."

"Come on, man! I've been shot! You gotta get me to the hospital."

"You must think we're idiots," Jimmy responds. "Quit screaming!"

"Ow!" He howls in pain.

Jimmy's face reddens as he fumes.

"I got just the remedy for you, pal," Anna-Lee says. She places two
long strips of gray duct tape over his mouth.

Jimmy glances at her and smiles warmly. "That's my girl."

I glance at Anna-Lee. "What's left in our bug-out bag?"

She sighs. "About a quarter of what was in it."

Jimmy looks down and notices the left heel of the thief's boot.
There's a chunk of the rubber missing. "See! Look at his boot. This
fellow's a liar. He is the same man who stole from us two nights ago.
I told you he'd come back with his buddies, didn't I?"

At these words, the thief squints in pain and turns his gaze to the dirt.

Anna-Lee's eye and cheek seems to grow more purple by the minute as she sits on the edge of the log bridge between the thief and the
others. Jimmy stands between the fire pit and the thief, aiming his
rifle at his chest. I sit beside Adam, keeping pressure on his wound.

We let Eli get the fire going, and Gracie skins the squirrels for
breakfast. Danny gathers the weapons and valuables from the gang
of thieves and brings them to the front of the tepee, announcing,

"Three guns. Two 30-ott-6's, one with a broken stock. But check out the third gun." He raises it into the air for us all to see.

It's Jimmy's Ruger 10/22!

"No way!" Jimmy reaches for it, admiring it. "So these guys were part of the raid the first day?"

"Or one of them was," Danny says. "It was that bald, big guy that hit Anna-Lee that had this one. He'd run out of ammo."

Jimmy turns to the thief.

"Did you attack us on the first day?"

The thief shakes his head violently side to side.

Danny piles up the guns, then sits and cradles his head with his hands for a moment.

"Head still hurting?" Anna-Lee asks.

He takes a deep cleansing breath but doesn't answer.

"What else do they have?" Jimmy asks.

Danny looks through the pile of things he removed from the thieves' backpacks. "A compass, two knives, a half-empty bottle of liquor, and a map. Plus a few boxes of ammo. I had a close look, and I don't think any of the raiders got away injured. No blood trails. Oh, check this out." He reaches into one of the thief's backpacks and lifts out a box of ammo. He raises it triumphantly into the air. "Subsonic 22, baby."

"Yeah." Jimmy reaches for the box. "Now we can hunt without waking the neighbors, but I'm curious as to why the guy didn't use the Ruger if he had ammo for it." Jimmy looks more closely at the action of his Ruger. "Ah, look at that. A jam." He shows the gun to Danny. "That's what happens when you don't clean your guns."

"Thank God it jammed," Anna-Lee comments.

"Plus," Jimmy adds, "subsonic doesn't have enough gunpowder to consistently push the action back all the way. They jam more. Danny, do you see my box anywhere in there?"

"Nope. Sorry."

Anna-Lee turns her attention to Gracie. "It's not every day a nine-year-old kills someone. How ya handling it?"

Gracie frowns. "I feel dirty."

I step toward her and kneel until we are eye level. "Gracie, you saved our lives, just like Dad and Mom did." Her eyes well with tears.

"With only one bullet too." Jimmy casts a wink toward Danny. "Unlike machine-gun Danny here."

"We're proud of you," Anna-Lee says, massaging Gracie's shoulders for a second.

Gracie nods dutifully. Faith, always coveting affection, inches closer to rest her head against Gracie's shoulder.

"Hey, look at this!" Danny holds up the thieves' map. "I think this thief"—Danny fastens his eyes on the bearded man—"hasn't been totally honest with us."

"What?" Anna-Lee step closer.

"Surprise, surprise," Jimmy says sarcastically.

"Our home has a red X on it." Danny searches the beady, shifting eyes of the hairy thief.

Anna-Lee appears confused. She studies the map over Danny's shoulder. "An X?"

My heart skips a beat. I snatch the map out of Danny's hands. "You mean, he targeted us?"

Jimmy steps around to look at the map more closely. He is immediately aghast, and his mood quickly shifts to passionately indignant.

He aims his rifle at the man's head. "You *were* there on the first day, you murderer! I can't believe it!" Beads of sweat coalesce down the man's dust-caked face. Jimmy turns to Anna-Lee. "We should have killed him instead of tying him up!"

Anna-Lee nods at Jimmy enthusiastically. Now, it appears she wants blood, much to Jimmy's satisfaction.

The bound and gagged thief begins to writhe.

"Ungag him," I instruct.

Jimmy looks at me like I'm an idiot. "He's just gonna lie and tell you a sob story. We have to do our own justice now. We need to just give him what he deserves and stop torturing the guy by putting off the inevitable."

The thief breathes rapidly from anxiety, sweat drenching his dirty white T-shirt.

"Ungag him," I repeat. "Danny, do it."

Danny finally removes the strips of duct tape from the thief's mouth.

The thief grows frantic. "My chest is hurting!" He wails with a contorted countenance. "I can't breathe!"

Jimmy brings his weapon closer to the thief's face. "Keep your voice down!"

"There's a red 'X' on the map where our home is." I speak calmly, shaking the map in his face. "Why?"

"Untie me, please—"

"Tell us!" I order him more forcefully. "Why did you target us?"

"I—I don't know. That's not my backpack."

"I got this map out of our bug-out bag." Danny points at the thief. "That's the one you had."

"That doesn't mean it's mine."

I step closer to the thief, showing him the map. I point to a scribbled name at the top of the map. It reads, "JACK."

"That's your name, right, Jack? I heard your friend call you Jack when you were fighting behind the tepee. Those two guys,"—I glance over at the two dead thieves—"you already said their names were Dillon and Big Rig. Why did you put these red X's on your map?"

The thief swallows hard, hesitating to answer.

Jimmy snarls at him. "You're not earning any sympathy with your lying, mister."

Finally, the thief responds, "Dillon and Big Rig had marked addresses of people they thought would leave town with the rioting, people who might leave stuff behind. I don't know how your house wound up on the list."

"Was it you that attacked us on the first day?" Anna-Lee asks.

He shakes his head vigorously back and forth. "No. I promise."

"What about your buddies?" Anna-Lee inquires.

"I don't know. If they did, I wasn't with 'em."

Jimmy isn't satisfied with his answer, so he presses his foot against the man's shoulder wound. "You're lying!" Jimmy screams. The thief grimaces and howls in pain.

"Jimmy! Stop it!" Gracie exclaims.

"Quit, Jimmy!" I shout.

Jimmy removes his foot and the thief continues to cry and tremble for fear and pain.

"Quiet!" I order. "Armed with weapons, you and your friends targeted us, stole supplies we needed for survival, and then came back to try to steal more. You tried to kill us!"

"We'd have starved to death, because of you," Danny snaps.

"What are we gonna do to him?" Gracie wonders aloud.

"What do you think?" Jimmy quips.

"That's a Bible there." The thief motions with his head to the red Gideon Bible that sets on the fallen log beside our tepee. "Don't it say to turn the other cheek?"

Anna-Lee and I laugh, and I'm amazed that the firm frown on his face reveals him to be serious.

"How dare you!" Jimmy barks.

"That verse refers to tolerating insults, not to letting murderers go free," I say. "We're turning you in, first chance we get."

Jimmy chuckles mockingly. "Turn him in to who?"

"Just let me go, please," the thief begs. "I'm injured."

Anna-Lee speaks up. "The Bible says that if you discover a thief while he's trying to steal from you at night, then you can kill him."

"But you can't kill him," I object, "if—"

Jimmy interrupts, "Hmm. Two plus two—I don't know the answer, so let's look it up in the Bible." He taps his index finger on his chin and his eyes roll heavenward. "Oh, I remember now. It's commandment number 'Duh!'"

I ignore Jimmy's mocking. "But you can't kill him if you catch him, and he has to pay you back."

"Even if we did have a criminal justice system," Anna-Lee says, "they wouldn't enforce that."

"Right." Jimmy turns to me. "That law presupposes that the thief could be forced to pay restitution."

"What about Zacchaeus?" Gracie asks. We all turn to her. "He repaid fourfold, and Jesus said he was forgiven."

"Yep." Danny nods. "That's what the law said. Fourfold."

"Unless it had sentimental value," Anna-Lee recalls, "and then it's five times the value of the object stolen."

"Like Jimmy's box?" Eli wonders. Anna-Lee nods.

"Danny, is my box in there?" Jimmy's question hangs out there for a minute as Danny finishes checking the last of the thieves' backpacks. Finally, he answers, "No. 'Fraid not."

"I'll bring back four times as much food and we'll call it even," the thief proposes, a faint hint of hope in his tortured countenance. "And ammo."

"But you're not just a thief!" Jimmy insists. "You've committed attempted murder. You can't trust him, Sophie. He'll return with his other gang-bangin' buddies and kill us all."

"I won't." The thief passionately promises, "I'll pay you back. I will!"

"He isn't going to pay you back," Adam assures us. "It's a waste of time even talking about it." He tries to sit up, and he immediately pales. He lays back down. "Oh boy, I'm gonna need some water."

"I'll get you some," Gracie says, reaching for the canteen.

"Did you find that coin box in there? In that red and black pack?" The thief glances at our backpack and then at Danny.

"You got it?" Jimmy's eyes widen. "Where is it?"

"I put it in a secret department between the first and second departments."

Danny picks up the backpack and rummages through it. "I think you mean *com*partment, not *de*partment."

"Yeah."

Danny reaches in and pulls Jimmy's treasure box out of the backpack. He lifts it up toward Jimmy with a smile.

Jimmy reaches for it in disbelief. "I can't believe it! Thank God!"

Thank God? Just the sight of that little wooden box makes me sick to my stomach.

"Ya see?" the thief says, wincing. "I didn't have to tell you about it, but I did." Jimmy kneels down, opens his box, and begins to sift through the coins.

"The lock of hair!" He leaps to his feet, and the coins tumble to the ground. "Where's the lock of hair?" He shoulders his rifle. "What'd you do with it?!"

"That lock of yellow hair?" The thief furrows his brow.

"What lock?" I ask Jimmy. He ignores me, and I tap him on the shoulder. "What's he talking about?"

The thief grows more horrified when he sees the rage in Jimmy's eyes. "I . . . uh, I—I cleaned it out, and I . . . uh . . . I threw away the dirt and junk . . . "

Jimmy moves his rifle to within a couple of feet of the thief. "What'd you do with it?" He grinds his teeth.

"I thought it was junk. I'm sorry . . . "

Jimmy explodes in uncontrollable fury and strikes the thief in his face with the butt end of his rifle. I step forward and push him back. "Jimmy!"

"It wasn't yours!" Jimmy screams at the thief, whose left cheek bleeds profusely.

"I-I-I-I . . . " the thief stutters, trembling for fear and shrinking as far away from Jimmy as his bonds let him.

I turn to Jimmy. "Get control of yourself! What lock of hair are you talking about?"

Spit flies out of the corner of his mouth as he screams, "It was Becca's!"

When our eyes meet, his whole countenance suddenly droops for embarrassment. He sighs heavily, holding back an uneasy sob. "It was

Becca's." He calms, his eyes turning toward the dirt, his rage quenched by his grief. "The morning. The morning it happened. She was cutting her hair in the bathroom. She was so mad she couldn't fix it. She asked me to help fix her crooked bangs. I tried to straighten it out, but it was a mess. Her hair was all over the bathroom. She begged me not to tell. I was going to sneak the scissors back in the closet when I walked into the living room. You remember. You were there . . . "

* * * * *

I remember it as clear as day. I was only nine.

I was sitting in the loveseat engulfed in *This Present Darkness* by Peretti. Mom was in the kitchen baking cookies with Anna-Lee. Dad had come home from the hospital after a 36-hour residency shift. He plopped down face first onto the couch and was out, sound asleep in a heartbeat, his stethoscope still wrapped around his neck.

Out of the corner of my eye, I saw little Jimmy tiptoe into the living room with a pair of kid's scissors, the dull ones that won't cut you. His twin sister was right behind him with her bright yellow hair.

"Shh," I whispered. "Don't wake him up." They quietly tiptoed toward Father.

I hear Becca say, "Don't touch it, Jimmy."

I thought she was referring to the scissors. I didn't even look up from my novel.

The next thing I know, Jimmy has retrieved Dad's concealed carry pistol from his ankle holster and pulled the trigger.

Dad's blood-curdling scream . . .

Mom's frantic shouting and rushing to get her little girl in the car and to the hospital as soon as possible . . .

The tears and blood everywhere.

I grabbed Jimmy by the shoulders. His eyes were open wide in shock. A splatter of blood on his face. "Bad boy! Bad boy!" He released a wail that invited my pity, but I gave him none. I shook him violently by the shoulders. "What have you done!"

The guilt and pain that saturated our home for weeks, for months on end, was inhuman. Life was difficult. My next breath was difficult. I couldn't even look at lil' Jimmy without hatred in my heart.

How much harder it had to have been for him. And for Dad.

At the funeral, Jimmy kept saying, "I'm sorry. I'm sorry." To Mom. To Dad. To the preacher. To Grandmother, visiting from Florida. "I'm sorry." To a couple of Dad's fellow residents. "I'm sorry." To the funeral director. "I'm sorry."

He wrapped his arm around Mom on the front row, while the preacher preached his sermonette. Mom kept her composure rather well, dabbing her tears with her tissue. Jimmy had scooped together a wad of Becca's cut hair from the bathroom counter and wrapped it in a pink rubber band. "I'm sorry," he uttered intermittently during the sermon, rubbing the hair between his fingers. Pastor lost control of his emotions at his pitiful interjections, and started crying. I think he concluded the sermon early.

Jimmy held the wad of Becca's hair in his hand for weeks, maybe longer. Even when he slept . . .

I never finished the novel.

* * * * *

Jimmy's obsession with his little treasure chest begins to make sense. That little box had more value to him than I could ever imagine.

"You kept a lock of her hair, all these years?"

He nods subtly, his eyes fixed on the thief, who cowers as Jimmy grieves.

"I was just a kid, Sophie. I loved her more than anybody." I have never seen anybody whose face showed so much rage, cry such pitiful tears. "You all still hold it against me. Every birthday. It's like living the funeral all over again. I saw it in your eyes when Dad gave me my Ruger. You still hold it against me. To this day . . ."

"I'm sorry, Jimmy." I place my hands gently on his shoulders.

"I was just a kid." He sobs. I've never seen Jimmy like this.

"Look at me, Jimmy. I'm sorry. It wasn't your fault."

"It was Dad's fault. Not yours," Danny suggests.

"I miss her too, Jimmy." Our eyes meet. "I miss her too. It's been so long though. You've got to let her go."

"I can't—"

Anna-Lee steps closer. "No, Jimmy. You have to."

"We've got to forgive ourselves."

Our words reinvigorate Jimmy's intimidating demeanor. "How?" He leans against the tree behind him, as if his legs have suddenly lost their strength. "Oh, God! Why!" he screams.

I lean close to him. "You were just a little, innocent boy."

Jimmy leaps to his feet. "Well, then whose fault is it?" He aims his rifle heavenward and shoots three shots, prompting the kids to put their hands over their ears from the volume of the blasts. "God's fault! It's God's fault, Soph!" He paces back and forth for a moment, mumbling to himself, and then collapses with his back against the tree, weeping.

"She's in heaven, Jimmy." Anna-Lee steps closer. "She's not suffering anymore. Be thankful for what God's given you. That's what she would want."

From the torrent of tears that stream down Jimmy's cheeks and nose, I know that this emotional splinter has haunted him for quite some time. He hasn't been able to let go of Becca. He and his twin sister were so close. Jimmy changed when she died. He grew harsh and abrasive. Unforgiving.

Anna-Lee leans in and whispers to him, "You need to stop being mad at God, Jimmy." He turns his eyes up to her. "Becca never belonged to you, so stop feeling like God's cheating you by taking her to heaven earlier than we would have liked. Thank God for the time you had with her, and move on. We only lost her for a little while. Trust God, and you'll see her again."

Jimmy turns away from us toward the thief. He wipes his tears roughly on his forearm, like he's mad at himself for crying.

The thief continues to groan in pain. There are genuine tears in his eyes. "Please untie me. I'm hurt. I've been shot."

"You're hardly bleeding at all," Danny rebuts.

"It's on the inside, man! My shoulder! On the inside . . . "

My eyes turn to Adam, sickly white, taking painful, shallow breaths.

"You think I'm the drama king? This guy makes me look like a statue." Jimmy raises his AR-15 heavenward. "Do you know how valuable these are in this lawless climate? Oh, he'll be back all right. With an overwhelming force of smelly, tattooed rapists and escaped convicts."

"Anyone will fake repentance if they get caught," Anna-Lee says.

"Didn't Jesus say to forgive those who sin against us?" Gracie's voice reveals her nervousness.

"Yeah, He did say that, and the thought of it has me feeling all warm inside." Jimmy's voice is full of sarcasm. "I even got a goosepimple right here." He raises his left forearm and points at it with his other hand. "Do you want to know what'll give me an even bigger goose bump?" He puts his rifle over his shoulder by its sling. "The verse that says, 'Cursed be he who keepeth back his sword from taking blood.' So, let's not waste a bullet on him." Jimmy grabs the handle of his sheathed sword.

Adam glances at Jimmy, shaking his head in frustration.

"Adam," I whisper to him, "say something. What do we do?"

"I don't know what to do. We can't keep him, and we can't let him go. And there isn't a 9-1-1 to call." He pauses and takes several deep breaths. He turns to me. "You'll have to deal with this on your own. I've been mortally wounded."

Mortally wounded?

"What?"

He nods. "Probably. The right side of my chest is starting to hurt, and I'm getting breathless."

I lean closer to him. "I'm sorry, Adam. Please don't die."

He smiles. "I will do the best I can." His eyes dim. He begins to breathe in short gasps through pursed lips.

I fetch a fresh gauze and apply firmer pressure to his wound.

Jimmy, in the process of unsheathing his sword, lets it slip from his grasp. He tries to grab it and cuts his hand on the blade. He jerks his hand back and presses it between a fold of his shirt to stop the bleeding.

"The sword cuts both ways, Jimmy," Danny comments.

Jimmy freezes, and turns to him. "What's that supposed to mean?"

Danny doesn't answer, but I get his point. The sword of vengeance belongs to civil authorities. If we wield it out of turn, then we may be cut by it.

"Gracie," I say, "fetch a Band-Aid for Jimmy."

"As long as he won't kill the thief," she responds.

"Oh, please, girls!" Jimmy turns toward them as he re-sheathes his sword. "Did Jesus take the thief from off the cross beside Him? Hmm? No. You don't let even saved murderers go free. If your fragile constitutions forbid you to do what needs to be done, at least spare us your wasted crocodile tears and leave for a bit so that I can do what must be done."

"Just untie his wrists, Jimmy!" Gracie pleads. "He's tied up everywhere else. He isn't going anywhere. He's been shot in the shoulder. You're torturing him!"

Jimmy turns to me, and seeing the sympathy in my eyes, he says, "Sophie? No! You're smarter than this. He's desperate. He'll try something."

While pressing on Adam's wound, I say to Jimmy, "Why do you have to contradict everything I say? Tie him in the front, Danny."

"What?" Danny acts like he didn't hear what I said.

"We're either gonna have to kill him, or retie his hands in the front—and we're not going to kill an unarmed man, so, retie him in the front!"

As Danny unties the thief, Jimmy mumbles his frustration. I can make out only one of every two or three of his words: " . . . moronic . . . dumb . . . idiotic . . . gonna get us killed . . . "

When the thief is able, he brings his arms forward, squinting away his tears, his shoulder in obvious excruciating pain. "Oh, thank you. Thank you."

With a deep sadness in her voice, Faith says, "He's really hurting." Without even looking at her, I shush her quiet.

Keeping my eyes fixed on the thief, I ask Adam softly, "What should I do, Adam?" He doesn't answer, so I repeat, "What should I do?"

"Uh-oh." Gracie has one look at Adam and points. I look into his eyes. "Adam?" His eyes are rolled back in his head. "Adam!" He begins to shake violently. "Oh no!" I put my ear to his chest as Anna-Lee comes and kneels beside me. "His heart's beating really fast, and, and . . ." I pause to listen.

"I'm sorry, Sophie." Anna-Lee's tone echoes hopelessness. Grief. The way her eyes keep staring into mine, it's as if she's trying to get me to accept the inevitable.

I shake my head side to side. "No. No, God. Not now. I haven't told him yet."

"Told him what?"

I close my eyes and begin to pray desperately for him to live.

Jimmy ties several more loops of rope around the thief's waist and the tree, putting the twine through the thief's leather belt to keep him from twisting free.

When I conclude my prayer, Adam has stopped shaking. His eyes are closed and his respiratory rate has slowed, but his heart's still beating 120 times a minute, and he's as white as can be.

"I'm sorry I stabbed him," the thief mumbles. We all turn to him. "It was self-defense. I ain't got no ill will toward him or anything. I just wanted to live."

Anna-Lee's words are sharp. "Did you have any ill will toward us when you tried to steal from us?"

"I—I just wanted to live. Surviving ain't easy out there."

I study the features of Adam's pale countenance, as he lies unconscious on the ground beside me. He got stabbed because he was trying to save my life. Greater love hath no man than this.

"Surviving, by killing others?" Anna-Lee walks around the fire pit and sits on the fallen log, grasping her 9. "Better to die and be right with God."

The thief drops his head, speechless.

Jimmy quotes a Bible verse, "'If man sheds man's blood, by man shall his blood be shed.' And if we don't, then the Bible says there's a curse on the land. Ain't that right, Anna-Lee?"

Danny stands to his feet. "It's the government's job to punish crime, not ours."

"And if the government's not doing it? What then? You ever heard of the avengers of blood in the Bible? Adam and I were just talking about it a few days ago. They weren't government agents; they were loved ones and family members of murder victims."

"Don't be foolish, Jimmy!" Anna-Lee exclaims.

"It's in the Bible," he insists.

"We don't have cities of refuge," she responds. "So it doesn't apply."

"What's a city of refuge?" Eli leans forward and clasps his hands around his knees.

Anna-Lee responds, "If someone kills another, then that person has to flee to the city of refuge until trial. If they are caught outside of that city, the loved ones of the victim can kill the accused and be guiltless."

"Oh." Elijah blinks hard. "So the city of refuge is like a prison then."

Anna-Lee nods. "Except it doesn't cost the taxpayers anything and the accused can live there with their family and work. Unless the loved ones of the victim bring a charge before a judge. Then the accused stands trial."

"That kind of justice system," Danny tells Jimmy, "may certainly be better than our godless system, but it cannot be applied without cities of refuge."

"Sure it can." Jimmy clears his throat. "Like Eli said, a city of refuge is like a prison. If the murderers are in prison,"—he motions southward, toward the city—"the avengers of blood can't kill 'em. But if we catch them outside of it, then we should be guiltless."

"Help me, God," the thief mumbles between grunts of pain. "Help me." The heels of his boots dig into the ground as he writhes, searching for a more comfortable position.

I take the duct tape and more gauze out of the bug-out bag, and begin to tie a tight bandage over Adam's wound. I bring my lips close to his ear. "You're not dead yet, and we have some unfinished business."

Anna-Lee hands each child a strip of deer jerky. "It'll be a while before the squirrels are done and cool."

Faith takes it slowly, her facial features drawn and gloomy. She puts the jerky in her pocket.

I grow concerned that the strife may be traumatizing the little ones more than I realize. "Gracie, please take Eli, Faith, and Joey, and y'all go bathe in the creek, in the shallow area where we can see you." I point toward the creek. "Keep Joey close."

Gracie picks up Joey. Faith reaches into the tepee for a Ziploc bag with a small bar of soap in it. Eli picks up a milk jug with the top cut open wide—his "crawdaddy bucket." Faith puts the strap affixed to the canteen of water over her shoulder, and they leave.

Ten feet away, Faith halts, turns and asks, "Are you gonna kill him?" The little ones beside her freeze, waiting for our answer.

"He might be the guy that killed Mom and Dad." Jimmy's countenance shows determination. "Of course, we're gonna kill him."

"Quit, Jimmy!" I respond. "You don't kill people because they *might* have committed a capital crime—"

"Attempted murder *is* a capital crime!" Jimmy objects. "He stole our food. We could have starved to death. He probably killed Adam. He was shooting at us, Sophie! We shouldn't reward murderers because they have lousy aim."

I motion toward the creek. "Gracie, y'all go."

Gracie nods and turns back toward the creek. "Come on." She looks way too old as she carries one-year-old Joey.

Jimmy turns to me. "Can you obey the Sixth Commandment in Exodus 20 and ignore the penalty for breaking it in Exodus 21?"

"You've got to have two or three witnesses to justify executing a capital criminal," Danny responds.

Jimmy points to him and Anna-Lee. "One, two,"—then he points to me—"three."

As we continue to debate what should be done to the thief, Faith takes matters into her own hands. She tiptoes up to him and hands him her strip of deer jerky. He reaches for it with his bound hands, but freezes when Jimmy sees them.

"Faith! What are you doing?"

Faith, undeterred by Jimmy's exclamation, puts the jerky to the thief's lips, and he takes it in his mouth.

The thief chews the deer jerky gratefully. "Hmm, good." He turns from eyeballing Jimmy suspiciously to wink at Faith. "Thank you, baby." "She ain't your baby!" Jimmy turns to me. "Don't you see the danger here?"

With Jimmy turned away, Faith tries to give him a sip from the canteen, but Jimmy sees her and places his hand on her shoulder to pull her away.

"Faith!" I exclaim. "No!" Giving him a stale strip of dried meat is one thing, but I don't want any of us to catch whatever poisonous pathogens this pale, jaundiced criminal may have floating around in his saliva.

"Get away from him!" Jimmy screeches. Faith stumbles and falls on her bottom with a grunt, snapping her neck back.

"Ow!" She grabs her neck in pain.

"Sorry, baby. I'm sorry." The thief is apologetic.

"Jimmy!" Anna-Lee reproves him. "Don't be so rough."

Jimmy nudges her away even further. "Stay away from him!"

Faith, holding her neck, has the look of fear on her face as her eyes dart back and forth between Jimmy and the thief.

"Calm down, Jimmy," Danny urges him.

"I didn't mean to push you down, Faith. But you need to respect that this man is our prisoner, and he's an evil man."

"As long as he's our prisoner," she responds weepily, "shouldn't we feed him?"

"That's exactly why we shouldn't keep him a prisoner!" With furrowed brow, he turns to us to forcefully make his case. "We're on the verge of starvation *without* having to feed him. It's not right, sacrificing our food and our time to babysit a murdering crook . . ."

As Jimmy makes his passionate argument for killing the thief, the thief whispers to Faith, "Thank you so much." His voice is quiet and tender. I pretend like I'm listening to Jimmy, but the thief and Faith have my attention. He wipes his grungy beard with the back of his twine-bound wrists. "What happened to your head?"

"I got shot on the day Daddy died."

The thief jolts, as if he's just been stung by a bee and is trying to conceal it from us. For a moment, I think he is going to reach for her. My heart skips a beat. I feel like a naïve fool, letting Faith come within his reach.

Surprisingly, the man's red eyes moisten. He looks down at his bound hands, trying to hide his emotion. I imagine the thief as an innocent boy, a seven-year-old being bullied in school, maybe a teenager in love with a girl, and I wonder what horrible things have happened to him to turn him into the hairy, smelly, tattooed monster he appears to be now.

"My name's Faith."

The thief stares into the fire. "Faith." He says her name slowly, as if it held some distant meaning for him, pulled from the recesses of a suppressed childhood memory. "I could use some of that right about now."

"Daddy named me after a patient who died on the day I was born."

The thief turns away from her, ignoring her. A rude response to her kind gesture in my estimation. Then he begins to cry. He brings his head forward and then slams it against the tree behind him with a *thud*. He shakes his head back and forth violently, as if he is struggling between two alternatives and is tormented with indecision. "I'm sorry. I'm so, so sorry."

His humility takes me aback initially, but I remember this is a hardened thief not to be trusted. He would probably say anything to get out of his predicament, especially to a malleable child. I can't let this monster continue to pull at Faith's heartstrings like this.

"My name's Jack," he whispers to Faith, oblivious to the fact that his life rests on the outcome of the debate Jimmy's moderating.

"Good to meet you." Faith grins widely.

"My chest is hurting real bad, Faith, and, and I need forgiveness for the bad things I do."

She raises her eyebrows. "Why don't you quit doing them, so God'll forgive you?" She flashes her dimples, like little exclamation points on the simplest but most profound of questions. I'm impressed with the effect her gentle admonition appears to have on him.

He stutters an answer, "I—I . . . um, I know I should."

She tilts her head to the side. "Do you want God's help?"

He nods, clearing his throat gruffly.

"Ask Him then."

She stares at him a moment, as if expecting him to simply ask and receive from the throne of grace right then and there.

The thief freezes as our eyes are fastened on him, awaiting his answer. A fine tremor becomes evident in his chin and lower lip. "I—I can't."

Faith smiles. "It's easy." Her voice is light and carefree, as if she's teaching her younger sibling how to add one plus one. "You can do it."

Jimmy turns to me angrily. "Are you gonna let this happen, boss? You gonna let them chat like this?"

"I've never been much of one for praying, baby." A twitch becoming evident in his left eye.

"Oh, it's easy. You just tell God you're sorry, and don't do it again. Jesus did the hard part."

For a long moment, Faith smiles at him with her head cocked to the side, as if fully expecting him to convert right then. "You want me to do it now?"

She giggles at his doubt and uncertainty. "Here, I'll ask Him for you." With a childish faith, she stretches forth her dainty hand and rests it softly on his uninjured shoulder, surprising him, startling us, and probably freaking out any guardian angels in the vicinity.

Jimmy takes a step toward her to stop them, but I grab him by the shoulder. He spins toward me. "But, Sophie—"

"Shh."

"This is stupid," he mumbles.

A moment's pause keeps us all patiently waiting with bated breath, anticipating something horrible or wonderful, but for a long moment, Faith and the thief are still, with her small hand still resting on his dirty shoulder. His eyes are squeezed shut as if in sincere prayer, holding his breath.

She finally opens her mouth to pray, "Dear Jesus—"

With those words, a dam of pride seems to shatter to pieces in Jack's heart, and his emotions break forth with full tears. After a deep breath, it transforms into a cacophonous sob.

"Faith, I told you!" Jimmy gets in between Faith and the thief, and pushes her away. "Go to the creek, now!" Faith backs away, keeping her eyes on the thief.

The thief takes another deep breath and tries to restrain his crying. "Thanks, baby, I mean, Faith." His eyes are full of tears, and his voice quivers. He takes another deep breath. "That was the best prayer I ever heard." The last of his breath is exhaled as a rumbling sob that trickles down to a raspy squeak. He takes several sharp breaths, trying to hold back the flood.

"Go, Faith!" Jimmy says forcefully. "He's a bad man."

Faith turns and looks up at Jimmy. "Everybody's bad without Jesus."

At hearing these words, the thief breaks out in weeping again, so bitter and irrepressible that my eyes dampen for him.

Faith turns to the thief, her eyes brimming with tears as she beholds him. A contagious frown appears in the midst of her fair facial features. "Sophie, he needs forgiveness too."

Too.

That word reminds me that the thief and I are in the same boat, needing the same Savior. He may have more to be saved from, but he who is forgiven much loves much. He's like the whore weeping at Jesus' feet, or the tax-collector beating his breast in self-spite, humbled on his knees at the altar, confessing his unworthiness in the temple. I feel like the snobby, starched Pharisee, righteously cold and bitterly critical, but inwardly full of rotting skeletons.

Faith speaks more forcefully. "Jack just needs forgiveness."

"I do need forgiveness," the man says, appearing to beg. "I—I do. Real bad."

"Yeah, that and a bath," Jimmy mocks him.

Without another word, Faith turns to leave.

"Wait. Faith, wait." Faith stops and comes back at the thief's urging. He takes a deep breath and looks up at us. "Please wait. I've gotta tell you something."

We pause to discover what the thief so desperately wants to tell us.

"You're probably gonna kill me for this, but I need forgiveness from you."

"We're gonna kill you anyway," Jimmy says.

"Not for what you think I've done, but for what you don't think I've done."

He needs forgiveness for what we don't think he's done? What in the world does he mean by that?

The thief studies his bound hands, a tear dripping from his crooked nose and disappearing into the maze of his straggly beard.

"What?" I finally blurt out to break the uneasy tension.

The thief suddenly extends a palm knife out toward Jimmy, holding it by the stainless steel blade. The three-inch blade is streaked with blood – fresh blood. It must be Adam's blood. Jimmy is initially taken aback. He steps away. The thief looks up at Jimmy and shakes the knife, motioning for him to take it. "Here." Finally, he just tosses it at Jimmy's feet. I gasp, realizing Faith was within his striking range.

"You see what I mean?" Jimmy has an I-told-you-so smirk on his face. "Where was it?"

"I grabbed it when you made me crawl around your shelter there. Put it in my boot. Then took it out of my boot when you retied me in the front. I'm sorry—"

"Save it!" Jimmy looks like he's about to shoot him.

"Wait!" he urges us. "Wait, wait, wait." He takes a deep breath, extending his palm toward Jimmy. "Your papa, he . . . " He pauses and looks down at the dirt, as if carefully weighing the consequences of what he's about to say.

"What about our father?"

After an uneasy pause, he finally answers in a whisper. "He saved my life."

9

TURN RIGHT AT THE Y

THE THIEF'S CHIN QUIVERS AND his bloodshot eyes well with tears. "Your dad didn't even know me, and he—he saved my life." He wipes his eyes with the back of his bound hands.

I prod him on with a wave of my handgun. "Go on."

The thief gulps hard and takes in a deep breath before continuing. "On the first day of the riots, I didn't wake up till 11. My head was splittin' with a massive hangover." He drops his forehead into his palms, as if recalling how bad his head hurt. "I was already halfway through my third Pabst, while Mac—he's my big brother—was hoggin' the remote, watchin' the riots on TV, and orderin' all of us around like a . . . like a prison guard.

"'Go change him, Jack!'" The thief screams at us at the top of his lungs, jolting us with his raspy holler. We flinch. "Sorry, but that's the way my big bro always talked to us."

"Change who?" I ask.

"Huh?"

"Who was he asking you to change?"

191

"Papa. He had a stroke 'bout a year ago and was in a wheelchair all the time now. I told Mac, 'I changed him last time!'

"'When was that? Last week?'" The thief speaks gruffly when imitating his brother. "Mac just stood there like a tower between me and the flat screen, one fist around his liquor and another around the remote, like he was king of the house. More like a slave-driver . . ."

I could tell right away the thief was a good storyteller, full of inflection and dramatic gestures.

"Get to the point!" Jimmy barks. "How did Dad save your life?"

The thief stretches his good arm toward Jimmy, palm out—as much as he could with his hands bound— as if trying to calm him. "I'm getting there. I was sitting on the couch wishing Mac would turn the station from morning news to something, you know, more entertaining, but he was fascinated with the reports of the riots. New York, Atlanta, Chicago, L.A.—the big cities were going up in flames." He motions toward the city. "What's going on in Zanesville is nothing compared to Columbus, or Cinci, or Cleveland, man, Cleveland's gone! On that first day, a lot of wealth was changin' hands quickly. There were prison breaks, and every cop and judge had a target on his back. Mac was schemin' to take advantage of the chaos.

"I could see a small puddle of Papa's, um,"—he pauses to bite his lip, I suppose, searching for a word that we wouldn't consider vulgar. "I could see a puddle of Papa's waste on the floor 'neath his wheelchair, where he was slumped over, his eyes half-closed, chin tremor swinging slobber against his chest, with food dribbling down his shirt." He winces as if in disgust, and I ponder that if this smelly, filthy beast thinks his father was disgusting, then he was disgusting indeed. "I grabbed onto the handles of his wheelchair to try to appease Mac, but I was fascinated with the news report about jihadists in Chicago and Seattle exploiting the crisis, beheading Jews, and crucifying Christians and Muslims of different sects, forcing people to convert. Mac raised the remote like it was some kind of king's . . . um, what do you call those things that kings have?" He acts like he's holding something in the air.

"Scepter," Anna-Lee says.

"Yeah. He raised the remote control like a scepter and said, 'Gotta keep Papa alive for his check, Jack. You want his check, don't you? Or, do you wanna work for a living to pay the cable bill? And the 'lectricity?'"

"What do you mean?" Danny asks with a furrowed brow. "What do you mean, 'keep him alive for his check'?"

"Mac and I always joked that we kept Papa's carcass warm for his monthly check and food stamps. You know, . . . social security. With that and Sissy's government check for her Downs, Mac's disability for his bipolar, and mine for my back, we made off pretty well. Sat TV, three Meals on Wheels a day, hours and hours of movies and online poker, partying with our pot-growing, meth-peddling buddies on weekends, and just enough of being sorry to make up with Candie after our fights. I thought we made off pretty well. It's the best of all I've ever known.

"When one of those government warnings came on TV, you know, the warning that starts off like a buzzing alarm clock, they told people to stay at home and not venture out. It made me a bit nervous. We weren't exactly in the best part of town, if ya know what I mean. I saw a half-drunk Schnapps pressed between the cushions of the couch, so I reached down and drank it fast. It buzzed me good.

Eased my nerves. It wasn't even lunchtime, and I was already growing numb with my poison of choice. Not fast enough, right?"

I smirk at his choice of words. At least he knows it's poison.

He heaves a raspy cackle that turns into a wet cough. We all take a step back, not wanting to catch whatever germs he's spewing into the air.

His eyes suddenly grow distant and the corners of his lips turn down, as if he is recalling even more painful things that transpired that fateful morning. "Candie—that's my girlfriend—she works at a topless bar. She stumbled down the hall of the trailer, knocking picture frames off the wall with her swagger. 'What's that stink?'" He imitates her with a shrill, effeminate voice. "Her words were still slurred from last night's party," he says, explaining his accent. "'Someone left some food out, and it's rotting. Can ya smell it?' With vomit on her OSU sweatpants and her tomcats stinking up the place, mating and peeing in the closets and drawers, she had no room to complain. The arrival of Candie's daily hangover always obliviated her . . . um . . . her grace, you know . . ."

I exchange a puzzled glance with Anna-Lee. *Obliviated?* I don't think that's a word.

"'Change Papa.'" His voice becomes even more high-pitched. "'Change Papa.' My Downs sister, we called her Sissy. She was Mac's echo, always saying whatever he said. Her seat was in the corner of the living room, where she played with her ripped-up teddy bears and plastic princesses.

"'No, it's not your papa,' Candie said. 'It's someone's puke in the sink.'

"'Well, shut ya' mouth and clean it up then,' Mac barks without lookin' at her.

"I toss my empty Schnapps bottle at the overflowing trash can in the corner of the kitchen. 'There's a hit a' somethin' on the kitchen table, Candie,' I told her. 'Help yourself.'

"She grunted at me—her way of thankin' me—and lifted the crack pipe to her lips.

"'Those are my rocks!' Mac hollered.

"'Aw, let her have one, bro.'

"'Please,' Candie begged.

"Mac finally gave in to our pesterin'. 'Alright, just one.'

"After several dry strikes of the lighter, Candie cussed and threw it at me. 'Lighter don't work!'

"I turned to cuss her back when Mac jumped up and stepped to within a couple inches of me. 'I told you to change Papa now!' He raised his right fist at me. 'Before I poke a boot-sized hole in the back end of your baggy blue-jeans!'

"Candie raised a finger in the air and flashed a toothless grin. 'That's a . . . uh, . . . a literation,' she said, sounding proud of herself. 'Nicely done, Mac.'

"'It's *illi*teration, woman!'" he screams in his gravelly Mac-accent.

"Candie used to be an English major before the hash done her in. That's when she got a job at the Infinity Bar and—"

"Our Dad!" Jimmy barks.

"Sorry. That's the A.D.D. I been outta my pills since the month after, um, and my mind is, a . . . Anyways, Mac says to Candie . . ." He pauses, and screams in his Mac-accent, "'It's *illi*teration, woman! And put your teeth in before you talk. You're disgusting!'" Jack pauses to chuckle, finding this humorous. "Mac was so rude to her. He was rude to everybody. He breathed out hate like oxygen . . . "

"Carbon dioxide," I corrected him.

"Huh?"

"Never mind. Continue."

"Mac speed-dialed a buddy while Candie flashed him a pair of middle fingers—when he wasn't lookin', of course. Candie flipped on the gas stove to light the pipe. While Mac was waitin' for someone to pick up on the other end of the phone, he took two steps closer to me and kicked me on the shin.

"'Ow! What did you do that for?'

"'Hello? Earth to Jack?'

"'I'm going, I'm going.' I finally wheeled Papa to the bedroom, taking every opportunity to make the trip as uncomfortable as possible for him, bankin' corners sharply to scrape his knees against the wood edges, hittin' bumps fast, you know. I tossed him onto the bed, stripped him, wiped him roughly, and powdered him. I left him naked on the bed as I put his wheelchair in the bathtub and sprayed it clean with the shower head. He grunted loudly, like he was in pain or hallucinatin' or something. Maybe he was upset for the way I jerked him around. I don't know. It had been more than a year since he spoke any sense, and I wasn't missin' it. My whole life, when he was sober, he was always mean, like a drill sergeant in the Army, you know. Any attention I got was, like, cruel, like the way you treat a dog you didn't want or like. He handled me like a gnat hovering between him and the TV, and would just as soon swat me out of the way as spray me with a can of Hot Shot. Know what I mean? He sprayed me with it one time, and it burnt my eyes for an hour." The thief laughs sadistically, but I don't find it that funny.

"When Papa was drunk, he teetered between rip-roarin' comical and insanely violent. Especially to Mom. I hated him for how he trampled on us." He snarls with bitterness as he describes his father. He despises him. I cannot imagine hating anyone as much as he appears to hate his own dad.

"I grabbed some rubbin' alcohol on the bathroom counter, held his head down, and poured some of it right down his open throat. He gagged and coughed and snorted up a storm. I grinned ear to ear as I towered over him like a—like the pimp tyrant he was to me. 'Who's the weak one now, Pop? Slap me now! Tell me how worthless I am now!'"

The thief pauses for a moment and continues, his voice gruff and gravelly as he imitates his brother. "'Hey! Jack! Get out here! We're moving out.' That's Mac, always screamin' out orders and bustin' heads if he thinks you're too slow.

"I left Papa on the bed and ran into the living room just as one of Mac's poker buddies showed up. Mac was rubbing his hands like he's got a full house at a table full of fat suckers, 'bout to strike it rich. Robby and Dillon had passed out some joints, and everyone was buzzin'. 'We're gonna go get some of this.' Mac was stoked, 'bout to jump out of his skin.

"My heart was just poundin' like crazy, 'cause I was seeing the clips of the rioting and the looting on TV, and I was thinkin', *What? We gonna do that?*

"'You gonna get yourself killed,' I said."

"Did he?" Anna-Lee interrupts, pointing to the two dead bodies about ten yards away. "Is Mac one of those dead guys?"

"Uh, no. He ain't there. I'm getting to it. Anyways, Mac's poker buddy, Robby, points at the TV. 'Just listen, Jack.'

"The news reporter was practically screamin' into her microphone—"

"Robby who?" Jimmy wonders out loud.

"Huh?"

"Robby who?"

"I dunno. Brown haired young 'un. Good with a gun. Bad at poker. But didn't throw a fit 'bout losin' money to Mac. He was a church kid till the crisis, and then did what he had to do, you know. Mac sold him dope to help him live with himself. Anyways, Robby points to the TV, and the news reporter was screamin' into her mic to be heard over the roar of the crowd around her. She goes on talkin' about the lootin' everywhere and the military and National Guard being MIA. The crowd behind her was cheerin' a dozen rioters who jumped up and down on an overturned police cruiser. It was crazy!

"This dude wearing a bandana and weighed down with all this loot in bags almost collided with the camera man. The reporter stuck the microphone in his face. 'Did you steal those shoes? Those DVDs?'

"'Nah, man, they're free. It's loot or be looted.'"

A sly grin creeps onto the thief's scraggly face. "Loot or be looted— that's a good argument, I'ze thinking . . . "

"Only if there is no God," I hear Anna-Lee mumble.

The thief continues, "Mac's friend egged us on with a wild grin on his face. 'It's free pickins.'

"'We're too late to the draw,' I tell him. 'Everything's already looted in town.'

"Mac lifts his Confederate flag T-shirt to reveal a black .38 revolver tucked under his belt. 'Let's loot us some looters then.'

"Suddenly, the 'lectricity went off in the house.

"'Wassup?' Candie squealed from the kitchen, where she had her head in the fridge, fishin' for something to eat."

His high-pitched accent of his girlfriend's slurred speech gets us chuckling, believe it or not. For all his faults, the thief is a master storyteller.

"'We've got to get going or we're gonna miss out,' Mac said. So we got the truck and got out of there like a bat outta . . . " He paused when he saw my disapproving glare. "Out of a cave," he concludes his sentence, giving me a wink and a sly grin, revealing for the first time a missing incisor tooth.

"Mac wanted to hit a sporting goods store in hopes of finding some guns and ammo. I wanted to hit a 'lectronics store to get this new shootin' video game, but Mac was convinced anarchy's days are here to stay and there'd be no 'lectric power for months. His muscles filled the gaps in his IQ, and my fear of his right fist kept me doin' what he wanted, if you know what I mean." He massages his left jaw as if he was recalling some former injury his brother had inflicted on him.

"We passed several burning cars and houses, and twice rioters pelted us with rocks and sticks. A bullet from Mac's .38, fired over the heads of those punks, sent them scurrying for easier targets.

"The looting of Gun Depot was just getting' underway when we got there. The parking lot was buzzin' with rednecks and hillbillies and gang-bangers fillin' their pick-ups and low riders, fightin' each other over stuff.

"Robby ran inside to see what goodies he could scrounge up. Mac picked a skinny loner in the parking lot, binding down this kayak and all this stuff with bungee cords in the back of his pickup. Mac pointed his .38 at the guy. 'Keys, dude.' I was scared out of my wits, but Mac was as calm as ever. The skinny dude acted like he ain't gonna give up anythin' without a fight, and Mac eased his tone even more even as he drew closer with his pistol. 'Now, dude.'

"The loner says, 'You don't want to do this, man. Just walk away.'"

In a gruff voice, the thief imitates his brother: "'Keys for your life. You got three seconds or I'll take them out of your hand when you're bleedin' out on the parking lot.' Mac cocked the trigger and squinted with his open eye lining up the fellow's torso down the sights. That skinny dude's courage flew right out the window, and he took off. I really didn't expect it to be that easy.

"I jumped into Mac's truck and followed him as he drove that loner's truck through the maze of vehicles and looters toward the parking lot's exit. We were about to turn onto the road when the same skinny dude came out from behind a car next to the road, firing a handgun at Mac through the window. Mac was immediately shot up."

The thief's voice grows anxious and fearful as he continues, "The, uh, the skinny fella opened the door and Mac fell out face first. He was seizing and blood was comin' out of his mouth. The way out of the parking lot was blocked—I couldn't get out without running over Mac. A knock on the glass beside my head was followed up by a swung brick, which shattered the glass and really freaked me out. I hit the gas pedal, colliding with the back of the skinny dude's loaded pickup that Mac was, um . . . He had his head and arms out the door, but his legs were stuck inside, and it was still movin' into traffic." He pauses, clears his throat gruffly, and his bottom lip begins to tremble. "Anyways, these guys opened my door, pulled me out onto the ground and started kicking me and beating me. One of 'em had a baseball bat and he busted me up really bad on my hip and back. If you'll lift my shirt on the right side, you'll see I'm all busted up. I wouldn't be surprised if I got Louisiana Slugger tattooed on my back." He raises his right elbow to display some black and blue swelling on his arm and tricep.

"I managed to get my hands on my butterfly knife from my pocket and tried to wedge my back up against the pickup to protect my blind side better, and I cut one or two of 'em on the legs while they were kicking me, but it ended up hurtin' me more than it hurt them, because one of 'em got mad that he got cut and with his steel-toe boots really started laying into me, knocking my knife out of my hand, bustin' me up bad."

In the brightening morning light, I can see some purple hematomas and old bloody scabs in the maze of his greasy brown hair.

"They kicked and beat me senseless until I thought I was gonna die. A luckier man woulda got knocked out, but Mac's and Papa's beatings must've toughened me up.

"A blast from your dad's gun brought me back to my senses. I look up, and there he is, hovering over me with his little silver handgun. I don't know how many shots he fired to get 'em off me, but his single-stack's barrel was smokin' and probably couldn't hold more than six bullets. My pockets were inside out. My wallet and my butane lighter was gone. My Marlboros were gone. They picked me dry. My blood was all over everything. I see a dead guy beside me. I assume your Dad shot him, but I don't know."

Imitating Dad's voice and pretending he is waving a handgun around, the thief says, "Get away from him! Now!" Surprisingly, he even sounds a little like Dad.

"He aimed his weapon at the redneck with those big old steel-toes. Those guys froze, staring him down. I was tryin' to catch my breath, grabbin' my stomach—it hurt so bad.

"Your dad reached down and grabbed me by the arm, trying to help me up. 'What good's your loot if you're not alive to enjoy it?' he said. I thought he was talkin' to me, but he was speakin' to the other guys.

"One of the looters removed a pistol from the small of his back— one of those two-shot Derringers—but your dad wasn't affected by it a bit. Not at all. He set his sights on that dude's forehead. I could see that the dude with the Derringer had these eyes that were totally glazed over, like he was drunk and stoned at the same time and wasn't scared of dyin'. Your dad took two quick steps toward him and caught his gun hand before he could aim it at him, then he brought his handgun to within two inches of that dude's face. That sobered him up quick. Another guy, this long-haired hippy, reached into his pocket like he was reachin' for a weapon, and your dad quickly shifted his aim.

"That made their knees as weak as water, and one of 'em got wise and said, 'Let's get outta here.' They scattered and your papa tried to help me to my feet. He practically dragged me to his SUV. I could barely see 'cause there was so much blood in my eyes.

"'Get Mac,' I said. He opened his back door for me, but I wouldn't get in. I pointed across the street. 'Mac, he's my bro.'

"'He's dead. Get in.' He threw aside a sack of horse feed to set me in the back seat."

The thief laughs as he recollects what happens next. "I called your papa an idiot. 'You should've shot that guy, you idiot,' I said. 'He could have killed us both faster than you could bag a joint and a 'tute on the corner of High and Luck.'

"He just stared at me like he didn't catch what I was sayin'—like you're staring at me now." He laughs. "Don't you guys know where High and Luck is?"

"Never mind it," I say. "Just go on."

"Okay. Well, then your dad said something that rocked my world. 'I was outta ammo,' he said. 'I shut the empty slide to make it look like I had a bullet in the chamber, but I was out. It was God who saved us.' That's what he said."

The thief pauses and turns his gaze skyward for a moment, and then continues, "When my pain eased up a bit about a mile or two down the road, I realized all around was like a war zone. Cars were burning, and looters were fighting over stuff in parking lots. Injured folks—old people and young Moms with their kids—were, like, trying to fight off the looters with whatever they had. Some folks had weapons, you know, and they got away or got shot tryin' to help other defenseless folks. The rioters were like a pack of wild hungry coyotes, and unarmed folks just couldn't get away.

"Your dad handed me a stack of napkins and told me to press it against my head, where I was bleedin'. My head didn't even hurt—not compared to the pain in my gut. Out of the corner of my eye, I saw a brick heading for the passenger front window. I didn't even see who threw it. It sprayed pieces of glass across the car onto your dad's lap. He swerved, I think, to avoid a staggering jay-walker, or maybe another brick. I got thrown against the door and my head smacked the window.

"Your dad looked back at me and asked me if I was all right. The thief brings his hands up to his forehead. 'Aw, man, I'm so dizzy.' He told me to put my seatbelt on. I started in on him for not saving Mac, but he was sure Mac had been killed already. I was pretty ticked off about that. He should have at least checked on him—"

"Then you'd both have been dead," Jimmy says. He appears slightly amused with the story, and his curiosity keeps his rage at bay.

The thief sighs. "You're probably right. I was stoned and drunk. Wasn't thinking right.

"'You're Jack, right?' He studied me in the rearview.

"I looked at him more sternly. Suddenly, I recognized him. 'You're that E.R. doc, right?'

"He nodded and turned back to the road. 'Never did get to tell you how sorry I am about what happened to your daughter. To you.'

"A gnaw started up in my stomach, bringing back all the pain . . ." His lip began to tremble, his fists clenched tightly, and he squinted his eyes shut and took several deep breaths, as if attempting to regain his composure.

"So you knew him?" Jimmy asks.

He nods, and continues with his recollection.

"Somebody started smacking the hood of the SUV and then the windshield with a hammer, and your papa put in another mag he had in his car and fired to get 'em off. Once we got clear, your dad asked me where he could drop me off, but I was on the wrong end of town and didn't have cell coverage. He didn't either.

"'That's what happens when ten thousand people dial 9-1-1 at the same time,' he said. He hit the 'Seek' button on the radio, and every station was broadcasting an emergency buzzing sound, then the government asked everyone to stay home. I realized he thought I was a victim, not an injured looter, so I played stupid.

"He said, 'I think that stock market plunge yesterday was more than a blip. The dollar's finally crashing for good.'

"'You mean, you figured this was gonna happen?'

"He looked at me in the rearview mirror like I was an idiot. 'You can't be that naïve.' I shrugged and he said, 'All peon bubbles pop.' I had no idea what he meant by that, but that's what he said."

"Peon bubbles?" Danny squints up his nose, confused.

"*Ponzi* bubbles," I say. "You misunderstood him. He said Ponzi bubbles."

"Huh?"

"A Ponzi bubble was Dad's way of describing what would happen if our country became so deep in debt it couldn't borrow any more money and couldn't afford to pay the minimum payments to its debtors. It would create a huge financial bubble like a Ponzi or a pyramid scheme that would eventually pop like a bubble."

"Oh. I thought he said peon bubble." The thief chuckles. "Anyway, your dad's voice cracks all gloomy-like as we pass a burning house. 'The U.S. may be big,' he said, 'but even big things can't defy the laws of mathematics. Or the law of God. Not and get away with it.' He was all highfalutin, like some kind of mutant newsman-preacher man. No disrespect."

Anna-Lee and Danny chuckle at his choice of words for Dad. Even Jimmy grins at this colorful description. But it saddened me, knowing Dad was gone.

"Anyways, I asked him if he could take me across town, and he said that he was in a hurry to get family and head for his secluded hunting cabin.'

"I was like, 'You prepared for this, huh?'

"He nodded and said, 'The best way to get prepared for the judgment we deserve is to get right with God. If you aren't right with God, this disaster ain't anything compared to what you're gonna face on Judgment Day.' I thought he was nuts. Nice, brave, but nuts. 'Then, when you're done getting saved and baptized, buy a gun and learn how to use it.'

"As we were bypassing two smashed cars goin' up in flames at an intersection, I said, 'Like my papa said, Hell's here on earth, man. Just look around.'

"'I'm afraid your papa was mistaken,' he said. 'This ain't nothing compared to the real thing.'

"Go on," I say.

His tone is low and melancholy. "He let me off on the side of Dresden Road. I got cell phone coverage long enough to call one of my meth-cookin' buddies, Cowboy. Least that's what we called him, because he used to train horses and always wore this dirty cowboy hat. He wanted to loot the mall, and then some homes. Said he had the locations mapped out of rich folks who may have left town in the crisis.

"'No, dude,' I said. 'The mall's been raked over already and was on fire when I passed it just ten minutes ago. Trust me, I got a better target.'

"Quick, man! Dresden and Vine, north of town. And bring some dope. I got beat senseless in a parking lot."

"How'd you know where we lived?"

"The horse feed in the SUV. And, I saw where he turned off the road. There was only one home with a barn on that dead-end road." He looks down at the dirt. Ashamed. "Dillon, Cowboy, and Craig picked me up in ten minutes. I was high as a kite in fifteen, and we were firing on your papa in your driveway within twenty . . ."

* * * * *

We listen to his story in stunned silence. The thief looks to his left and fastens his eyes on Faith. He says something that seems to stop my heart. "Faith, I'm sorry, but . . ." He pauses, his voice shaking with grief. "It's my fault you got shot. Your papa died because of me."

Faith's eyes suddenly widen in fear. She reaches up with her right hand and touches her scalp, as if remembering all she had suffered in the early days of the crisis from that bullet graze and the subsequent loss of blood and infection. She takes a step back while Jimmy inches closer to the thief. With clenched teeth, Jimmy shoulders his rifle and presses his finger against the trigger.

"I didn't mean to hurt anybody, but when your papa started firing back, well, I'm, I'm sorry . . ." The thief speaks hurriedly, as if he knew that any breath might be his last. "I just wanted to scare y'all off . . ."

I'm so close to walking up to him and kicking him square in the face! I would do it, but I can't decide whether to slap him or kick him, and Anna-Lee beats me to the punch. Crying in a rage, she punches him across the face and kicks him hard in the calf. "How could you!" She slaps him once more, and he shrinks back away from her, tucking his chin and raising his bound hands to defend himself. "How could you do this to us?!"

Danny, with tears dripping down his face, darts between her and the thief, restraining her.

I see Jimmy raise his weapon at him again, his finger against the trigger.

"Wait, Jimmy." I stretch a hand out to him, motioning for him to lower his weapon.

"What happened to Mom? Tell us about Mom."

His face went blank. "The woman?"

"Yes, the woman."

His bottom lip quivers. "I don't . . . why it, it never occurred to me that—"

"What happened to Mom?" Jimmy shouts.

"I'm sorry." He bows low to the ground and claws the dirt and stubble for grief. "I didn't know that was your momma."

"How could you not know she was our mom?!" Anna-Lee screams.

"I was stoned!"

"What'd you do to her?!" Jimmy asks, trembling with rage.

"Your boy there, Adam, he knew. Cowboy would have killed her if it wasn't for him. When they ran out of ammo, Cowboy was fumin' that Craig had been shot in the gut, and he was out for blood. Adam stepped up to the plate, promising help and money and guns if they'd set your mom free. He opened his dad's gun safe as payment to free your mom."

We all turn to look at Adam, who appears to be resting comfortably.

"Why didn't Adam recognize you?"

"I suppose, the beard. I didn't have much of a beard on the first day. And, and I was so busted up."

"What happened to her?" Jimmy asks.

"They didn't set her free, but they didn't kill her either. She got shot, and they took her." At hearing these words, we all break out in tears. "One of Craig's friends, he—he showed up late. I . . . I don't know him. He took her. I don't know where." He raises his palms, shaking with anxiety at our grieving. "Oh, God, I'm so sorry." He begins to weep almost as bitterly as we all do.

I check on Adam. He's still comfortably unconscious, but tears collect on his eyelashes. I lean closer to him and whisper, "Adam? You awake?" He doesn't move a muscle. His respiratory rate has quickened a bit, but he doesn't seem to be suffering. He is in a coma.

Jimmy shakes the gun in the thief's face. "Where is our mom?!"

"I don't know where she is! I don't know! Craig was one of the guys you shot on the first day. He survived for a few days, then died. Uh, the only other guy I know, Dillon, he's dead over there." He motions toward the two carcasses ten yards away. "I don't even know the others or where they went." He clenches his hands together and pleads with us, practically begging us for forgiveness. "I'm so sorry. You have to believe me."

Just when I think Jimmy's about to shoot him in the head—as I sit idly watching without protest—Faith steps between Jimmy and the thief.

"Move!" Jimmy yells. "Faith, move!"

Faith ignores Jimmy, and turns to the thief. "It's all right. Mommy and Daddy are in heaven with Jesus. I'm not mad anymore."

He looks up at her, his eyes red and wet with tears. His face is smeared with dirt from rubbing his filthy hands against his wet cheeks in grief. "It's all right." She smiles at him—a smile so warm and sincere, it makes me wish I was the recipient of her grace. Although I admire her compassion, I am quite fearful of her being so close to this monster. I point to the creek. "Faith, leave, and don't come back till I call you."

As she obediently turns to leave, a thin smile beams from her face that puts a lump in my throat. I watch Faith disappear down the deer trail, and I sense a strange feeling of déjà vu.

* * * * *

Dad paused to read the sign beside the sidewalk at the foot of our town's famous bridge. "'Now in its fifth incarnation, the bridge spans the Licking River to the west and the Muskingum River to the east. Zanesville's Y Bridge is the only place in the United States where you can cross a bridge but stay on the same side of the river.'"

"Cool." Jimmy trotted past us up the bridge's sidewalk with a handful of rocks he intended to toss into the water.

"Kids," Mom instructed us as she pushed the stroller, "no climbing on the side rail."

I'm more interested in history than my immature brothers, so I tarried to read it one more time. "Wonder how many Y bridges there are?"

"I don't know," Dad said. "But there's only one Y City, named, I suppose, after this bridge."

"Nope," I told him with a sly grin. "Arkansas has a Y City."

"Oh. I didn't know that."

"I did a report on it." As I ascended the bridge with Dad, that all-too-familiar fear began to grip my heart with its icy fingers. "Oh, man, I hate heights." I had that eerie feeling that the bridge was moving under my feet, threatening to topple into the water. My heart sped up and my brow broke out in a cold sweat. "Aren't these kinds of bridges . . . uh, rare and . . . like . . . experimental?" I was trying to set Dad up for my request to wait in the van.

"Sophie, wait." Dad let the other kids behind us go on ahead. "Y'all catch up with Mom, I want to talk to Sophie alone for a minute." When several feet separated us from the others, he urged me to walk beside him. I hesitated for a moment, then reluctantly caught up to him on the southwestern side of the Y Bridge. We walked slowly.

"Sophie, I've been noticing that you've been afraid of a lot of things recently. Why is that?"

I shrugged, embarrassed.

"Everybody was sound asleep at midnight last night, but you were still awake, fearful of a distant storm."

"It shook the house, Dad."

He smiled at me. "Not quite, Sophie. And you were scared of it before ever a raindrop fell. Everyone else could sleep through it, but you were awake for two hours, trembling like a leaf. You worry about every bump and scab on your body. You have a lot of fears, irrational fears at that."

Shamed by his keen observations, I looked away, down river, studying the bubbling water as it rushed over the shallows. "Sister Martha says I have panic attacks and can't help it. It's a chemical imbalance."

Dad sighed. "Don't you wear that label, Sophie. Joy and peace are fruits of the Spirit. The Bible wouldn't tell you to 'Fear not' and 'Be anxious for nothing' if it were impossible for you. There are hard times a-comin' and more things to be afraid of than Y bridges and thunderstorms, but if you trust God, you will receive the peace that passes all understanding. God promises to give you perfect peace if you keep your mind fixed on Him."

I am consumed with my own thoughts, so I do not respond. Dad patted my shoulder warmly. "When Becca died, I wished I could've died. But you know what that was?"

"What?"

"Selfishness." His eyes moistened. "It was my own foolish heart trying to worship the created more than the Creator, holding the gift above the Giver." He shakes his head, appearing frustrated with himself. "Cling loosely to the things of this world, Sophie. It's all so fragile. Jesus is the solid rock of this life." I kept glancing at passing cars and passersby on the other side of the bridge, oblivious to the emotion in my father's demeanor. "Circumstances are quicksand, Sophia. Temporary. Fleeting. Unreliable. Don't let your faith be poisoned by circumstances, however dire. If you've run with the foot soldiers, and they have wearied you, then how can you contend with the cavalry?"

"I've read that verse."

He smiled proudly. "What does it mean?"

I swallowed hard. My mouth felt dry. "I suppose it means that if in the times of plenty you can't trust God, what will you do when the really, really hard times come?"

Dad nodded. "Unbelief. Sin. Fear. Those are paths to misery, Sophie. The devil will appeal to your circumstances to justify your sin and despair, but trusting God is always the path to peace."

I tried to stare at my feet to distract me from my surroundings, but the sounds of the river and the constant traffic would not release me.

"Look at that." At the top of the bridge, Dad stopped and pointed to some blooming magnolia trees across the river. "Isn't that the most beautiful sight in the world? And smell it." He took a deep breath and smiled broadly. "Magnolia blossoms. Ah, I love it."

My stomach turned as I beheld the trees across the river, and I squinted my eyes shut. "Don't close your eyes," he urged me. "Relish the beauty. It's evidence of God's love. His goodness. Thank God for it."

I took a deep breath, inhaling the spring scents deeply, trying to enjoy the rich aroma of the tea olive, the bubbling of the rushing rapids downstream, and the bright color of the pink dogwoods intermingled with magnolias and overhanging the river. But my feelings forbade me from enjoying it. My fear took the facts and used them like weapons to keep me bound up in the prison cell of my unreasonable mind. It felt like I was teetering over a precipice, about to fall off. I hate that dropping feeling deep down in my gut. Dad told me I had a choice, that I didn't have to give in to fear but could fight it with faith. What if I really did have wings, like a bird, and could just leap off this precipice and fly over the vast expanse below? How foolish it would be for me to shiver away the best moments of my life fearing what I didn't need to fear. Right then, in my heart, I leaped off the precipice. I tried to ignore my racing heart, and I opened my eyes and gave thanks to God for the beauty around me.

A smile broached my frowning face, and that smile plunged down into my heart till it began to race for a different reason. "It *is* beautiful, Dad. It is."

"If God so clothes the flowers, which don't toil or spin, which tomorrow falls to the ground, if God feeds the sparrows—are you not of much more value than them? Oh ye of . . . " Dad paused to let me finish the passage from Jesus' Sermon on the Mount.

I laughed. "That's a pretty bad misquote, you know."

"Come on, you homeschooled geek. Give us public-schooled Christians a break."

"Hey!" Jimmy called out from the peak of the bridge. "Dad! There's a huge fish by the piling! We gotta bring our fishing poles." As the kids leaned over the side rail to see what had so enraptured Jimmy, Mom warned them not to fall. Dad grabbed onto Jimmy's and Danny's belts as they leaned over the railing to watch the fish below.

Mom exclaimed worriedly, "Don't you let them go, Hon."

Dad smiled broadly, his eyes shifting back and forth between me and Mom. "Oh ye of little . . . "

* * * * *

Faith disappears down the short trail to the creek's bubbling waters.

As Jimmy squints down his sights prepared to shoot the thief, I realize at any moment I will hear a loud gunshot and see the murderer of our father and the one most responsible for the loss of our mother—the one who is the cause of so much of our suffering— slump over dead. The thief no longer begs to live. It appears he is beginning to accept his fate. Instead of posing as a victim, he acts like one who accepts that he's going to get what he deserves. Instead of excuses, he begs God for forgiveness under his breath.

I step forward until I am beside Jimmy. He mumbles his anger under his breath as beads of sweat form on his reddened brow and cheeks, yet he appears hesitant. "We gonna have to clean up the mess if we kill him here. Whatcha think about taking him to the edge of our property?"

"Yeah," Anna-Lee says. "Good idea."

Danny, however, seems less confident that this is what they should be doing. Shooting someone who is firing at you, trying to steal the last of your food, is one thing. Shooting someone who is injured and bound, who has just humbly and tearfully confessed murder to the ones most likely to kill him for it, is quite another. One is self-defense. One is justice.

I study the repentant thief for a moment. Anyone can fake remorse when facing justice. Yet his repentance appears so sincere.

"Unbiblical justice is *in*justice, and can be just as dangerous as unbiblical mercy," I say. "Avenge not yourselves, but give place unto wrath. 'Vengeance is mine,' says the Lord."

Anna-Lee frowns, disappointed. "What?"

I keep my gaze fixed on Jack. "When your enemy hungers, feed him. We're not going to kill you now, Jack. We're not going to make decisions based upon fear. Fear of an atheistic future that doesn't exist—"

"What?!" Jimmy is flabbergasted.

"We're gonna give it some time and see if God gives us an opportunity to turn you in to the proper authorities. If no opportunity arises, we'll elect a judge among us and have a trial."

Jimmy lowers his weapon and turns to me. "You have got to be kidding me!"

I put a palm on Jimmy's shoulder. "We're not wielders of that sword, Jimmy." With my other hand, I lower his weapon. I touch the handle of his sword. "We may be one day, but not yet."

"You're just weak," Jimmy says to me. "I'll wield it right now." He turns to the thief. "Do you have any final words?" He shoulders his weapon, aiming it at the thief's chest.

"Do it," Anna-Lee mutters. "I'll drag him away. Kill him now!"

"Anna-Lee!" I object. "No."

The thief's hushed prayers grow louder and more demanding. "Oh, God have mercy on me. Save me, Jesus . . ."

I attempt to take the AR-15 away from Jimmy, but he jerks it out of my grasp. "Give me the rifle now, Jimmy! We're not going to kill him without some kind of trial."

"Shame on you then." Jimmy levels his sights on the man's chest again. "Wartime justice is different than peacetime justice. Call the cops if you don't like it—"

I grab and push down the barrel of his gun.

Blam!

The bullet strikes beside the thief's left leg, throwing dirt up on his chest.

"Ahh!" the thief screams with fear and from the concussion of the blast so close to his face. He pulls violently and futilely against his wrist ties, and the rope around his waist, gasping and mumbling inaudibly.

The little kids by the creek gasp. I glance over at them and see Gracie's fearful eyes looking through the leaves toward us. She's covering her ears with her hands.

Jimmy pushes me away with the hot barrel of his gun. "I'm tired of you hovering over me like you're my momma!" His finger is on his trigger as he briefly waves it past my torso. For the first time, I feel personally threatened by him.

"Jimmy, calm down!" Danny says.

"You just can't go killing people in cold blood, Jimmy!" I insist.

"It's not cold blood," Anna-Lee responds. "He deserves it."

"Well, it's not self-defense," I rebut.

"Whose meager rations are you going to sacrifice to feed him?" Anna-Lee motions to the other children. "Eli's? Hmm? Joey's? Faith's? Or are you going to let him starve to death? Is that more compassionate than just killing him quickly like the Bible says you should do to murderers?"

"Yes, it should be done, but not by us!" I exclaim.

Danny stands and raises his voice. "God's already put Sophie in charge of us, Jimmy! We may not like her decision, but it's her call."

Jimmy keeps his sights on the thief, but his eyes fixed on me. "Delayed justice is injustice, Sophie. Doesn't the Bible say that because a sentence is not executed speedily, the heart of man is fully set in him to do evil?"

Anna-Lee nods. "Yes, it does say that. In Ecclesiastes."

I glance at Anna-Lee. I can't believe she's turned against me so strongly. The knowledge of the thief's premeditated raid of our home and the killing of our father and kidnapping of our mother has made her thirst for vengeance far transcend any previous disposition she had to agree with me for the sake of unity and peace.

Jimmy sighs wearily, puts his rifle over his shoulder by its sling, and turns his back to us. He bends down, takes the last of the jerky and two loaded AR-15 magazines out of our backpack, and half of what remains of our .223 ammo. He shoves the boxes of ammo in his backpack.

"What are you doing?" I can't believe he's taking half our ammo.

He enters the shelter, and exits in a moment with his backpack. He unzips it to ensure his box is inside.

Danny speaks with a trembling voice. "Jimmy, you disobeyed Dad when you went back into the home for your box didn't you? You have been carrying this guilt, and it's been tearing you up inside."

Jimmy does not respond.

"The quickest way forward is to go back to where you took a wrong turn, and make it right," I counsel him.

"I'm outta here," Jimmy says flatly.

"Why, Jimmy?" Danny chokes with sadness. He stands slowly to his feet. "Why are you leaving?"

"God has forsaken us." Jimmy turns to walk through the thicket away from us. "We're on our own."

When I fix my gaze on the thief, hands clasped in prayer, I think I hear Jimmy's name on his lips. I lean closer to him. Sure enough, he's praying for Jimmy. I feel a stab of guilt in my heart. Here is this man who Jimmy was about to kill, praying for Jimmy to return to his family, praying for him to be safe, praying for him to have peace.

One prodigal has come home, and another is leaving.

Would Dad have considered his death an acceptable cost for the redemption of this sinner? I think so.

"Help that boy find his way home," the thief pleads in prayer, his hands clasped tightly together, his head bowed low.

Home.

The thought resurrects grief in my heart. How I miss home, at least where home used to be. Our new home is this dirty, stinky, damp shelter right here by this narrow creek. If home is where you are loved, then for all its moldy discomfort, this is our home. Yes, Lord, help Jimmy find his way home.

I need to pray for Jimmy like this broken prodigal. I fear Jimmy's path will only grow darker. He will need our prayers to survive.

What am I supposed to do with the thief now? Now that he's confessed to killing Dad, shooting Faith, allowing the kidnapping of our Mom, trying to steal the last of our supplies, and now that he appears to have repented, what are we going to do? Can I trust him, or does my duty to care for my younger brothers and sisters preclude any hope I have that his conversion is genuine? Should I feed him of my own meager rations? If he has to go to the bathroom, I will have to untie him and guard him. If he flees, should I shoot him? Was Jimmy right all along? If law and order collapses, does the duty to do justice fall to the unelected jurisdiction of those with the courage to do it? To the "avengers of blood"? I don't know what to do. I fear my path, like Jimmy's, will only grow darker.

I remember that God only gives us enough grace for today's troubles. Tomorrow will take care of itself. "Be anxious for nothing," I whisper the verse, "but in everything through prayer, with thanksgiving, let your requests be made known to God. And the peace of

God that passes all understanding will keep your hearts and minds through Jesus Christ our Lord."

I am distracted by the breath-snatching sight of the bright orange illumination of untempered flames through the shallow tepee entrance! Black smoke rushes from the smoke hole in the top of the shelter.

"Fire!" I shout. "Jimmy, you set the tepee on fire!"

He hasn't even made it twenty feet down the trail when he turns and runs back. Smoke billows from the entrance to our tepee. "What happened?" he asks.

"Fetch water!"

"Hurry!"

"Use the bucket!" I hold my breath, reach inside the shelter, and pull out the sack of ammo before it explodes. Part of the thick fabric of the sack is already on fire. I take it and heave it into the creek. It lands partly on the sandy bank and partly in the water. Danny dumps a muddy bucket full of water all over me – whether on purpose or accidental, I don't know. The smoke burns my eyes, and I get a chest-full of it, which provokes a hard coughing spell. "Put it . . . *cough, cough* . . . put it out!" I yell at Danny, pointing at the ammo sack on the creek bank.

"I got it." Danny takes his bucket of water and pours it on the sack to douse out the flames. I take the thieves' backpacks and toss them toward the creek to keep them from catching fire.

Jimmy rushes past me with a bucket of water to try to salvage the shelter, shouting, "I didn't do it, Sophie!"

With my coughing and the burning in my eyes so painful, I am little help in putting out the fire, but it has no effect on my ability to argue with Jimmy.

"Try to get the bags of clothes!" Anna-Lee yells from the creek, keeping the stunned little ones close in shin-deep water. I can barely see them through the smoke.

Jimmy and Danny sprint back and forth from the creek to the shelter, coughing from inhaling the growing swellings of smoke. Jimmy lugs water in the five-gallon bucket, and Danny, in the pan we boiled water in.

"The smoke!" the thief squeals, coughing vigorously. "Untie this rope around my waist! Please!" He pulls with all his might at the twine around his waist, but he cannot break it. "I can't breathe!"

We all ignore him, as he seems to be a safe distance away from the fire. The smoke seems to stay low to the ground, not rising and disappearing into the sky as is usual. A layer of smoke forms like a low-lying fog, but the thief's head is just below the thickest layer, and he isn't coughing as badly as I am.

To my surprise, Adam jerks awake from his coma and begins to cough. "Adam!" I rush to his side. His eyes wince in pain, and he's breathing rapidly.

"Sophie," I hear him utter between painful coughs.

"Adam!" With my hands under his arms, I try to drag him away from the fire toward the creek. "Stay with me, Adam!"

Danny tries to help me, but I push him away. "No! I've got him. Put out the fire!"

When I finally reach the creek, I fall to my knees beside him. I look into his eyes, and I see death. His lips are pale, opening in short gasps, taking in as much air as he can. I can see that every breath is excruciating. "Sophie." He gasps. "Sophie . . . "

Tears flow down my eyes. "Oh, Adam."

"Sophie."

"Don't talk." I put my fingers to his lips.

I lower my face close to his until we are eye to eye. "Adam, you are a man of God. I do trust you." My tears fall, easing the burning in my eyes and landing on his cheeks. "I do forgive you. With all my heart."

His eyes lower. I think he is closing them, but then he reaches into his front right pocket, and removes my ring. He tries to place it on my ring finger, and I let him. He rubs the tip of his index finger against the diamond. "Sophie . . . will you . . . marry . . . me?"

A sob rises in my throat, but I don't have time to let it out. I nod. "Yes, Adam. Yes."

Anna-Lee comes near with the little ones. I can hear their gentle cries behind me.

"With . . . this . . . ring . . . " He pauses and tries to take deeper breaths. His eyes flutter. Death pulls at him.

"With . . . this . . . ring . . . " He swallows hard. His mouth is dry, and the words barely audible. "I . . . thee . . . wed."

I look into his eyes. "Until—"

He takes one more breath, then his eyes raise to heaven. I see the corner of his lips turn up a bit. Then he's gone.

I wrap my arms around him and weep.

Anna-Lee drops to a knee beside me. We cry in each other's arms as the little ones surround us, trying to comfort me.

Just when I think that the shelter is completely lost and the flames will burn the tepee frame until it is all useless, Jimmy and Danny finally begin to win the battle with the fire.

"Oh no," Anna-Lee utters. "Now the whole neighborhood knows we're here."

I look up. The cloudy skies have cleared, leaving a baby blue color overhead. We're certainly gonna have to move now.

"Where's the thief?" Jimmy asks, his chest heaving from exertion and adrenaline. My hair stands up on end. I look and see that the ropes that tied him to the tree have been cut. "Anna-Lee, please tell me you've tied the thief up over there by the creek."

"No." She draws near the tepee. "Where is he?"

Danny turns to Gracie, who stands stiff in the ankle-deep water beside the little ones. The guilty look on her face belies her confession. Her pocket knife is still open in her hand. "What did you do, Gracie?"

She shuts her knife, shoves it into her pocket, and immediately bursts into tears. "He was coughing so bad. He said he wouldn't hurt us—"

"You might've just killed us all!" Jimmy screams at her. "That was so stupid!" Gracie cowers at his threatening posture.

"You shouldn't have done that, Gracie," Anna-Lee scolds her.

"And you shouldn't have threatened to kill him!" she rebuts.

Joey begins to complain about his cold feet, from standing in the frigid creek water. Anna-Lee picks him up.

"And where's my bow?" Danny wonders. "It was hanging on that branch." He points at a broken branch about eye-level height.

Jimmy asks Gracie, "The thief took the bow and arrows, didn't he?" Gracie remains speechless.

"You think what you did was loving," I say to Gracie, "but it wasn't. You should have trusted our decision."

"*Our* decision?" Jimmy turns and marches right up to me until he hovers over me. "It was *your* decision, not ours, and your decision's to blame! You should've let me kill him when we had the chance! Now he's out there drumming up support in town from all the friends of the two crooks we shot!"

I lay Adam's head down on the creek bed, but I cannot rise to my feet. I'm not done mourning him.

"I'm outta here." Jimmy places his gun over his shoulder by its sling, picks up a canteen and his ammo sack. He also has the Taurus under his belt. How'd he get that? It's usually in Anna-Lee's holster. It must have fallen out in the chaos, and he picked it up.

"Don't go," Danny says. "Jimmy!"

Jimmy ignores him and walks away from us on the trail toward the Y.

"Jimmy? That's it?" Danny takes several steps toward his brother. "Please don't go!" With tears dripping down his cheeks, he chases him and catches up to him twenty feet down the trail. "Jimmy, please." He grabs Jimmy's shirt tail, and Jimmy turns to face him. He places a hand gently on Jimmy's shoulder. "Please stay. You're my buddy."

He shrugs off Danny's hand like a drowning man foolishly shaking off a life preserver. "If I'm your buddy, then come with me." He turns toward the tepee. "Anna-Lee! Come with us. You don't have to live under Sophie's thumb anymore."

Anna-Lee sighs and turns away from us, toward the woods, still holding Joey. She's mad at me.

"Anna-Lee?" I say. "Please don't—"

"I'm not going anywhere," she interrupts, shifting Joey to her other hip. "I disagree with your decision to not kill that scumbag, but Danny was right, it was your decision. Now you're going to need my help moving camp to another spot."

Danny turns toward us. Even from this distance, I can see his pale blue eyes through the leaves, welling with tears, facing the most difficult decision in his life. I pray silently for him.

Seeing Danny's struggle, Jimmy turns toward us. "You're all going to starve to death in these woods, or freeze to death when winter comes! And that's if you survive the looters and murderers that could be on their way here right now! And all for one sick drug-addict who killed Dad and tried to kill us all!"

"Jimmy, please stay," I say. I finally stand to my feet and wipe my tears. "I'm sorry for everything, Jimmy. You and Adam got ninety percent of our food. We really need you."

Our pleadings seem to have no effect on him. He turns to Danny and speaks invitingly. "Come with me, Danny. We don't need them."

"But *they* need *us*, Jimmy. Only the unforgiven won't forgive . . . "
I can't hear everything Danny says, but I see him pat the ammo bag that holds Jimmy's coin collection and what may be half of the last of our dry ammo. Jimmy jerks his bag away from him. I cannot hear Danny's final few words to him, but I sigh with relief when he turns and walks back toward us. He sits by the dimming fire, and drops his head against his knees. Jimmy turns away with a frustrated huff, his pace quickened by our silent spurning of his dark invitation.

Gracie, Eli, Faith, and then Joey burst into tears as they watch their family get painfully torn apart one more time. Now I know why the Bible says through the bitterness of one many are defiled. Now I know why Jesus kicked the crowd of unbelievers out of the house before he raised that girl from the dead. Unbelief is contagious, and Jimmy is saturated with it. I struggle between despising him and pitying him, but I have never been one for natural tenderness. Or forgiveness.

"You did the right thing," Anna-Lee whispers. She reaches for and squeezes Danny's shoulders gently. "I'm proud of you."

"I almost left with him," Danny admits through his tears. "I can't believe he's going to be by himself out there. What is he thinking?" His eyes search the shadows of the trail down which Jimmy departed, as if hoping he will return any moment.

"You can't make sense of it," Anna-Lee says. "Sin is by definition unreasonable and malicious."

Danny stands to his feet, cups his hands around his mouth to amplify his voice. "Jimmy!" He's refusing to give up on him. "Jimmy! Come back!"

We are silent for a moment as the echo of Danny's bellowing voice reverberates throughout the valley. Except for the crackling of the burnt remnants of our beloved shelter and the gentle breeze that sways the branches of the tall trees over us, the forest is silent.

Jimmy is gone.

10

NEW BEGINNINGS

ANNA-LEE LETS ME MOURN BESIDE Adam for several more minutes. Then she comes to stand beside me and rest a gentle hand on my shoulder. "I'm sorry, but we need to get out of here. The thief could be coming back, and this fire has attracted a lot of unwanted attention."

I look up and see the plumes of smoke from our burnt shelter, rising thick and high into the blue sky.

Eli and Faith, who are about twenty feet away downstream, celebrate the capture of a large crawdaddy. Anna-Lee's gaze drifts toward them. "We've got to tell the little ones what happened."

"They overheard, I'm sure. They probably already know."

I stand to my feet and join the others packing up what is worth carrying to another location. When you have so little, it is hard to leave anything behind. Every foot of burnt rope or piece of broken pottery may have some undiscovered use. I, however, cannot seem to stop gazing longingly down the trail which appears to have swallowed Jimmy. I am speechless. Aghast. I wonder what I could have said or done differently to alter this sad outcome. I cannot believe it has come to this. We have barely survived *with* Jimmy's remarkable gift of snaring and killing animals, and gathering wild edible fruit and plants. How will we fare without him and Adam, especially now that we have to relocate?

I hear a noise behind me, and I suspect it is the children returning from the creek with their difficult questions. My mind immediately buzzes with the various ways to explain what has happened. I glance at Danny, hoping he will help me comfort them somehow. His eyes dart rapidly and curiously in the direction of the creek and his mouth widens with a blast of fright, speeding my heart. Uh-oh.

I reach for my holstered handgun and turn quickly to see someone approaching wearing a black hoodie, flanked by two gunmen in camouflaged hunting outfits. The gunman on the right has a beard and a ripped brown shirt tied around his scalp to hold back his long black hair. He holds a sawed-off shotgun and has a shoulder belt full of red and green shotgun shells. The other is holding an assault rifle with a thick, long barrel. The lead hooded gunman clutches Joey tightly, with the other three younger children hovering around them. Gracie's eyes are bloodshot from crying.

They are using the children as shields!

Everything appears to go in slow motion. I raise my weapon, reminding myself that I must be extremely careful with my aim lest I strike the children. But I must not let them be captured. Better to die fighting and go to heaven than to be captured and abused.

The camouflaged gunmen startle when they see me raising my handgun toward them.

"Wait!" the man with the shotgun shouts, raising his hands.

"Don't shoot!" Gracie calls out, wiping her tears.

I realize the little ones appear to be crying with happiness, not fear. Little Joey clutches the neck of the lead gunman, whose weapon still sits in a thigh holster, and who walks with a limp. Gracie affectionately holds onto his waist. I stand still, confused, paralyzed with trepidation.

Backdropped by the giddy laughing of Faith and Eli, Little Joey's the first one who introduces our unexpected company.

"It's Mommy!"

Mother pulls back her hoodie and falls to her knees with tears streaming down her freckled cheeks. I hardly recognize her. Her face is so thin.

Mom's alive! I can't believe it!

We lunge for her like thirsty souls for cups of water that may disappear if we hesitate. We surround her with tearful hugs. She kisses us with tears of joy and utterances of gratitude to God.

I am so happy, I cannot even speak. I just hug her and cry. It was a test. It was all a test. I just wish Adam was alive to enjoy this happy ending.

"I didn't mean to startle you," she finally tells us. "I heard some yelling near your shelter, and I saw the dead man by the creek. I wanted to be sure everything was okay."

"That's Adam," I inform her. "He was captured trying to save you. He was killed trying to save me."

Mother places her palm gently on my cheek. "I'm so sorry."

We hug and then she takes a knee, gently pushing Faith's curls behind her ears.

"Who are those guys?" Eli asks.

"These men are Christians." She pulls a dried flake of mud off Eli's cheek. "This is Deputy Dave"—the man with the long bolt-action rifle nods, "and his brother Jase"—Jase gives half a wave. "They rescued me from the bad guys who took me. They're gonna take us to a safe place." I realize that Dave and Jase look just alike. They are twins.

Mom glances affectionately at us, trembling with joy. "Oh, I thank God you're alive. I can't believe how skinny you are all." She runs her fingers through Eli's disheveled hair. "And tall!"

"Are those real shotgun shells?" Eli asks Jase, admiring the red and green shells on his bandolier.

Jase nods while his brother Dave leans in closer to Eli. "I know what you're thinking, little buddy. Why in the world would you drape Christmas lights across your chest like that?" He motions to Jase's bandolier. "Especially when you're trying to stay inconspicuous in the woods?" Dave chuckles at Jase's feigned embarrassment. "It's like screaming, 'Shoot me! Shoot me!' every twenty feet."

"Anything's better than a rifle that weighs 50 pounds." Jase motions to Dave's massive sniper rifle. "Look at that thing! It's like you've got small-man syndrome, and you need a bigger gun to make you feel better about your small self . . ."

"Small self?" Dave, who does appear about fifteen pounds lighter than his twin brother, raises his right sleeve and flexes his bicep. "You call this small?" Eli gasps and puts his hands on Dave's bicep.

Jase flexes both of his biceps. "All right, kids, who's bigger?" Dave quickly pulls his sleeve back down. Jase teases him, "What's the matter? It's because you're smaller, admit it. It's too hard for you to compare. Too traumatic to your, you know, your ego."

"It's because I'm more humble than my baby brother," Dave says with a bashful grin.

"Being five minutes younger doesn't make me a baby brother. The better bread has to bake just a bit longer than that cheap stuff . . . "

The kids all laugh at their joshing, but I cannot. I'm still grieving the loss of Adam.

"We caught a thief that stole our bug-out bags, but he got away," Eli announces.

"He shot Dad," Danny adds.

"And Adam," Eli glances to me.

Mother's brow furrows. "What thief?"

Before we can answer Mom's question, her kind countenance contorts into an anxious grimace. She looks around her and, with furrowed brow, asks, "Where's Jimmy?"

Anna-Lee and I trade a troubled glance. I leap to my feet, turn, and shout at the top of my lungs in the direction Jimmy had fled.

"Jimmy!"

* * * * *

Jimmy breaks out of the trail into a field with corn stalks almost five feet high, mostly devoid of edible ears. He thinks he hears something behind him. A scream of pain? A shout of anger? The noise is vague through the creaking trees and rustling brush.

Jimmy runs through the corn stalks until he comes to a clearing where heavy rain and torrents of erosion have destroyed the seedlings, leaving plateaus of red dirt and shallow ditches. He keeps running, anxious to get out of the nakedness of the clearing and back into the cover of the stalks and the woods across the field.

Sprinting over the bare ground, with his eyes scanning the horizon, he hears it before he feels it—a loud *whack* of metal jaws slamming down on bone—followed by extreme pain in his right ankle. He falls to the ground, gasping. He screams out when he sees a bear trap has clamped down on his right lower leg. He claws the dirt in panic, clenching his teeth for pain as the hot blood soaks his jeans.

He takes a deep breath, and screams, "Help!" He turns the direction of the shelter, and bellows at the top of his lungs. "Help me!"

Thinking he hears a gunshot in the field in the direction of the city, he forces himself to be silent. The only sound is his labored breathing and the gusty wind rustling the leaves on the stalks. He is in the center of the clearing and the greenery provides little cover.

He examines his leg and realizes he will bleed to death if he cannot get help quickly. He screams in the direction of the shelter, "Sophie! Anna-Lee! Danny! Help!"

Silence. Desperate, he shoots his rifle in the air twice. "Help!"

There is no answer besides the dauntless whispering of the stiff, increasingly erratic gusts of wind.

He removes his belt and forms a tourniquet just below his right knee. He takes his sheathed sword and inserts it inside the loop of belt. He twists the sheath, slowly tightening the tourniquet to shut off the blood supply to the wound.

The tourniquet is painful, but he continues to twist until the bleeding trickles to a standstill.

He hears a familiar voice behind him.

"Don't move, Jimmy."

He turns. It is Robby, aiming a rifle at him. Robby's eyes are glossed over, like he's intoxicated on drugs.

"Robby! I was on my way to you and got my leg—"

"Well, somebody call 9-1-1," comes the slurred words from behind Robby. A short man, sloppily dressed and wearing a greasy green cap, enters the clearing. Another one is right behind him. He is a black man with a beard and a blue bandana around his head. They all point weapons at Jimmy.

Jimmy reaches back for his rifle, but a boot presses it against the ground.

"Whoowee!" It's the skinny guy in the cowboy hat that was with Robby, with his foot on Jimmy's rifle. "I've had my eyes on this bad boy!" Cowboy reaches down to pry Jimmy's fingers off the rifle.

Before Cowboy can even pick up the rifle, Jimmy unholsters his handgun and aims it at Cowboy's face.

Cowboy ducks the first bullet and crawls like mad for the cover of the stalks. The others begin to fire at Jimmy, and he turns his handgun on them and unloads all his rounds as fast as he can. Robby takes a shot in the chest and falls hard. More shots are fired at Jimmy, striking the ground and throwing dirt up on him. A fallen brown, dried corn stalk explodes from the impact of a bullet and drops shards of the dehydrated plant on him like confetti.

When Jimmy's mag is empty, all is silent for a moment except Robby's death rattle. Jimmy turns and crawls for his ammo bag a few feet away. The trap clamping on his leg is chained to a metal pole that is twisted into the ground, keeping Jimmy an inch from his ammo bag. Before he can reach it, Cowboy, now hatless, rushes in and gives Jimmy a swift boot kick in his side.

Jimmy has the breath knocked out of him.

"He shot Robby!" one of them shouts angrily.

"Patience," Cowboy declares, reaching down and picking up Jimmy's handgun.

Blam!

Jimmy's pain in his already crippled leg worsens when he is struck with a few shotgun pellets.

"Hey!" Cowboy turns angrily toward the man in the blue bandana. "Watch where you're shootin' that thing!"

"He shot Robby!" The man in the blue bandana marches right up to Jimmy, furious. He ejects a shotgun shell and loads another round.

"And why's that a good reason to shoot me, moron?"

"Sorry."

"Use the sights, and stop shooting that scattergun from the hip."

"Ah, man!" The man with the green ball cap enters the clearing, cradling a bleeding elbow. "He got me too."

The bearded fellow with the blue bandana kicks away Jimmy's backpack as Cowboy frisks Jimmy for weapons.

The injured man with the greasy green ball cap approaches slowly. He grasps a machete in his left hand and has a stainless steel handgun in a hip holster. He manages a scornful threat with charisma, "Oh, you are so gonna regret that!" He shakes his machete at Jimmy.

"Found me a new weapon, boys," Cowboy says with an intoxicated grin, showing his brown teeth. He puts Jimmy's AR over his shoulder by its sling. "Plus, a new 9." He pats Jimmy's 9 mm handgun, now shoved under his belt. Then he bends down and removes Jimmy's sheathed sword, thereby loosening the tourniquet around his leg. "Move over, Jet Li! Looky, looky!"

Cowboy unsheathes the sword and raises it proudly, carefully examining the blade. "Nice."

The spasming in Jimmy's gut eases, and he can finally speak. "I was on my way to join Robby."

"Little late." Cowboy swings the sword in a figure eight position, grinning widely, looking as out of place as a Chinese Samurai at a bull riding competition.

"But Robby invited me to join y'all."

"Robby's not in charge anymore." Cowboy shoves the sword back into its sheathe and puts it under his belt. "Especially now that he's dead."

Jesse steps on Jimmy's wrist and raises his machete above Jimmy's elbow. "Now, for a taste of your own medicine."

Cowboy stops him. "Wait a sec."

Jesse, through clenched teeth, strongly objects. "Why?"

"Jesse's gotta right to pay back," the bearded fellow with the blue bandana insists.

"Please don't kill me," Jimmy begs between groans of pain.

Cowboy laughs as he fetches his hat. "We can make better use of him, Jesse. Have some fun with him." He smacks it to get the dust off it.

The man with the bandana grins from ear to ear. "Bad day for you, kiddo."

Cowboy repositions his hat and walks past Jimmy till he's between Jimmy and the tree line. "Sophie, Anna-Lee, and Danny. Ain't that who he cried out for? The older ones, I suspect. What's the name of your little brothers and sisters?"

The fellow with the bandana laughs sadistically at the fear evident in Jimmy's eyes. Jesse, however, is in too much pain to find the scenario entertaining. The man with the blue bandana begins to wrap Jesse's wounded elbow with an elastic bandage.

"And it looks like things aren't going so well with them," Cowboy says, pointing at the horizon. Jimmy looks at what he is pointing to. It's a plume of smoke ascending into the sky from the shelter fire.

"Please leave them alone," Jimmy pleads. "Please."

"Oh, stop acting like you care about them. You were leaving them to join Robby, right?" Cowboy snickers. "What do you think their chances of survival were without you?"

Cowboy looks down at the blood pooling under Jimmy's injured leg. "The way that leg's gushin', it might be death-by-bear-trap, huh? Not a bad way to go."

"We can't let him die of blood loss," the man in the bandana says.

Cowboy opens up Jimmy's backpack. Finding more ammo, he celebrates, "Jackpot!" The others cheer their friend's discovery. "Oh, what's this?" he exclaims, removing Jimmy's box of old coins and trinkets. He opens it up. "Sweet!" He pats Jimmy's shoulder. "We're not going to kill you yet, buddy. You're too fun. Full of surprises."

Cowboy dumps the contents of Jimmy's box on the ground, and begins to pick some coins.

"You want to tell me why you think those weapons and that booty's all yours?" Jesse says.

"We'll divvy it out later," Cowboy responds. "I'm just separating the junk from the good stuff."

"Should we bring the kid to the party?" the man in the blue bandana asks.

"Definitely," Cowboy responds. "BYOB."

Jesse's brow furrows.

Cowboy sees the confusion in Jesse's grimace. "You should get out more, Jesse."

"I'll take that third, right there." Jesse thrusts his machete into the dirt, splitting the coins and treasure by a third. Cowboy jerks his hand back with a curse.

"Whoa. Watch the fingers."

As the men argue over the loot, Jimmy fixes his eyes on the coins and thinks for a moment he sees the lock of blonde hair amidst the trinkets. The pink rubber band. The dirty, cruel fingers searching greedily for loot, appear to move around the fibers of yellow hair blowing in the breeze. He blinks, and realizes he is seeing things. The lock of his sister's hair, he remembers, was discarded in the trash by the thief.

"But who's gonna carry him?" the man with the bandana wonders aloud, standing and dumping a handful of coins into his pocket. "He ain't gonna be able to walk with that busted leg."

"Not me." Cowboy shakes his head side to side.

"He'll be dead by the time we get there," Jesse says. He leans down closer to Jimmy with a sadistic grin on his sweaty face. "I'm not only going to kill you, I'm gonna enjoy it!" He cocks his revolver and coldly aims it at Jimmy.

Jimmy's face, already pale from blood loss, contorts with the fear of the moment. He raises a palm between his face and the weapon. "No, please, don't."

"'No please don't?' That's it? Those are your final words?"

"Yeah. Got any final words better than that?"

Jimmy closes his eyes. He remembers asking the thief the same question less than half an hour earlier. Now, he's the one with the weapon aimed at him. He's the one in need of mercy. Jimmy recalls the thief's tearful prayer. He repeats the words. "Oh, God, have mercy on me . . . "

The stress suddenly dissipates from Jimmy's tortured countenance. He comes to grips with what appears to be his imminent death. Now, his only fear is dying and not being right with God. He closes his eyes and feels the breeze blowing gently against his flushed cheeks.

"I'm sorry, God," he mumbles, his heart breaking over his sin. The others laugh nervously as Jimmy bows his head in reverence. "Save me, Jesus . . . " A tear drifts down his cheek.

Jesse taps the pistol against Jimmy's forehead, hoping to induce the fear in him again, but Jimmy doesn't even look up at him. He's more concerned about his eternity than in gratifying the cruel beast thumping the barrel of a loaded pistol against his scalp.

"Religion in the fox hole," the man with the blue bandana says, chuckling.

Jesse places his hand over his heart. "So touching."

"So predictable," Cowboy adds, as he inserts a pinch of tobacco between his lower lip and his teeth.

Jesse cocks the pistol and bites his lip. The nail of his index finger whitens as he gradually increases the pressure against the trigger.

Suddenly, a gunshot resounds. Jesse's body convulses and collapses violently to the ground.

Jimmy jolts, expecting to have been shot, but feels no pain.

Cowboy looks to his left. "What in the—!"

Blam!

Cowboy ducks a bullet, and the man in the blue bandana is shot behind, his head snapping back as he crashes hard to the ground. Cowboy crawls for the cover of the stalks, cursing and threatening.

* * * * *

We are walking along the edge of the cornfield beyond the boundaries of our woods, looking for Jimmy, when the two gunshots prompt us to all drop and hug the ground. One of the bullets sounds like it whizzes right past our heads!

"Down," Dave orders.

I steady the rifle on a branch of a small tree and begin to study the field through my scope, while Anna-Lee climbs a little higher and begins to scour the cornfield through the binoculars.

Danny guards Gracie, Eli, Faith, and Joey back by the tree line where the trail spills out into the field.

"Do you see Jimmy?" Mom asks. "Who fired those shots, Sophie?"

"I don't know."

Anna-Lee points. "There he is. I see him. In that clearing in the middle of the cornfield."

I reposition my rifle, as does Dave beside me. Dave twists the knobs on his large scope affixed to his massive rifle.

I study Jimmy through the binoculars. His breathing rate appears rapid. He looks confused. "He's hurt. I think Jimmy's hurt."

Momentarily, Mother takes off running into the stalks toward Jimmy. "Jimmy!" she exclaims. "Jimmy!"

"Kate!" Dave shouts. "No! Get down, Kate."

Jase rushes after her. "I'll stay with her!"

A flurry of gunfire suddenly resounds, transforming Jimmy's location into a cloud of brown dirt. I struggle to see through the haze. I make out the flashes of at least three different guns through the dust.

What in the world is happening?

"Jimmy!" Mother cries out as she runs through the stalks toward the clearing. "Jimmy!"

"I saw Jimmy just a few seconds ago," I tell Dave and Anna-Lee, keeping my eyes focused through the scope, looking for a target in the dusty clearing.

A moment later, Dave announces, "I can see your brother now. And there are our targets."

"Oh, I see them," I respond. "There's three of them."

"We've got to do this at the same time, Sophie. You take out the one closest to Jimmy, in the green cap. On the count of three."

"All right," I respond. "I'm ready."

"One, two, three."

We pull the trigger at the same moment and our two targets go down.

"Where's the other?" Dave asks as he ejects the brass and loads another round into the chamber. "Where'd he go?"

"He ran into the cover of the stalks," Anna-Lee says.

Dave sees the man in the green hat jerking on the ground. "Die already," he says as he pulls the trigger again.

The explosion of his gun is so loud it hurts my ears.

"Man, I'd hate to get shot by those bullets," Anna-Lee comments, still looking into the field through her binoculars. "Uh-oh. Jimmy's aiming a pistol at Mom." Anna-Lee lowers the binoculars. "Dave, tell Mom and Jase to watch for friendly fire."

Dave unholsters his handheld radio and taps a button. "Hey Jase, watch for—"

Blam!

Dave pauses. "Jase? You alive?"

"Yes, I'm alive. Barely. That went right by my ear. What were you telling me to watch for again?"

"Friendly fire."

"Thanks for the warning, Mr. Sleep-Till-Noon. How in the world did you ever come out first?"

"Hey, Dave, I can't find Mom!?" Anna-Lee says, looking at the field through her binoculars. "Where is she?"

Worried, I leap off the tree and run toward where I last saw Mom. When I finally reach her in the stalks, she says, "I'm fine. Who's shooting at Jimmy?" I shrug.

Braving the gunfire, Mom continues toward the clearing again. Jase and I follow, scraping our arms and face from the sharp-edged, broad green leaves of the stalks.

As we crest the hill, I can't see Jimmy, but through the dust and greenery I can make out the man with the cowboy hat stepping out from the stalks into the clearing. He crouches low to the ground. He has a smirk on his face as he raises his rifle, preparing to shoot at someone to my right.

Suddenly, an arrow shot from the other side of the clearing pierces the man's head. He falls to the ground, dead.

We step into the clearing, and I can see Jimmy. He is looking away from us.

"Jimmy!" Mother runs to him, holding her handgun with two hands. With my handgun at the ready, I follow.

"Mom?" Jimmy sounds like he doesn't believe his own eyes. "Mom?" We run to Jimmy's side. Mom holsters her handgun and embraces him with both arms.

"I'm so sorry, Mommy." Jimmy weeps as he confesses, "I went inside for my sword and my coin collection when Dad told me not to . . . " She begins to tighten the tourniquet around his broken leg.

When the cloud of dirt settles, a man rises from the stalks the far side of the clearing, holding a bow. He wears a backpack over his right shoulder.

The sun is to his back. I feel threatened and aim my handgun at him, but Jimmy raises his hands and urges me not to shoot, shouting loudly, "No, Sophie! Don't shoot." The man drops his bow and raises his right hand. "He saved me!" Jimmy shouts.

Something about this bystander troubles me, so I take a step to the side to get a better look at him without the sun to his back. Then, I realize who it is.

It's Jack!

The thief takes another step toward us. I raise my handgun at him. "Stop! Don't move."

The others come into the clearing as Jimmy pours out his confession to Mom. Jase checks on the fallen, to be sure they have expired, while Anna-Lee implores Jimmy to drink from a canteen.

Dave sees I'm pointing my handgun at the bystander, and he draws near. "Whoa."

Jase's hands are outstretched. "Jimmy said he's a friendly, Sophie. What are you doing?"

"I did save him," the thief says, handing his bow to Jase. "I came back to return the stuff I stole from the kids, and these dudes were tryin' to kill Jimmy."

Jack, with his good arm, tosses his backpack to Anna-Lee. "I brought your stuff back."

"Will somebody tell me what's goin' on?" Dave inquires.

Anna-Lee tells Jase who Jack is and what he's done.

"Fourfold." There is an anxious tremor in Jack's raspy voice. "Like Zacchaeus. That's what you said, right?" Upon Dave's insistence, he drops to his knees. "Open the backpack, and see for yourself."

"You killed our Dad," Anna-Lee reminds him. "How can you make amends for that?"

"I-I-I can't," he stutters, "but I wanna try." He lowers his head, ashamed, while Jase tries to cuff him behind his back. The pain is too much for him because of his wounded shoulder, so Jase ties his wrists in the front and ties those bonds around his waist.

Mother looks at Anna-Lee, puzzled. "Who killed your father? That man?" She motions at Jack. "The one Jimmy says saved him?"

Before anyone can answer, the thief's eyes suddenly brighten, and he exclaims, "And your sister's lock of hair! Jimmy, I found it."

Jimmy, his face as pale as snow, still manages an enthusiastic raising of his eyebrows and a faint smile. "You found it?"

The thief motions to the backpack with his head. "It's there. Front pocket."

Anna-Lee unzips the bag to look for the lock of Becca's hair.

Mother, with her arm still around Jimmy, turns toward the thief. "He killed your father?"

Anna-Lee finds the lock of yellow hair bound together with a weathered, pink rubber band. She brings it to Jimmy, and he takes it reverently in his hands.

"Thank God." Jimmy takes a deep breath, exhausted. "Come closer, Anna-Lee." Jimmy pulls her down to her knees beside him and Mom. "I'm so sorry. Will you forgive me?"

"Why won't someone answer my question?" Mother stands, unholsters her handgun, and stomps toward the thief. "Did you murder my husband?"

"Forgive him, Mom!" Jimmy cries out.

I am in awe as I behold my brother who tried to kill this thief in a vengeful rage less than two hours ago now plead for his pardon.

"Mom?" Jimmy grows dizzy and falls to his back. His eyes dim.

"Stay with me, Jimmy." Jase gently smacks Jimmy's pale cheeks.

"I've changed!" The thief's eyes fix on Mom as she marches up to him. "I ain't the same man."

Anna-Lee examines the contents of the backpack. "He returned what he stole. Fourfold." She glances at me. "It's all here."

Suddenly, Mom recognizes Jack as one of the men responsible for her kidnapping. "You!" She is overcome with horror. "You monster!"

She takes the handgun off safety and pulls back the slide slightly to ensure a bullet is in the chamber. She aims the 9 mm at his face. Her countenance, so merciful and tender just a moment ago when she reunited with Jimmy, is now red and blazing with rage.

"Kate, put it down." Dave takes a step closer to Mom. "Kate?"

She isn't dissuaded in the slightest, keeping her handgun aimed at the thief and her finger tight against the trigger. The weapon shakes in her hands as she seethes.

"I'm sorry." The thief is trembling for fear. "Faith, it was Faith."

Mother appears surprised by the thief's words. "Faith?"

"She won my heart. Jesus got through to me through her."

Mother turns her eyes to me, as if expecting me to take her side. I desperately wish I could. But my heart tells me what I must do. "He's right, Mom. Don't do it."

"Isn't he the one who killed Adam? How on earth can you forgive him?"

All eyes turn to me for a long moment. "Because God forgave me." Mother winces, as if my words do not register with her. I fix my eyes on the thief, the author of so much of our suffering. "Jack, I forgive you."

My words drop a thick blanket on all of the fiery rage and everyone calms. Everything becomes still, like all creation holds its breath, as we stare at Mother for a long moment. She is immovable, keeping her weapon aimed at Jack's face. He clamps his eyes shut, and I see his lips mumbling a silent prayer.

"I forgive you too," Anna-Lee says. "Thank you for bringing our stuff back, Jack."

He smiles at Anna-Lee, and nods.

Danny arrives with the little ones. As soon as Faith sets her eyes on Jack, she squeals for joy. "Jack!" She runs toward him as if she was going to hug him, but then she sees Mother pointing the handgun at his face. She freezes and stares at the weapon in Mom's quivering hands.

Dave stretches his hand to Mom and demands, "Kate, give it to me. Now."

Mom doesn't even acknowledge his order. She appears indecisive.

To our surprise and Mom's horror, Faith steps right in between the barrel of Mom's weapon and Jack's face, and wraps her arms tightly around his neck.

Jack begins to sob. "Faith! Thank you, Faith."

Mother, breathing rapidly and shaking like a leaf, lifts her finger from the trigger and lowers her weapon.

Dave takes a step closer and rests a hand gently on Mom's shoulder. He looks back at us. "You may forgive him for the crime against you. So may your mother. But you may not pardon him for the crime of murder against another. For murder, he'll need to stand trial."

Dave gently pats Mom's shoulder. "Let him stand trial. Better him than you." He reaches for her handgun.

Mom refuses to surrender it to him, but instead, she puts it in her hip holster and walks slowly back to Jimmy, speechless.

After Dave and Jase pry the bear trap jaws off Jimmy's leg, they begin to give copious amounts of water to him. Upon our insistence, he drinks down much more than he wants while Anna-Lee applies a tight field bandage. They give him a pain pill and an iron tablet, and I'm amazed how quickly it rejuvenates his personality.

We carefully carry him back to the concealment of the dense woods at our burnt-out shelter. Danny and I wrap Adam's body in a tarp and drag him back to the shelter.

I begin to dig Adam's grave beside the creek as the two militia deputies bandage Jimmy's lacerated leg. They carefully sterilize his wound and remove three shotgun pellets. Jack begs me to let him dig the grave for Adam, but I do not respond to him. Tears flow down my face as I dig, oblivious to everything except my breaking heart.

The deputies don't trust Jack at all, so they keep him bound while Dave treats his shoulder wounds. He appears to accept his fate peacefully. Faith expresses concern that the rope binding his hands is too tight.

"It's okay, Faith," Jack says softly. "I've been in and out of the slammer my whole life, but I've never been free." He appears to try to enjoy every moment he has left to the max. He especially seems to love conversing with Faith, who tells him every story about Jesus she can remember, treating him as warmly as a long-loved babysitter.

When I'm done digging by the creek, everyone surrounds the grave as the two deputies cover Adam's body with dirt. Mother comforts me from one side, while Anna-Lee puts her arm over my shoulder on the other. Danny and Eli prop a flat slab of stone at the head of the grave, and Dave gives me a thick black marker to inscribe Adam's name on the stone. Upon my request, they leave me alone for a bit by the grave beside the bubbling creek.

When my weeping calms, I write on the slab of stone at the head of Adam's grave. Then I go sit beside Mom around the fire.

Mom rests her arm over my shoulder and fastens her eyes on mine. "Are you going to be all right?"

I nod, but do not speak. I worry that if I utter a word I will begin crying again.

While some of the jerky and rice Jack returned to us boils in a pan over the fire pit, the children listen intently as the two deputies tell us how they saved Mom from her captors. These men are two appointed deputies in an autonomous, self-sufficient Christian community that has been formed in Warsaw, thirty miles north. Their mission is not only to protect the innocent from roving bands of lawless thugs, but also to expand their community of peace and justice into surrounding areas of unrest, and to prepare everyone to resist the government's predictable tyrannical remedy for the prevalent anarchy. There's no more separation of God and government, they assure us. Not in Warsaw.

"Once I'm better," Jimmy asks Dave, "can I train to be a deputy like you?" His face is pale, and he has to lie down to prevent from getting dizzy, but I can see he's feeling much better.

Dave nods and says, "Once you're older, Jimmy, if you keep loving God and honoring His law, I don't see why not. As long as you don't wear Christmas tree lights across your chest."

Jase grins and punches Dave playfully in the shoulder, and Joey squeals and jumps on Dave's back, trying to choke him. Eli tries to tackle Jase, and Jase shouts, "Stop!" He and Dave hand their weapons to Mom, and then the wrestling match commences. For several minutes the little kids have fun trying to pile on the two deputies, and we all have a good laugh.

Perhaps we have not begun the last chapter of America as I thought. Just when things never looked bleaker, a brighter day dawns. The Promised Land never looked so far out of reach to Israel as when they were right on the edge of it on the banks of the Jordan, listening to the ten false spies. How close I was to despairing, when I was only steps away from celebrating at the finish line!

While we enjoy our last meal around the stone fire pit, Dave converses in whispered tones with Jack beside the creek. Mother seems quiet and distant, always turning to glance at the thief, as if she suspected at any moment he would turn on us.

After dinner, Dave announces he's going to baptize Jack. With Jack's hands still bound, Dave and Jase plunge him into the shallow muddy water in Jesus' name. Not once, not twice, and not just three times. At first, I think they are doing it three times for each of the three persons in the Trinity, but no, they aren't done. They dunk him six or seven times, and quite vigorously! Every time they bring him up out of the water, Jack howls for joy. After a half a dozen times, however, he's squealing, "I'm clean already! I'm clean!"

"You're clean on the inside," Jase replies. "It's the outside we're worried about."

"Nah, that wasn't it," Dave says in a serious tone. "You wouldn't quit thrashing your legs out of the water, Jack, and I wanted to get you all in at the same time." He glances at Jase. "Stop making fun of the brother's odor, will ya? That's the skunk calling the diaper stinky." We all roar with laughter at their impromptu joking.

As Jack walks out of the shallow creek, showing his big smile with his missing incisor, Dave acts like he's gonna baptize Jase, but Jase pulls away. "Get your paws off me!"

"You're right," Dave says. "We'd need to baptize you in the Pacific Ocean, you're so . . . " He pauses, searching for the right word as he rubs his belly. "Protuberant! You know?" The kids laugh. "Even then we'd have to do it slowly or we'd risk a tsunami in Africa."

"That's the Atlantic Ocean, not the Pacific, dufus."

I laugh so hard I cry as I watch the solemn ceremony venture into the comical. I've never been so enraptured nor so thoroughly entertained with a baptism. Nor had I ever seen the one being baptized so thoroughly enjoy it.

Just when I think it is impossible to squeeze one more drop of drama out of this day, Jimmy hobbles on his crutches to the water.

"My turn."

After a plastic bag is tied tightly over his leg to keep his wound and cast dry, he hobbles with his crutches into the deepest part of the water. Dave and Jase invite me and Anna-Lee to do it. With Jimmy's permission, I am honored. We dunk him only once.

I glance at Mom on the edge of the fire pit and see her tense countenance ease with a warm smile as she watches Jimmy's baptism. When Jimmy is helped out of the creek and onto the bank, he totters with his crutches toward Jack and wraps an arm around him. With Jack's hands tied, he cannot reciprocate, but he whispers something in his ear that makes Jimmy cry.

This appears to soften Mother's heart, and she breaks out in full tears. She doesn't say anything, but I can tell her rage has settled and her desire for retaliation has abated. Love truly covers a vast multitude of seemingly unforgiveable sins.

Around the fire over which the last of our food boils, Dave and Jase tell us stories about how they helped restore justice in the small town of Warsaw, and how their government spread to other areas of lawlessness. "Without justice, there can be no peace." Dave nibbles on a granola bar that was in the bug-out bag Jack returned. "And no blessing. If we want God's blessing— freedom being one of the greatest of them—there's got to be justice. For everybody. The weak and helpless. The preborn. The elderly. If we're going to be victorious over the federal government's predictable remedy for anarchy—which will be disarmament and tyranny —we must have God's favor."

"Disarmament?" Jack doesn't believe his ears. "How can the government disarm the people? We got too many guns—"

"It'll start in the big cities, where fearful and frazzled hungry folks are begging the feds for food and defense. A godless people will beg for cages to keep them safe. Oh, the feds will get the guns. Then from there, the troops will move into places most damaged by the lawlessness. They'll take the criminals down by force, or co-opt them into helping get the guns from others. It's just a matter of time. But first things first. If we don't do justice in Warsaw, we don't deserve liberty. We don't deserve freedom . . ."

Using Adam's crutch, Jimmy stands and tries to put his sheathed sword inside his belt. Dave stretches out a hand.

"I'll take that."

Jimmy stares at him for a moment and then hands the sword to him. Jimmy hobbles down toward the creek and stops beside Adam's grave.

Curious, I follow him. I overhear him mumble, "Thank you." I don't realize who he's speaking to at first, but then I see he's holding Becca's lock of hair in his hand. He looks at it with heartfelt sentiment, running his thumb over the yellow strands, still wet from his baptism. He lowers himself to the ground with a grunt, and digs a hole with his hands in the dirt beside Adam's grave. He kisses the lock and gently drops it into the hole.

"It's time I let you go."

He covers the hair with dirt and presses the mound flat against the ground.

Still standing behind him, I reach into my pocket for my folded magazine page, the one with pictures of models in wedding dresses. I study it for a moment. Every dress, every face, every crease of the familiar white square streaks, where the folds have worn away the waxy ink, is etched into my memory. It seems like yesterday when

I drew a circle around the wedding dress I had picked and wrote in black marker the words, *This is the one!*

My tears begin to flow, and my heart struggles. The tug of the Spirit pulls me to my knees, and I finally succumb. I plop down beside Jimmy, dig a hole about two inches deep, and drop my folded precious heirloom into the bottom of the hole. I hold my breath as I cover it with soil. Feeling Jimmy's hand on my shoulder, I turn to him. "We're gonna be all right, Jimmy."

He throws an arm over my shoulders, and we dampen the soil with our tears.

I hear a noise behind us, like a sniffle. I look back. It's Mom.

In one quick jerk, she unholsters her handgun, ejects a round, and catches the bullet. She sticks the weapon back in her holster. She sits down next to me and studies the bullet for a moment.

"That was the bullet that almost killed Jack."

She digs a hole with her hands and drops it in without another word. A lump rises in my throat as she covers it with dirt.

That was a hard bullet to bury.

Jimmy gets in a stretcher Jase and Danny made for him, and everyone puts on their packs and picks up their loads for the journey. I venture once more to where my heart keeps pulling me—Adam's grave.

In a few minutes, Jase calls my name. "Sophie, I'm sorry, but we've got a lot of ground to cover before night falls."

I glance over my shoulder at him as he pours a bucket of water over the embers, releasing a cloud of steam. He's the last one here. Everyone else is heading down the trail already. I raise a finger. "I'm coming."

Facing Adam's grave, I kiss my palm and touch the tombstone playfully. "There. First kiss." I smile briefly and take a deep breath. "Oh, Adam." I finally rise and follow my family down the trail.

The headstone reads:

ADAM BRANSON

LOVED

FORGIVEN

FRIEND

HUSBAND

Jimmy has stuck three stems of jewelweed into the ground over the little miniature graves we have dug for Becca's lock of hair, the picture of my dress, and Mom's bullet of vengeance.

Jewelweed. Perfect.

As we begin our trek toward Warsaw, Dave leads the way. Jack, with his hands tied in the front, and carrying as heavy a pack as he can stand, walks behind Dave. Anna-Lee offered to carry Faith on her back, but Faith prefers to walk next to Jack, jabbering away a million miles an hour. Danny follows, holding the front of Jimmy's stretcher. Jase holds the back of the stretcher. Anna-Lee is next with Joey on her back. Mom follows with Eli and Gracie beside. They let me take up the rear.

When we come to the Y, Jack halts. He motions to something on the ground just left of the crook of the Y. The guard doesn't see it, but Faith does. She bends over to pick up Jimmy's lost survival knife.

"Hey Jimmy," Jack says. "Look what we found."

Jimmy's face beams as Faith hands him his lost knife. "I was wondering where I lost it." He fastens the lost weapon in its sheath.

Being the very last in the line of our group to leave these familiar woods that I've called home for the last three months, I pause at the crook of the Y. With the five-trunk tree to my back, I gaze one last time down the trail that leads to our shelter. It is completely obscured by the trees of the forest, but I still can see a thin wisp of smoke from our last fire in the stone circle, slivering past the branches and leaves, climbing toward the misty sky above. I'll never forget the bubbling waters of that shallow creek, the heartfelt prayers before bedtime as we clasped hands around the dimming embers in the stone circle, and the sweet singing as heavenly comfort descended upon us with the night's damp chill. The look of the crescent moon as it peeked at me through the tepee's smoke hole. The thrill of being reunited with Mom. Those awe-inspiring baptisms. I will never forget the delight I felt when I gave forgiveness. When I received it. The hope and comfort that washed over me when I called on Jesus' name as I grieved the untimely death of the man I had grown to love so deeply. The celebration of new life birthed beside his shallow grave.

Ain't God a wonder? Isn't that just like Him to bring such happiness out of so much pain? So great a peace out of such an ugly storm.

The north trail steepens into unchartered territory. I don't know what lies ahead, but I know God loves us, and if we trust in Him, everything will be all right.

I hum the tune of a song that Anna-Lee wrote. I cannot remember the words, but dependable as ever, Anna-Lee's crystal voice soon takes up the melody.

You have been a shelter, Lord,
To every generation, to every generation.
A sanctuary from the storm.
You have been a shelter, Lord.

Other novels by Dr. Patrick Johnston:

Body by Blood

Naomi's Sacrifice

The Revolt of 2020

The Lesser Hills of Kinder County

Johnny and the Mystery of the Rusty Musket

Beating Grim

"Like" The Johnston Family on Facebook and sign up to receive their E-newsletter through their website www.JohnstonFamilyMinistry.com.

To keep current with the progress on the full feature movie "The Reliant," "like" us at www.facebook.com/TheReliantMovie.

For more information about

Dr. Patrick Johnston
and
The Reliant
please visit:

www.JohnstonFamilyMinistry.com
www.ProLifePhysicians.org
www.PersonhoodOhio.com
www.Facebook.com/docjohnston
Email: DocJohnston@yahoo.com

For more information about
AMBASSADOR INTERNATIONAL
please visit:

www.ambassador-international.com
@AmbassadorIntl
www.facebook.com/AmbassadorIntl